The
Foreign Classical Romances

Complete in Twenty Crown Octavo Volumes

With Introductory Essays by

HAMILTON WRIGHT MABIE, L.H.D., LL.D.
Co-Editor N. Y. Outlook.
Author of "Norse Stories," "Essays on Books and Culture," etc.

PROF. MAURICE FRANCIS EGAN, A.M., LL.D.
Catholic University of America.
Author of Studies in Literature," "Modern Novelists," etc.

PROF. LEO WIENER
Harvard University. Translator of Tolstoy's Complete Works.
Author of "Anthology of Russian Literature," etc.

BARON GUSTAVO TOSTI
Doctor of Laws, Naples University. Royal Consul of Italy at Boston

WOLF VON SCHIERBRAND
Former Berlin Correspondent N. Y. Evening Post. Author of "Germany," etc.

A. SCHADE VAN WESTRUM
Licentiate Amsterdam University. Literary Editor N. Y. Mail and Express

General Editor: **LIONEL STRACHEY**
Compiler of "Little Masterpieces of Fiction."
Translator of Stories by Balzac, Sudermann, Serao, etc.

Frontispieces and Biographical Sketches

T

DOÑA
PERFECTA

PÉREZ GALDÓS

TRANSLATED FROM THE SPANISH

A FRONTISPIECE AND A BIOGRAPHICAL SKETCH

P. F. COLLIER & SON
PUBLISHERS   :   NEW YORK

DOÑA PERFECTA

CONTENTS

	PAGE
LIFE OF GALDOS	5

CHAPTER I
VILLAHORRENDA—FIVE MINUTES ... 7

CHAPTER II
A JOURNEY IN THE HEART OF SPAIN ... 11

CHAPTER III
PEPE REY ... 29

CHAPTER IV
THE COUSIN'S ARRIVAL ... 39

CHAPTER V
WILL THERE BE DISCORD? ... 46

CHAPTER VI
DISCORD ARISES THAT MIGHT HAVE BEEN PREVENTED ... 53

CHAPTER VII
DISCORD INCREASES ... 62

CHAPTER VIII
IN ALL HASTE ... 69

CHAPTER IX
DISAGREEMENT INCREASES AND THREATENS TO END IN DISLIKE ... 80

CHAPTER X
THE EXISTENCE OF DISLIKE IS EVIDENT ... 96

CHAPTER XI
DISLIKE INCREASES ... 109

CHAPTER XII
THE TROYAS ... 124

CHAPTER XIII
A CAUSE FOR WAR ... 138

CHAPTER XIV
DISLIKE IS STILL ON THE INCREASE ... 145

CHAPTER XV
DISLIKE INCREASES UNTIL IT ENDS IN A DECLARATION OF WAR ... 155

CHAPTER XVI
NIGHT ... 160

Contents

CHAPTER XVII
LIGHT IN DARKNESS.................................... 168

CHAPTER XVIII
THE TROOP.. 182

CHAPTER XIX
TERRIBLE COMBAT—STRATAGEM........................... 195

CHAPTER XX
RUMORS—FEARS... 211

CHAPTER XXI
FEAR IS EXCITED...................................... 220

CHAPTER XXII
INDIGNATION.. 236

CHAPTER XXIII
MYSTERY.. 247

CHAPTER XXIV
THE CONFESSION....................................... 252

CHAPTER XXV
UNFORESEEN SUCCESS—AN UNDISCOVERED FUGITIVE......... 257

CHAPTER XXVI
MARIA REMEDIOS....................................... 273

CHAPTER XXVII
A PRIEST'S TORMENT................................... 285

CHAPTER XXVIII
FROM PEPE REY TO DON JUAN REY........................ 299

CHAPTER XXIX
PEPE REY TO ROSARITO POLENTINOS...................... 307

CHAPTER XXX
THE ACT.. 308

CHAPTER XXXI
DOÑA PERFECTA.. 312

CHAPTER XXXII
THE END.. 322

CHAPTER XXXIII
L'ENVOI.. 333

LIFE OF GALDÓS

IT is said that the novelist Valdés, when he depicted the good town of Sarrio—see "The Fourth Estate"—so humorously, was aiming at Santander. Whether or not the Sarrian celebrities one reads of in the tale had actual counterparts in the place supposed to be described, we have no means of knowing, though it is certain that at least one eminent Spaniard of our day has graced that little city by residing there. This is Benito Pérez Galdós, the author of "Doña Perfecta," who went to live at Santander, which is pleasantly situated on the Bay of Biscay, some years ago. Though his chosen vocation is novel-writing, he still indulges himself as an amateur painter, and clings faithfully to the study of history. Indeed, a quarter of a century back he made a deep impression on the Spaniards by his "National Episodes," a series of historical romances dealing with Spain's emancipation from the Napoleonic yoke through British armed assistance, with an account of Joseph Bonaparte's rule at the Escurial included. Such titles as "Trafalgar," "Salamanca," "Saragossa," would be highly significant to the countrymen of

Life of Galdós

Galdós, and would be interesting to Frenchmen and Englishmen as well.

There is virtually nothing to say about the private life of this author. He was born in the year 1845, at Las Palmas, in the picturesque Canary Islands. After studying law for a few years at the Spanish metropolis, he became a writer for the press, contributing, especially, to "La Revista d'España" and "El Contemporaneo." His first novel, "The Fountain of Gold," appeared when he was about twenty-five, and was at once well received, like favor awaiting his "Glory," "The Unknown," "Leon Roch," and "Doña Perfecta." The subject of "Doña Perfecta" (1894) Galdós also utilized for a play, which enjoyed a long, prosperous career on the boards. Another dramatic venture, "Reality," was, however, not attended by success. But his novelistic work has continued to secure him admirers everywhere. As among the most notable of his later productions may be cited the trilogy of "Torquemada" (1890), "Marianela" (1893), "The Nazarene" (1895)—and the book now open before the reader.

DOÑA PERFECTA

CHAPTER I

VILLAHORRENDA—FIVE MINUTES

WHEN the mixed train No. 65 (it is unnecessary to name the line) drew up at the small station situated between kilometres 171 and 172, nearly all the second and third class passengers remained sleeping or yawning within their compartments, for the piercing cold of the early morn did not invite one to take a walk on the dreary platform. The only first-class passenger who had traveled by the train briskly descended, and, advancing toward the porters, inquired if that were the station of Villahorrenda. (This name, like many others, as will afterward be seen, is fictitious.)

"We are at Villahorrenda," replied the conductor, whose voice was almost drowned by the cackling of some hens, which, at that moment, had been put into the freight car. "I had forgotten to call you, Señor de Rey. I believe they are waiting you yonder with the horses."

"But it is devilish cold," observed the traveler, wrapping himself up in his cloak. "Is there no place where one can rest and obtain refreshment before taking a journey on horseback across this frozen country?"

He had not finished speaking when the conductor, recalled to the urgent duties of his office, walked off, leaving our unknown cavalier with the words on his lips. This latter perceived another of the employees approaching him, with a lantern swinging in his right hand, which moved to the measure of his step, projecting geometrical series of luminous undulations. The light fell on the ground, forming a zigzag similar to that described by a shower from a watering-pot.

"Can one find a place in which to eat or sleep at Villahorrenda?" demanded the traveler of the man with the lantern.

"There is nothing here," replied he, dryly, running toward those who were loading, and letting off such a volley of oaths, curses, blasphemies, and atrocious invocations that the very fowls, scandalized by such gross brutality, protested from within their baskets.

"The best thing I can do is to get away from here as quickly as possible," said the gentleman to himself. "The conductor told me that the horses were yonder." He was reflecting thus, when he felt a subtle, respectful hand gently draw him from the shelter. He turned round, and saw a dark mass of gray cloth, and through its principal fold he

discerned the nut-brown, astute countenance of a
Castilian laborer. He noted that the man was
of that tall stature which distinguishes the poplar
from the rest of the vegetable kingdom; he saw
the sagacious eyes which sparkled beneath the
broad brim of the old velvet hat; he saw the
tanned, hard hand which grasped a green twig,
and the broad foot which, when he walked, caused
the spur to jingle.

"Are you Señor José de Rey?" he asked, taking
off his hat.

"Yes; and you," replied the gentleman, joyfully,
"are Doña Perfecta's servant, who has come in
search of me to conduct me to Orbajosa?"

"The same. When you are ready— The pony
runs like the wind. I should suppose Señor de
Rey to be a good horseman. It is true that the
race he comes of—"

"How do we go out?" questioned the traveler,
impatiently. "Come, let us get away, sir— What
is your name?"

"Pedro Lucas," replied the gray bundle, again
raising his hat; "but I am called Lycurgus. Where
is the Señor Don's luggage?"

"I see it there under the clock. There are three
lots. Two trunks and a world of books for Don
Cayetano. You take hold of the end."

A moment later cavalier and squire turned their
backs on the cabin, termed station, and turned into

a road which, dividing there, became lost among the neighboring naked hills, whence one obtained a vague glimpse of the miserable village of Villahorrenda. Three horses were in attendance to transport all, men and luggage. A fairly good pony was destined for the gentleman. Lycurgus rode a venerable, somewhat exhausted, though sure-footed hack; and the horse, which a stout young man, with active limbs and of zealous disposition, led by the bridle, was loaded with the luggage.

Before the caravan got under way, the train started, creeping along with that parsimonious sluggishness peculiar to mixed trains. Its passage, resounding each time from a greater distance, seemed to produce deep subterranean rumblings. On entering the tunnel of kilometre 172, it flung out a volume of steam, and a shrill shriek reechoed through the air. The tunnel gave forth white vapor from its black mouth, clamored like a trumpet, and at the sound of its powerful voice, villages, towns, cities, provinces awoke. Here crowed a cock, there another. Day had dawned.

CHAPTER II

A JOURNEY IN THE HEART OF SPAIN

THE journey commenced; they left the wretched huts of Villahorrenda to one side; and the gentleman, who was young and handsome, spoke in these terms:

"Tell me, Señor Solon—"

"Señor Lycurgus, at your service—"

"That is, Señor Lycurgus, I would say that you are a wise legislator of olden times. Pardon the mistake. But, to the point. Tell me, how is my aunt?"

"Ever sprightly," replied the laborer, making his horse advance. "Years seem to leave no mark on Doña Perfecta. Truly it is said that the good God grants her a long life. This angel of the Lord might live thus a thousand years. If the blessings showered on her on earth were feathers, the señora would require no other wings with which to fly to heaven."

"And my cousin, Señorita Rosarito?"

"There is one whom her friends love much!" responded the villager. "What can I say of Señorita Rosarito, but that she is her mother's living

11

portrait? A fine jewel you will carry off, Señor Don
José, if it be true, as reported, that you have come
to marry her. Every one with their mates, and the
young lady will have nothing to complain of.
There is much difference between man and man."

"And Señor Don Cayetano?"

"He is always toiling among his books. He has
a library which is larger than the cathedral; he
likewise scratches up the earth to seek for stones
full of fantastical scrawls, which 'tis said the
Moors wrote."

"At what time shall we reach Orbajosa?"

"At nine o'clock, God willing. The señora will
soon be gratified with the sight of her nephew—
And Señorita Rosarito was busy yesterday preparing your room— As they have not seen you, both
mother and daughter were excited, wondering
whether Señor Don José would be like this or that.
Now the time has arrived when letters are silent,
and tongues shall speak. The cousin will see her
cousin, and all will be glory and rejoicing. 'God
will appear, and we shall prosper,' they remarked
to each other."

"As my aunt and cousin do not know me yet,"
said the gentleman, laughing, "they are not prudent in laying plans."

"True, for 'tis said that one feeds the steed and
another saddles it," answered the laborer. "But
the countenance does not deceive— What a treas-

ure you will win! And what a nice young man
will she!"

The cavalier did not hear Lycurgus's last words,
for he became somewhat meditative. They had
reached an angle of the road, when the peasant,
changing his course, said:

"We must now turn off in that direction. The
bridge is broken, and we can only ford the river
by the Cerrillo de los Lirios."

"The Cerrillo de los Lirios?" [the Hill of the
Iris] said the gentleman, roused from his reflections. "How poetic names abound in these very
ugly places! Since I started for this country, I
have been surprised at the horrible irony of names.
Such a spot distinguished by its wild aspect, and
the desolate sadness of its black landscape, is termed
Valleameno [Pleasant Vale]. Such a tiny hamlet
of mud cabins, which is miserably situated in an
arid plain, and proclaims its poverty in different
ways, has the insolence to call itself Villarica
[Rich Town]; and then a stony, dusty fissure, where
even thistles will not grow, yet designates itself
Valdeflores [Valley of Flowers]. And is that the
Cerrillo de los Lirios which we have before us?
But where are the irises, man of God? I see but
stones and discolored grass. Were they to call this
the Cerrillo de la Desolación [Hill of Desolation],
then would they call it aright. Excepting Villahorrenda [Horrid Town], which appears to have

received its name and form at the same time, all else is irony. Fine words, prosaic, miserable reality. The blind should be happy in this country, which to the tongue is a paradise, but to the eyes a hell."

Lycurgus either did not hear Señor de Rey's remarks or did not pay any heed to them. When they had forded the river, which, impatient and turbulent, rushed on with great precipitation, as though fleeing from its own banks, the peasant stretched out his arm toward some lands, which lay to the left, of large, denuded extent, and said:

"Those are the Poplars of Bustamente."

"My lands!" exclaimed the gentleman, gaily, gazing on the sad fields, lighted up by the first rays of the morning sun. "It is the first time that I look upon the patrimony inherited from my mother. The poor woman thought so much of this country, and related such wondrous things about it to me, that I, being but a child, believed that to live here meant to live in glory. Fruit, flowers, game—both large and small—mountains, lakes, rivers, poetic rivulets, pastoral hills, all these were at the Poplars of Bustamente, in that blessed land, the best and most beautiful of all lands— The deuce! The inhabitants of this country live by imagination. If, in my childhood, carried away with my good mother's ideas and enthusiasm, I had been brought hither, these denuded hills, these dusty or submerged plains, these very ancient peasants' houses, these exhausted wells, this wretched, slothful desolation on which I am gazing, might also have proved to me enchanting."

"It is the best land in the country," declared Lycurgus, "and for chickpea there is none equal to it."

"Then I commend it, for since I inherited these celebrated lands they have never brought me in a peso."

The wise Spartan legislator scratched his ear, and heaved a sigh.

"But I am told," continued the gentleman, "that some contiguous landowners have put their plow in these large estates of mine, and, little by little, will deprive me of them. There are no landmarks, no boundary, no true proprietorship here, Señor Lycurgus."

The laborer, after a pause, during which his subtle mind seemed occupied in profound examination, expressed himself in this manner:

"Uncle Paso Largo, who is known as the 'Philosopher,' so great is his prudence, plowed the Alamillos, above the hermitage; and, let them say what they will, has gathered six measures."

"What an incomparable school!" exclaimed the cavalier, laughing. "I will bet that he has not been the only—philosopher."

"Well," said the other, "he who knows, plays, and if the dovecot is not deficient in food, neither will it be in doves— But I might tell you, Señor Don José, that the master's eye fattens the cow, and you are now here to see whether you can recover your rent."

"It may not be so easy, perhaps, Señor Lycurgus," replied the gentleman, as they were about to enter a path, on the sides of which might be seen some beautiful wheat that, by its exuberance and early ripeness, delighted the eye. "This field appears to be better cultivated. I perceive that all is not sorrow and misery in Los Alamillos."

The peasant's face took an expression of pity, and he, affecting a certain disdain toward the fields praised by the traveler, said, in a very humble tone:

"Señor, this is mine.'"

"Excuse me," responded the gentleman quickly; "I feel like putting my sickle to your field. It seems that the philosophy of the place is contagious."

They immediately reached a glen which was barren, and where there was a checked rivulet; and, this passed, they entered a very stony field, without the slightest signs of vegetation.

"This is very bad ground," remarked the gentleman, turning his face round to look at his guide and companion, who loitered a short distance behind. "It would be very difficult to make anything of it, for it is nothing but mud and sand."

Lycurgus very meekly responded:

"This—is yours."

"I see that all that is bad here is mine," remarked the gentleman, laughing jovially.

As he spoke they gained the road again.

Now daylight, entering in joyous irruption by all the windows and skylights of the Spanish horizon, inundated the fields with clear splendor. The immense cloudless sky seemed to grow larger, and to become more distant from the earth, to gaze upon it, and rejoice in the contemplation from a greater altitude. The desolate, treeless earth, at intervals of straw color, chalky in places, divided into triangles and yellow and blackish quadrilaterals, gray or slightly greenish, in a certain manner resembled a ragged cape, spread out in the sun. Over this wretched cape Christian and Islamite had fought epic battles. Glorious fields; yes, but ancient combats had rendered them horrible.

"I fancy that the sun will be very hot to-day, Señor Lycurgus," observed the gentleman, disembarrassing himself partly of his cloak. "What a sad road! I do not see a single tree in sight. Here all is contrariwise. There is no cessation to the irony. Why, since there are neither short nor tall poplars, are these called Alamillos?"

Lycurgus did not reply to this question, for his whole mind was centred on distant sounds which had just become perceptible, and which, moreover, rendered his hack restless; while he explored the road and distant hills with sombre gaze.

"What is the matter?" questioned the traveler, likewise halting.

"Do you carry arms, Señor Don José?"

"A revolver— Ah! I understand. Are there robbers?"

"Maybe—" replied the peasant with reserve. "I thought I heard a shot."

"We will go and see—forward!" said the gentleman, spurring on his nag. "They can not be so formidable."

"Be quiet, Señor Don José!" exclaimed the villager, detaining him. "These people are worse than devils. The other day they killed two gentlemen who were going to catch the train— Let us leave them to their fun. Gasparon el Fuerte, Pepito Chispillas, Merengue, and Ahorca Suegras shall not look on my face. Let us take the footpath."

"Forward, Señor Lycurgus."

"Retire, Señor Don José," responded the peasant, in a dolorous tone; "you do not know these men. They are the same who last month robbed the Carmelite Church of its cibory, the Virgin's crown, and two candlesticks; they are the same who two years ago sacked the Madrid train."

Don José, on hearing these lamentable antecedents, felt his intrepidity give way slightly.

"Do you see that high hill some distance off? Then, it is there that these rogues hide in caves, which are known as the 'Retreat of the Cavaliers.' "

"The Cavaliers?"

"Yes, sir. When the Civil Guard becomes careless, they come down to the highway proper, and rob whom they can. Do you not remark a cross at the turn of the road, which was erected in memory of the murder of the Justice of Peace of Villahorrenda during the elections?"

"Yes, I see the cross."

"There, there is an old house where they lie in wait for travelers. We designate that place 'The Delights.' "

"The Delights?"

"If all who have been murdered and robbed on passing there were to come back to life again an army might be formed of them."

As they were conversing thus, shots were heard nearer, which somewhat disturbed the travelers' valiant hearts, but not that of the young fellow who attended the luggage, who, dancing for joy, begged Lycurgus's permission to advance, that he might see the battle which was raging so near. Observing the young fellow's decision, Don José, ashamed of having felt afraid, or at least some little respect for the robbers, exclaimed, spurring on his pony:

"Then we will all go. We may, perhaps, be able to render some assistance to the unhappy travelers who are in such dire distress, and to make these Cavaliers bite the dust."

The peasant tried to convince the young man of the danger attending his proposal, as of the uselessness of his generous idea, for the robbed, robbed would be and perhaps dead, and in that case would be beyond all help.

The gentleman insisted in spite of such judicious counsel; the villager replied, making the most lively resistance, when the presence of two or three wagoners, who advanced tranquilly along the road, leading a wagon, decided the question. The danger could not be great when these came so carelessly singing gay couplets; and this was really the fact, for the shots, so these men declared, had not proceeded from the robbers, but from the Civil Guard, who, by these means, desired to clip the wings of half a dozen footpads, whom they were conducting in a body to prison.

"Now I knew it would be so," said Lycurgus, pointing to some smoke which rose on the left-hand side of the road, and at regular distances. "They have peppered them there. This was sure to happen one day if not another."

Doña Perfecta

The gentleman did not understand.

"I assure you, Señor Don José," added the Lacedemonian legislator, energetically, "that it serves them right; for it is of no use to take these rogues' part. The judge imprisoned them for a time, and afterward liberated them. At the end of six years' consideration, they would be sent to the house of correction, to escape better, or pardoned, and would then return to the 'Cavaliers' Retreat.' It is better to act thus—fire on them! They might convey them to prison, and when passing a place, purposely— 'Ah, dog! you wish to escape—pum! pum!—' That was done summarily, the witnesses called, the view commended, the sentence given— all in a minute. It is truly said: 'The fox knows much, but he that traps him knows more.' "

"Then, forward, and let us hasten, for this road, though wide, has nothing to recommend it," said Rey.

On passing near to the "Delights," they saw, at a short distance from the road, the Guards who, some minutes before, had executed the curious sentence, as the reader knows. The boy was much grieved, because he was not allowed to go to see the palpitating corpses of the robbers, which formed a terrible group in the distance; and all continued forward. But they had not proceeded twenty paces ere they heard a horse's gallop behind them, traveling so rapidly that it soon overtook

them. Our traveler looked round and beheld a
man, or rather a Centaur, since no more perfect
harmony could be conceived between rider and
horse; the rider was of fair, sanguine complexion,
large, ardent eyes, fine head, black mustaches,
middle-aged, and of general brusk, provoking
appearance, with indications of great personal
strength. Mounted on a superb horse of fleshy
breast, like to those of the Parthenon, and capari-
soned according to the picturesque fashion of the
country, he carried a large leathern portmanteau
on the croup, on the strap of which might be seen
in large letters the word "Courier."

"Hullo! good-day, Señor Caballuco," said Lycurgus, saluting the horseman, when he drew near.
"We had the advantage, but you will arrive before
us at that rate."

"Let us rest a short time," replied Caballuco,
accommodating his animal's step to that of the
travelers, and attentively observing the chief of
the three. "You are in good company—"

"The gentleman," said Lycurgus, smiling, "is
the nephew of Doña Perfecta."

"Ah! Very pleased!"

Both bowed. Caballuco, it may be remarked,
performed his urbanities with an expression of
haughtiness and superiority, which at least revealed the consciousness of great worth or high
position in the district. When the proud horseman

left them for a short time to speak with the two
Civil Guards who had come up, the traveler questioned his guide:

"Who is that curious chap?"

"Caballuco."

"And who is Caballuco?"

"What!—have you never heard him mentioned?" inquired the peasant, astonished at Doña
Perfecta's nephew's supine ignorance. "He is a
very valiant man, a great horseman, and the first
gentleman in all the country-side. We love him
dearly in Orbajosa: then he is—and truly do they
affirm it—as good as God's benediction. When
he goes yonder he is a power, and the Provincial
Governor raises his hat to him."

"When there are elections—"

"And the Madrid Government inscribes official
letters with many 'Your Excellencys' therein—
He shoots like a St. Christobel, and can wield all
weapons as we can our own fingers. When anything is the matter we can not manage without
him, and shots are heard every night at the city
gates. He is a man worth some money; he is as
ready to scour kitchen utensils as to sweep. He is
very good to the poor, but any outsider who comes
and dares to touch a hair of one of Orbajosa's sons
must settle with him. Madrid soldiers rarely
come here; when they were stationed in this locality, blood was shed every day, because Caballuco

sought quarrels with one if not with another. Now it seems he lives poorly, and is satisfied with the position of courier; but it is like an incitement to the corporation that another revolt take place, and an end be put to him. I can not understand how it happens that you should have never heard him mentioned in Madrid, for he is the son of a famous Caballuco who took part in the revolt, who was likewise the son of another Caballuco, who also formed part in a still more ancient revolt. And as 'tis now reported that revolution is again showing itself, for all is twisted and in revolt, we fear that Caballuco will join it, thus finishing the exploits of his father and grandfather, who, to our honor, were born in this town."

Our traveler was surprised to find a species of knight errantry existing in the places he was about to visit, but found no further opportunity for new questions, as he who was the subject of them rejoined them, saying, ill-humoredly:

"The Civil Guard has despatched three. I had already cautioned them. We shall talk to the Provincial Governor to-morrow, and I—"

"Are you going to X—?"

"No, the governor is coming here, Señor Lycurgus. Do you know that a couple of regiments are to be stationed at Orbajosa?"

"Yes," said the traveler, quickly, smiling. "I heard it said in Madrid that there was a fear of some party rising in this country. It is as well to be prepared."

"They talk nothing but rubbish in Madrid!—" exclaimed the Centaur violently, accompanying this declaration by a string of those vocables which raise a blister. "There is nothing but knavery in Madrid. Why should they send soldiers to us? To levy more contributions and conscripts? By the life of . . . if there be a revolt, must it necessarily be here? As to you," he added, glancing slyly at the young horseman, "so you are Doña Perfecta's nephew?"

The man's tone and insolent look vexed the young fellow.

"Yes, señor. Does it matter to you?"

"I am a friend of the señora, and love her as I do the children of my eyes," said Caballuco. "As you are going to Orbajosa, we shall see each other there."

And, saying no more, he put spurs to his charger, which, setting off, disappeared in a cloud of dust.

After another half-hour's journey, during which neither Señor Don José nor Lycurgus appeared very communicative, an old village, situated on a hill, appeared to both, from which stood detached some black towers and the ruinous fabric of a castle at the highest point. A medley of deformed walls, of gray mud cottages, dusty as the soil, formed the base, with some fragments of embattled walls, under the shadow of which rose a thousand humble cabins, with their miserable clay frontispieces, like to the bloodless, famished faces which beg an alms of the passer-by. A poor river encircled, like a tin girdle, the town, refreshing some orchards in its course—the only spots of verdure which delighted the eye. Men on horseback or on foot entered and issued, and the human movement, though little, gave a certain vital appearance to that great abode whose architectonic aspect was rather that of ruin and death than of progress and life. The innumerable repulsive beggars who crawled along on either side of the road, begging charity of the traveler, offered a most piteous spectacle. Impossible to conceive existences more in unison and benefiting that sepulchre where a city was not only interred but also corrupted.

When our travelers approached, some bells were ringing discordantly, indicating by their expressive sound that the mummy yet possessed a soul.

This was Orbajosa, a city in no geographical map if not in that of Spain, having 7,324 inhabitants, a corporation, an Episcopal seat, a judicial district, a seminary, a stud-farm, an institute for instruction, and other official features.

"They are ringing for High Mass at the cathedral," said Lycurgus. "We have arrived sooner than I expected."

"The aspect of your country," observed the gentleman, examining the panorama before him, "could not well be more displeasing. The historical city—Orbajosa—the name of which is doubtless a corruption of 'Urbs Augusta,' is like a large rubbish-hole."

"You only see the suburbs from here," affirmed the guide in disgust. "When you enter the Calle Real and the Calle del Condestable, you will see buildings equal in beauty to the cathedral."

"I have no desire to speak ill of Orbajosa before I know it," replied the gentleman. "That which I said was not intended as a sign of depreciation; humble and wretched, even as beautiful and arrogant, this city will ever be dear to me, not only because it is my mother's country, but because it is the home of some whom I love, even without knowing them. Let us then enter this august city."

They now proceeded down a causeway proximate to the main streets, and round by the mud walls of the orchards.

"Do you see that large house at the extremity of this large orchard, the wall of which we are now passing?" asked Lycurgus, pointing to an enormous thick wall adjoining the only dwelling which had a comfortable, pleasant aspect.

"Ah! is that my aunt's residence?"

"Exactly. It is the back part of the house that we see. The front faces on the Calle del Condestable, and has five iron balconies which resemble

27

five castles. The beautiful orchard enclosed by this wall pertains to the house, and were you to raise yourself in your stirrups you could see over."

"Then we are at home now," said the gentleman. "Can not we go in this way?"

"There is a small door, but the señora has ordered it to be closed up."

The gentleman raised himself in the stirrups, and, stretching out his neck as far as possible, peered over the wall.

"I can see all the orchard," he declared. "There, beneath some trees, is a woman, a little girl—a young lady."

"That is Señorita Rosario," said Lycurgus.

And he also raised himself in his stirrups to look over.

"Ah! Señorita Rosarito!" he shouted, making very significative gestures with his right hand. "Here we are. I have brought your cousin."

"She has seen us," said the gentleman, stretching out his neck to the utmost. "But, unless I am mistaken, there is a priest with her—a sacerdotal gentleman."

"It is Penitentiary," replied the peasant, frankly.

"My cousin saw us—she has left the priest alone, and has run into the house—she is pretty."

"As the sun."

"She is ruddier than a cherry. Let us go, let us go, Señor Lycurgus."

CHAPTER III

PEPE REY

BEFORE proceeding further, it may be as well to explain who Pepe Rey was, and what business took him to Orbajosa.

When Brigadier Rey died in 1841, his two children, Juan and Perfecta, had just married, the latter the richest proprietor in Orbajosa, the former a young girl from the same town. Perfecta's husband was known as Don Manuel Maria José de Polentinos; and Juan's wife as Maria Polentinos; but, notwithstanding the similarity of surname, their relationship was but a very slight one, one of those rarely recognized. Juan Rey was a worthy jurisconsult, had been graduated at Seville, and exercised the calling of barrister in that same town for thirty years with as much honor as profit. In 1845 he became a widower with an only son, who was already growing mischievous, and who found his sole amusement by constructing in the courtyard attached to the house viaducts, dikes, reservoirs, dams, aqueducts, and letting the water flow through these fragile works. His father allowed him his own way and said: "You will be an engineer."

Perfecta and Juan lost sight of each other when they married, as she went to live in Madrid with the very wealthy Polentinos, who had a ready hand to squander their great opulence. Gambling and women captivated Manuel Maria José's heart to such an extent that he would have wasted all his wealth had not death seized him before he could quite dissipate it. In a night of debauchery, the days of that very rich man were suddenly ended. He had been sucked so voraciously by the Court sharpers and the insatiable vampire of play that his only legacy was a daughter of a few months old. On the death of Perfecta's husband the family experienced no further dread, but a great conflict began. The Polentinos' house was ruined; the landed property in danger of being seized by the usurers; all was in disorder; enormous debts, lamentable administration in Orbajosa, discredit and ruin in Madrid.

Perfecta appealed to her brother, who, coming to the poor widow's aid, acted so diligently and skilfully, that in a short time the greater part of the danger had disappeared. He, first of all, persuaded his sister to reside at Orbajosa, administering her vast property herself, while he settled the formidable claims of the creditors in Madrid. Little by little the house was relieved of the heavy burden of its debts, for worthy Juan Rey, who was the best man in the world for such matters, fought valiantly; he made contracts with the principal creditors, arranged times of payment; and the result of this clever management was that the Polentinos' rich patrimony was saved from wreck, and would continue, for long years, to shed splendor and glory on the illustrious family.

Perfecta's gratitude was so lively that on writing to her brother from Orbajosa, where it was decided that she should live until her daughter grew up, she said, among other endearments:

"You have been more than a brother to me, and to my daughter more than her own father. How shall we repay you for so much kindness? Ay! dear brother, from the moment my child begins to lisp and to pronounce a name, I will teach her to bless yours. My obligations will endure my whole life. Your unworthy sister feels that she will never find an opportunity of showing you how much she loves you, and of recompensing you in a manner befitting the greatness of your soul, and your heart's immense goodness."

When this was written Rosarito was two years old. Pepe Rey, shut up in a Sevillian college, drew lines on paper, and was busy in proving that *"the sum of the interior angles of a polygon is equal to twice as many right angles, less four, as the figure has sides."* These vexatious truths greatly puzzled him. Years upon years rolled by. The boy grew and continued to make lines. At last, he drew one which he named, "From Tarragona to Mount Blanc." His first formal plaything was the 120 metres bridge over the Francoli River.

Doña Perfecta resided at Orbajosa during the greater part of this time. As her brother never quitted Seville, some years passed by without their seeing each other. A quarterly letter, as punctually written and as punctually replied to, formed the communication between two hearts whose affection neither time nor distance could cool.

In 1870, when Don Juan Rey, satisfied that he had worthily fulfilled his mission in society, retired to live in his beautiful house at Puerto Real, Pepe, who had for some years been working with various constructing companies, undertook a journey with a view to study in Germany and England. His father's fortune (as large as it might well be in Spain, when its noble origin was a writing-desk) allowed him short periods of freedom from the yoke of material work. A man of high ideals, and with an immense love of science, he derived the greatest pleasure from the observation and study of the prodigies that the genius of the century had worked in the culture, physical well-being, and moral perfection of man.

On his return from his journey his father revealed a most important project to him, and Pepe, who believed that he was referring to a bridge, harbor, or at least to the reparation of lakes, was apprised of his error when Don Juan gave vent to his thoughts in these terms:

"We are in March, and Perfecta's quarterly letter has come as usual. My dear son, read it, and if you can conform with this holy and exemplary woman's wishes, my dear sister's, you will bestow upon me the greatest happiness possible in my old age. If you do not approve of this project, then reject it at once, although I should feel grieved; but there shall not be the shadow of a command on my part. It would be unworthy of us both were this realized by an obstinate father's compulsion. You are free to accept it or not, and should you feel the slightest disinclination, arising from an affair of the heart or any other cause, I do not wish you to do violence to your inclinations for my sake."

Pepe placed the letter on the table, after glancing over it, and observed quietly:

"My aunt is desirous that I should marry Rosarito."

"She replied, gladly accepting my idea," said his father, deeply affected. "For it was my idea . . . yes, some time ago, I conceived it some time since, but did not care to mention it to you before hearing my sister's opinion. As you see, Perfecta is overjoyed with my plan; says that she had also thought of it, but dared not mention it to me, for you are . . . does she not say so? You are a man of singular merit, while her daughter is a village maiden, who has not received a brilliant education, and who possesses no worldly attractions. So she says. Poor sister! How good she is! I see that you are not angry; I see that you do not consider my project absurd, although it somewhat resembles the officious arrangement of parents in olden times, who married their children without consulting them, and often made premature, unequal marriages. God willing, this would be, or promises to be, one of the happiest. It is true that we do not know my niece; but you and I feel assured of her virtue, discretion, modesty, and noble simplicity. For she lacks nothing, even good looks. My opinion," he added gaily, "is that you should take the road to this remote Episcopal town, and there, in my sister's and her graceful Rosarito's presence, make up your mind if she is to be something more than a niece to me."

Pepe again took up the letter, and perused it carefully. His countenance neither expressed pleasure nor disgust. He looked as though he were examining a plan for the dovetailing of two iron roads.

"Certainly," continued his father, "in this distant Orbajosa, where, between parentheses, you have property which you might survey, life passes with the peacefulness and sweetness of the idyls. What patriarchal manners! What nobleness in such simplicity! What rustic, virginal peace! If, instead of being a mathematician you were a Latin scholar, you would exclaim, on entering there, the *ergo tua rura manebunt!* . . . What an admirable spot for the dedication of one's self to the contemplation of one's own soul, and for the preparation for good works! There, all is goodness and honor; there, falsehood and farce are not known as in our large cities; there, are regenerated those holy inclinations which the bustle of modern life has stifled; there, sleeping faith awakens, and one feels a lively, undefinable impulse within one's breast, resembling a puerile impatience which cries from the depth of one's soul, 'I wish to live.' "

A few days after this conference Pepe left Puerto Real. Some months before he had refused a Government commission to examine, from a mining point of view, the bed of the Nahara River, in the valley of Orbajosa. But the projects laid before him at the aforesaid conference gave rise to these reflections: "I must make the best of my time. God alone knows how long this courtship with its tediousness may last."

Going to Madrid, he solicited the commission to explore the bed of the Nahara, which they granted him without any difficulty, in spite of his not belonging officially to the mining corps; and he then set out, arriving by the mixed train, No. 65, as has already been seen, and received by Lycurgus's loving arms.

This excellent young man's age bordered on thirty-four years. He was of manly, herculean build, with rare perfection of form, and so haughty that, had he worn a military uniform, he would have presented the most warlike mien and figure that could possibly be imagined. He had reddish hair and beard, but his features did not possess the phlegmatic imperturbability of the Saxon race; on the contrary, they had such a lively expression that his eyes looked black, without being so. His person might have passed for a beautiful and finished model, and had he been a statue the sculptor would have engraved these words on the pedestal: "Intelligence, valor." If not in visible characters, yet were they vaguely expressed by the keenness of his glance, the powerful charm which was peculiar to his person, and by the sympathy invited by his endearing traits.

He was not a great talker; only on hearing insecure ideas and inconstant criticism was he propelled to verbosity. This worthy young man's profound moral feeling rendered him sparing of words in the disputes which the men of the day constantly held on different subjects, but in friendly conversation he displayed a piquant, discreet eloquence, always replete with good feeling, and a measured, just appreciation of worldly affairs. He would allow no false statements, no mystification, no playing upon words such as some intelligent people were fond of indulging in, and sometimes to uphold the privileges of reality Pepe Rey employed, not always kindly, the weapons of jest. This was almost a defect in the eyes of a large number of persons who esteemed him, because our young friend appeared somewhat disrespectful in the presence of the multitude of common feats in the world, which every one admitted. He was courageous then at the risk of diminishing his prestige. Rey knew not the gentle tolerance of the complying century, which had invented singular pretexts of language and of deeds to cover that which might prove displeasing to the vulgar eye.

This, and this alone, whatever calumniating tongues might say, was the man that Lycurgus introduced to Orbajosa at the time that the cathedral bell was ringing for High Mass. After looking over the wall and seeing the young girl and the Penitentiary, and remarking the former's swift course toward the house, the horsemen urged on their beasts and entered the Calle Real, where numerous vagrants paused to stare at the traveler as being a stranger trespassing in the patriarchal city. Turning to the right, in the direction of the cathedral, the bulky edifice of which seemed to dominate over the whole town, they arrived in the Calle del Condestable, which was narrow and paved, and resounded with the strident noise of the horses' shoes; so alarming the neighborhood that people appeared at the windows and balconies to satisfy their curiosity. The lattices were opened with a peculiar jerk, and divers faces, nearly all belonging to the fair sex, looked out from above and below. When Pepe Rey reached the architectonic threshold of the Polentinos' home a multitude of commentaries had already been made on his figure.

CHAPTER IV

THE COUSIN'S ARRIVAL

THE confessor, on Rosarito quitting him so abruptly, glanced up at the wall, and, seeing the heads of Lycurgus and his companion, muttered: "Behold! the prodigy already here!"

He remained reflecting a short time, holding his cloak together with both hands crossed over his abdomen, looking on the ground, with his gold spectacles gently sliding down the bridge of his nose, his under-lip protruding and moist, and his grayish black eyebows slightly knit. He was a holy, merciful man, of no common wisdom, of confirmed clerical habits, somewhat more than a sexagenarian, with an affable expression, sagacious and polite, a great distributor of advice and warnings to men and women. He had been for many years the master for Latin and rhetoric at the institute, which noble profession brought him a great wealth of Horatian quotations and flowery tropes, which he used gracefully and opportunely. It is unnecessary to add anything further about this personage, except that, on hearing the trot of **horses hastening** down the Calle del Condestable, he regulated his mantle, straightened his hat, which did not fit his venerable head at all well, and, walking toward the house, muttered:

"Let us go and see this prodigy."

In the meantime Pepe had dismounted from his pony, and was received in Doña Perfecta's loving embrace—even on the doorstep, her face bathed in tears, and only able to utter short, stammering words—sincere expression of her affection.

"Pepe . . . but how tall you are! . . . and bearded. It seems to me but yesterday since I nursed you on my knees—now you are a man, quite a man. How the years roll by! . . . Jesus! here is my daughter, Rosarito."

Speaking thus they had reached a room on the ground floor, usually used as a reception-room, and Doña Perfecta presented her daughter.

Rosarito was a young girl of delicate, weak appearance, which announced inclinations termed by the Portuguese "saudades." Something of pearly softness, such as the majority of novelists bestow on their heroines, and without which sentimental gloss neither Enriqueta nor Julia would seem interesting, was perceptible in her fine, pure features. But the most striking thing about Rosarito was her expression of sweetness and modesty, which, however, did not hide the fact that she was not perfect. Not that she was ugly; but it is equally certain that it would have been hyperbolical to have called her beautiful, taking the word in its literal sense. Doña Perfecta's daughter's real beauty consisted in a kind of transparency, resembling mother-of-pearl, alabaster, ivory, and other materials used in the descriptive composition of human faces; a species of transparency, I say, through which the depths of her soul were clearly seen; depths, not cavernous and horrible as those of the sea, but like those of a gentle limpid river. But material was wanting for the completion of her person; she was deficient in depth, in surface. The vast wealth of her spirit overflowed, threatening to destroy its narrow banks. On her cousin saluting her, she blushed furiously, and only uttered silly words.

"You must be exhausted," said Doña Perfecta to her nephew. "We will prepare you some breakfast immediately."

"With your permission," replied the traveler, "I will rid myself of some of this dust from the road."

"Well thought of," said the señora. "Rosarito, show your cousin to the room prepared for him. Make haste, then, nephew, I am going to give my orders."

Rosarito took her cousin to a beautiful room on the ground floor. As soon as he entered it, Pepe recognized the diligent, loving hand of a woman in every detail. All was arranged with singular taste; and the comfort and freshness invited one to repose in so charming a nest. Everything was so superfluously exact, that it was almost amusing.

"Here is the bell rope," remarked Rosarito, taking hold of it, the tassel of which fell over the head of the bed. "You have but to extend your hand. The writing-table is placed there in such a manner that the light falls to the left. See, you may throw scraps of paper in that basket. Do you smoke?"

"I have that misfortune," replied Pepe Rey.

"Then you can throw your cigar-ends here," she said, touching a gilded utensil, filled with sand, with her foot. "There is nothing uglier than to see the floor littered with the remains of cigars. There is the lavatory. For your clothes, you have a wardrobe and a chest of drawers. I think the clock is not well placed here, and should be near the bed. If the light annoys you, you have but to draw the blind down by the cord—do you see?"

The engineer was enchanted. Rosarito threw back a window.

"See!" she said, "this window opens on to the orchard. The afternoon sun enters here. We have hung up a canary in a cage, which sings like a mad thing. If it annoys you, we will take it away."

She opened another window on the opposite side.

"This other window," she continued, "is on the street. Look! the cathedral can be seen from here; it is very beautiful, and is full of precious things. Many English come to visit it. Do not open both windows at once, as drafts are injurious."

"Dear cousin," replied Pepe, his soul inundated with inexplicable delight, "in all that is before me I perceive an angel's hand, which can be no other than yours. What a charming room this is! I could fancy that I have lived here all my life. It is conducive to peace."

Rosarito made no reply to these loving expressions, and, smiling, went out.

"Do not delay," she said from the door; "the dining-room is also on this floor—in the centre of the gallery."

Lycurgus entered with the luggage. Pepe rewarded him with a fee, to which the peasant was altogether unaccustomed, and he, after humbly tendering his thanks, placed his hand to his head, like one who would neither raise nor put on his hat, in an embarrassed tone, chewing his words, as though he were undecided whether to say or not to say something, and expressed himself thus:

"When would it be most convenient for me to speak with Señor Don José on a—on a small matter?"

"On a small matter? Why, now," replied Pepe, opening a trunk.

"No, it is not opportune," said the laborer. "Let Señor Don José rest; we have plenty of time. There are more days than sausages, as 'tis said; and one day follows another. You must rest, Señor Don José— When you care for a turn— The pony does not step badly— With that, good-day, Señor Don José. May you live a thousand years— Ah! I had forgotten," he added, returning to the doorway after a few minutes' absence, "if you have any message for the municipal judge—I am going now to speak with him respecting our little matter."

"Give him my compliments," replied Pepe gaily, not meeting with any better formula to relieve himself of the Spartan legislator's presence.

"Then God be with you, Señor Don José."

"Be off!"

The engineer had not taken off his things, when the sagacious eyes and brown physiognomy of Lycurgus again appeared.

"Excuse me, Señor Don José," said he, showing his white teeth as he laughed; "but I should like to tell him that you wish the matter arranged by friendly arbitrators. Although, as 'tis said, take your egg to law, and some will say 'tis white, and others, black."

"Man! will you go away?"

"I said so because I do not want to go to law. I want nothing with justice. To the wolf a blow,

and that in the forehead. God be with Señor Don
José. God preserve you to be good to the poor."

"Good-by, man, good-by."

Pepe locked his door and remarked:

"The people of this town seem to encourage
lawsuits."

CHAPTER V

WILL THERE BE DISCORD?

SHORTLY after Pepe entered the dining-room.
"If you take much breakfast," said Doña Perfecta to him, in a kind tone, "you will have no appetite for dinner. We dine here at one. The
country fashions will not suit you."

"I am enraptured with them, dear aunt."

"Then say which you would prefer; to make a
hearty breakfast now, or to take something light
that will stay your hunger until dinner time?"

"I should prefer a light refreshment, that I
may have the pleasure of dining with you; and,
could I have met with anything in Villahorrenda,
I should take nothing now."

"I presume there is no necessity to tell you to
make yourself at home. Here, you may give your
orders as you would in your own house."

"Thanks, aunt."

"But how much you are like your father," added
the señora, gazing at the young man with the
greatest admiration while he was eating. "I could
fancy that I am looking at my dear brother Juan.
He sits as you do, and eats even as do you. Indeed,

you and he are as alike in every way as two drops of water."

Pepe partook of the refreshments very frugally. The expressions, manner, and glances of his aunt and cousin inspired him with such confidence that he verily believed himself at home.

"Do you know what Rosarito said to me this morning?" asked Doña Perfecta, looking at her nephew. "Well, let me tell you: She said that you, a man accustomed to Court pageantry and etiquette, and to foreign fashions, would be unable to support this rather rustic simplicity in which we live, which is wanting in *bon ton,* for all here is very homely."

"What a mistake," replied Pepe, glancing at his cousin. "No one detests the deceit and nonsense which is termed 'High Society,' more than I. Believe me, there are times when, as some one, I know not who, says, I should like to lave my whole body in Nature; to live far from the bustle, in the solitude and calm of the country. A vehement desire for the repose of a life, free from strife, free from anxiety, neither envying nor being envied, as the poet says. My studies first, and my works afterward, have taken up so much of my time that I have not had the rest which was necessary, and which both my body and mind reclaimed; but as soon as I entered this house, dear aunt, dear cousin, I felt myself encompassed by the atmosphere of peace for which I had so longed. Do not then talk to me of high or low society, for gladly would I barter all for this corner."

He had scarcely finished speaking when the panes of the door, which formed the means of communication between the dining-room and the orchard, became obscured by the interposition of a large, black opacity. Some mirrors became illumined by a stray ray of light from the sun, the latch clicked, the door was opened, and the Penitentiary walked gravely into the room. He bowed, and almost swept the floor with the brim of his hat in doing so.

"This is the confessor of the cathedral," said Doña Perfecta, "a gentleman whom we much respect, and with whom I hope you will be friendly. Sit down, Señor Don Inocencio."

Pepe shook hands with the venerable priest, and they both took a seat.

"Pepe, if you are in the habit of smoking after eating, do not refrain from doing so," remarked Doña Perfecta, benevolently, "nor the confessor neither."

Good Don Inocencio seasonably drew forth from his cassock a large leather tobacco-pouch, which bore indisputable signs of long use; he opened it and took out two large pipes, one of which he offered to our friend. Rosarito found some matches in a large cardboard box, termed ironically by the Spaniards a "wagon," and soon the engineer and priest were both smoking.

"And what does Señor Don José think of our cherished town, Orbajosa?" questioned the canon, closing his left eye, as was his custom when smoking.

"I have not yet been able to form any opinion about the town," said Pepe. "But, from the little I have seen of it, it appears to me that it would not be a bad idea to sell Orbajosa to half a dozen large capitalists, and to employ two intelligent heads, who would direct the renovation of this country, and some thousands of active hands. From entering the town, even to the moment I arrived at the door of this house, I saw more than a hundred beggars. The majority are healthy, robust men. It is a pitiable sight, and oppresses one."

"For this was charity intended," affirmed Don Inocencio. "But for all that, Orbajosa is not a miserable town. You already know that the best garlic in all Spain is grown here. And more than twenty rich families reside here."

"True," remarked Doña Perfecta; "but the last years have been detestable owing to the droughts; but even then the granaries have not been empty; and, lately, many thousand strings of garlic have been in the market."

"During the many years that I have lived in Orbajosa," declared the clergyman, frowning, "I have seen innumerable persons here from Court, some attracted hither by the electoral conflicts, others to visit some abandoned piece of land, or to see the antiquities in the cathedral, and all have spoken of the English plows, of steam thrashing-machines, of weirs, banks, and I know not what other nonsense. The burden of the songs is, that this is very bad and might be improved. Better would it be to be carried off by a thousand demons than that gentlemen from Court should visit us; much better than to hear this continual clamor about our poverty and the grandeur and wonders of other parts. But the fool knows his house better than the wise man does his mustard-field; is not that so, Señor Don José? For, supposing that I do not believe in the least what you say, then that is sufficient. I know that we have before us one of the most eminent young men of modern Spain; a man capable of transforming our arid plains into a rich district. Neither am I vexed because you sing the old song about English plows, and horticulture, and agriculture. Not at all; men of so much, so very much talent can be excused showing so much depreciation of our humility. No, my friend; no, Señor Don José, you are authorized to do anything, even to tell us that we are little better than savages."

This declamation terminated with a marked tone of irony, and almost of impertinence, so that the young man felt annoyed; but he abstained from manifesting the least disgust, and continued the conversation, refraining from those points which might possibly wound the canon's susceptible patriotism, and thereby procure him an easy motive for discord. The latter rose when her ladyship began speaking to her nephew on family matters, and walked down the room several times.

The apartment was extensive and light, covered with paper of an ancient date, the flowers and branches of which, although discolored, preserved their primitive design, thanks to the care which pervaded the whole establishment. The clock—wherein the immovable weights and fickle pendulum were revealed to the eye, saying perpetually, "No"—occupied, with its variegated horary, the preeminent position among the solid dining-room furniture; a series of French copperplates, representing the exploits of the conqueror of Mexico, with prolix explanations at the foot, in which were mentioned a "Ferdinand Cortez," and a "Donna Marine," as improbable as the figures depicted by the ignorant artist, completed the decoration of the walls. Between the two glass doors which communicated with the orchard was a brass apparatus, which it is almost impossible to describe other than as serving as support to a parrot that stood there with the seriousness and circumspection peculiar to these animals, observant of all.

The ironical, harsh physiognomy of parrots, their green coat, red throat, yellow boots, and, lastly, the burlesque, hoarse words they learn to pronounce give them a wondrous, repulsive aspect— between the sublime and ridiculous.

The Penitentiary was the parrot's great friend. When he left the señora and Rosarito in conversation with the traveler, he approached the bird and allowed it to bite his little finger with the utmost complacency, saying:

"Cunning rascal! impostor! why do you not talk? You would be worth little were you not a prattler. The world is full of prattlers, both men and birds."

He then took in his own venerable hand some chickpea which was near him, and gave it to the parrot to eat. The bird began to call the servant, begging for chocolate, and distracted the two ladies and their guest in a conversation which could not be other than important.

CHAPTER VI

DISCORD ARISES THAT MIGHT HAVE BEEN PREVENTED

PRESENTLY Don Cayetano Polentinos, Doña Perfecta's brother-in-law, entered, with open arms, crying, "Come to me, my dear Señor Don José;" and they cordially embraced.

Don Cayetano and Pepe knew each other, as the distinguished savant and bookworm sometimes went to Madrid when a sale of books left by some deceased collector was announced. Don Cayetano was tall and thin, middle-aged; but continual study or suffering had much weakened him. He was sparing in his speech, kind, amiable, sometimes almost to exaggeration. Respected for his vast fund of knowledge, who would dare to insinuate that he was not a veritable prodigy? He was always mentioned with respect in Madrid. Had Don Cayetano resided in the capital, he could not have escaped belonging, in spite of his modesty, to all the existing academies and those likely to exist. But he liked a quiet spot; and where vanity holds sway in others' souls, his possessed a pure passion for books, love of solitary, recollected study, without any other ulterior attraction than those same books and study.

He had formed in Orbajosa one of the richest libraries in Spain, and there he passed the greater part of the day and night compiling, classifying, making notes, and sifting matters of precious worth; or, perhaps, realizing some unheard of, undreamt of work, worthy of so grand a head. His habits were patriarchal. He ate little, drank less, and his only dissipation consisted of a luncheon at Alamillos on fine days, and daily walks to a place known as Mundogrande, where he had recovered from the earth twenty centuries of Roman medals at least, and pieces of architrave, rare relics of unknown architecture, and other things of inestimable value.

Don Cayetano and Doña Perfecta lived in such harmony, that the peace of paradise was nothing to it. They never disputed. Assuredly, he never interfered in household affairs, nor she in those pertaining to the library, further than having it swept and cleaned every Saturday; respecting with religious admiration the books and papers on the table and their disposition.

After the questions and replies usual on such occasions Don Cayetano remarked:

"I have already seen the box. I am sorry that you did not bring me a 1527 edition. I shall have to go to Madrid for it myself. Are you going to remain here some time? The longer the better, dear Pepe. How pleased I am to see you here. Between us we will arrange part of my library, and will make an index of Gineta's writings. One can not always meet with such a talented man as you. You shall see my library. You will be satiated with reading. All that you could wish for. You shall behold marvels—veritable marvels, inappreciable treasures, rarities, which I alone possess—I only. But, truly, it seems to me that it must be dinner time. Am I not right, José? Am I not right, Perfecta? Am I not right, Rosarito? Am I not right, Señor Don Penitentiary? You are doubly Penitentiary, to-day. I say so, because you will help us to do penance."

The priest bowed, and, smiling sympathetically, displayed acquiescence.

The meal was cordial, and in all the dishes the disproportionate abundance of public banquets was manifested, at the cost of variety. There was provision for more than double the number of persons present. During the conversation various subjects were discussed.

"You must visit our cathedral," said the priest. "But there is little to see, Señor José. Certainly, you who have seen so many wondrous things in foreign lands will meet with nothing noteworthy in our ancient church. We, the poor clowns of Orbajosa, consider it divine. The great master,

Lopez de Berganza, in writing about it, termed it in the sixteenth century, *Pulchra augustina.* Nevertheless, men who are as learned as yourself may not find it meritorious, and may consider an iron market-place more beautiful."

Pepe Rey became each time more disgusted with the sagacious priest's irony, but resolved to contain himself, and dissemble his anger. He only replied vaguely.

Doña Perfecta then continued the discussion, and gaily expressed herself in these terms:

"Gently, Pepito; I warn you that should you speak ill of our holy church, our friendship will suffer. You know much, and are an eminent man; this we all understand; but if you do not declare this grand edifice to be the eighth wonder of the world, you will do well to reserve your judgment, and not to stuff us with nonsense."

"Far from thinking that the edifice is not beautiful," responded Pepe, "the little of the exterior that I have seen appeared to me exceedingly so. Do not be afraid, aunt, I have no wish to startle you; neither am I so very learned."

"Gently," said the priest, extending his hand, and allowing his mouth a brief respite, for, in talking, he had left off eating. "Halt there; I can not have you pretending modesty, Señor Don José; it is enough that we know your great worth, the great fame you enjoy, and the very important paper which proclaims it wherever you go. Men like you are not to be seen every day. But now, as I am praising your merits—"

He paused to proceed with his dinner, and then shortly after continued thus:

"Now as I am praising your merits, allow me to express another opinion, with my usual frankness. Yes, Señor Don José; yes, Señor Don Cayetano; yes, señora; and you, my child; science, as it is studied and propagated in modern times, is the death of sentiment and sweet illusions. With it the life of the soul is diminished; all is reduced to fixed rules, and even Nature's sublime enchantments disappear. Science destroys the marvels of art as it does faith in the soul. Science says that all is false, and it wishes to arrange all in ciphers and strokes, not only *maria adterras,* where we are ourselves, but also *coelumque profundem,* where God is. The admirable dreams of the soul, its mystic rapture; even the inspirations of the poets are false. The heart is a sponge, the brain a breeding maggot."

All laughed, while he swallowed a draft of wine.

"Come, will Señor Don José gainsay me?" continued the priest; "will he deny that science, as taught and propagated to-day, is going the right way to make of the world and human species a large machine?"

"That depends—" said Don Cayetano. "Everything has its *pro* and *contra.*"

"Will you take more salad, Señor Penitentiary?" asked Doña Perfecta. "It is seasoned with mustard to your taste."

Pepe Rey did not like to sustain silly disputes; he was not a pedant, nor vain of his learning; he particularly did not like to show it off before women and in a friendly reunion; but the priest's importunate, aggressive verbosity necessitated, he thought, a rebuke. To allow the priest to believe that he agreed with him would be to flatter the cleric, and he decided to express the most contrary opinions, and those most likely to mortify the sarcastic confessor.

"You wish to make fun of me," he said. "You shall see how bad I am to deal with."

And then in a louder tone he added:

"Certainly all that the priest said in a joking tone is true. But it is not our fault that science destroys with blows of the hammer, day after day, some vain idol—superstition, sophism, the thousand delusions of the past, some beautiful, some ridiculous, therefore all pertaining to the Church. The world of illusions, which is, as he would tell us, a second world, comes tumbling down with a clatter. The mysticism in religion, the routinary in science, the mannerism in art, fall, as fell the pagan gods, among scoffs. Adieu, stupid visions, mankind awakes and its eyes see light. Vain sentimentality, mysticism, fever, hallucination, delirium disappear; and that which was formerly diseased is to-day healthy, and revels in the inappreciable delight of the just appreciation of things. Fantasy, that terrible crack-brained woman, mistress of the house, becomes but the servant. Cast your eyes round on all sides, confessor, and you will see the admirable conjunct of reality, which has taken the place of the fabulous. The sky is not a vault; the stars are not lanterns; the moon is not a restless hunter, but an opaque mineral body; the sun is not a lazy vagabond coachman, but a fixed incendiary. The quicksands are not nymphs, but two shelves under the sea; the sirens are sea-calves; and, as regard persons, Mercury is Manzanedo; Mars is an old man with a thin beard, Count von Moltke: Nestor may be a gentleman in a greatcoat, who is known as M. Thiers; Orpheus is Verdi; Vulcan is Krupp; Apollo is some poet. What would you have more? Well, Jupiter, a god fit for the house of correction, should he still exist, does not discharge the thunderbolt, but the thunderbolt falls when electricity so disposes. There is no Parnassus, no Olympus, no Lake Stiria, no other Elysian Fields—Champs Elysées—than those in Paris. There is no descent now to the lower regions than that of geology, and this traveler, who is always returning, says there are no condemned souls in the earth's centre. There is no other ascent to heaven than that of astronomy, and that, to its regret, assures us that it has never seen the six or seven steps mentioned by Dante, nor the visions and mysteries of the Middle State. Only stars, distances, lines, enormities of space are to be met with, and nothing more. There are no false computations on the state of the world, because paleontology has counted the teeth of the skull in which we live, and ascertained its true age. Fiction, which is known as Paganism or Christian idealism, now no longer exists; imagination represents it. All the miracles possible reduce themselves to that which I am able to do when in my cabinet with a galvanic battery, an inductive wire, and a magnetic needle. There is no other multiplication of loaves and fishes than that effected by industry with its molds and machines, and printing offices, which imitate Nature, drawing millions of copies from a single model. In fact, my dear priest, the command has gone forth that all absurdities, falseness, illusions, visions, sensibilities, and preoccupation, which obscured man's understanding, shall cease. Let us celebrate its success."

When he had finished speaking a slight smile wreathed the priest's lips, and his eyes expressed extraordinary animation. Don Cayetano busied himself in making various forms, some rhomboid, some prismatic, with a piece of bread. But Doña

Perfecta was pale, and her eyes were fixed on the priest with persistent watchfulness. Rosarito contemplated her cousin with astonishment. He bent toward her and whispered:

"Take no notice, little cousin. I only said it to vex the cleric."

CHAPTER VII

DISCORD INCREASES

"Is it possible," asked Doña Perfecta, with a slight accent of vanity, "that Señor Don Inocencio is going to sit down quietly without contesting all and each one of these points?"

"Oh, no!" exclaimed the priest, arching his eyebrows, "I shall not measure my poor forces against so valiant a commander, and, moreover, one who is so well armed. Señor Don José knows everything—has the whole arsenal of exact sciences at his disposition. I well know that the doctrine he upholds is false, but I have neither the talent nor eloquence to combat it. I should employ the weapons of sentiment; I should employ theological arguments taken from revelation, faith, the Divine Word. But, ay! Señor Don José, who is an eminent *savant,* would laugh at faith, theology, revelation, the holy prophets, the Gospel— A poor, ignorant priest, an unfortunate man who is no mathematician, and who understands no German philosophy about the 'I' and the 'not I,' a poor dominie who knows but the lore of God and something of the Latin poets, can not enter into the lists."

Pepe Rey laughed openly.

"I see that Señor Don Inocencio," said he, "has taken all the nonsense that I uttered as serious— Come, Señor Don Inocencio, let us lay down our lances and terminate it. I feel sure that my real ideas and yours accord. You are a pious, well-instructed man, I am the ignorant one. If I have been pleased to jest, you must all pardon me, it is my nature."

"Thanks," responded the priest, visibly annoyed. "Shall we settle this now? I know well, we all know, that you have advanced your own ideas. It can not be otherwise. You are the man of the age. I can not deny that your knowledge is prodigious, truly prodigious. While you were speaking, I confess it, ingenuously, I, in deploring inwardly such great error, could not help at the same time admiring the sublimity of expression, the prodigious fecundity, the surprising method of your ratiocination, the strength of your arguments. What a head, what a head, Doña Perfecta, is your young nephew's! When I was at Madrid, and was taken to the Atheneum, I own that I was absorbed on beholding the wonderful genius with which God has gifted atheists and Protestants."

"Señor Don Inocencio," said Doña Perfecta, glancing alternately at her nephew and her friend, "I think that you, in judging this boy, go beyond the limits of benevolence— Do not be vexed, Pepe, nor heed what I say, because I am neither learned, philosophical, nor theological; but it seems to me that Señor Don Inocencio gives a proof of his great modesty and Christian charity in not replying to you, as he might do, did he feel so inclined—"

"Señora, for God's sake!" exclaimed the ecclesiastic.

"It is so," continued the lady. "Ever feigning to be vanquished— And he knows more than seven doctors. Ay, Señor Don Inocencio, how well your name suits you! But let us have no importunate humility here— If my nephew has pretensions— If he knows that which he has been taught and nothing more— If he has learned error, what could he desire more than that you should save him from the hell of his false doctrine?"

"Exactly. I desire nothing else but that the Señor Penitentiary should rescue me—" murmured Pepe, understanding that he had, without intending it, involved himself in a labyrinth.

"I am a poor cleric who only knows ancient science," averred Don Inocencio. "I recognize the immense worldly scientific value of Señor Don José, and before such a brilliant oracle I observe silence and prostrate myself."

So saying, the priest crossed his hands on his breast, and bowed his head.

Pepe Rey was troubled on account of the disagreeable position his aunt was placed in, from the silly dispute that he had entered into on the spur of the moment. He believed that the most prudent course he could pursue in so dangerous a predicament was to let the matter drop. And with that end in view he addressed a question to Don Cayetano, who, rousing himself from the lethargy which had overtaken him after dessert, offered to the diners the indispensable toothpicks, which stood in a china turkey.

"Yesterday I discovered a hand which clenched the hilt of a dagger, traced with curious figures. I must instruct you in them," observed Don Cayetano, delighted at being able to introduce his favorite theme.

"I suppose that Señor de Rey is also an expert in archeological things," remarked the priest, who, always implacable, followed up his victim, even to his most secret refuge.

"As to supposing," said Doña Perfecta, "are we to hear nothing all day but these childish quarrels? All the sciences are carried at one's finger ends. Universities and academies teach them as parrots are taught, granting patents for wisdom."

"Oh! that is unjust," replied the priest, noticing the pained expression on the engineer's countenance.

"My aunt is right," affirmed Pepe. "To-day we learn a little of all, and quit school with the rudiments of different studies."

"I should say," continued the priest, "that you are a great archeologist."

"I know nothing of that science," responded the young man. "Ruins are ruins, and I have never cared to sprinkle myself with their dust."

Don Cayetano pulled a very expressive grimace.

"I do not intend to condemn archeology," declared Doña Perfecta's nephew quickly, sorrowfully aware that he could not utter a word without wounding some one. "I well understand that the dust is historical. Those are precious, useful studies."

"You," said the Penitentiary, picking his last tooth, "prefer controversial studies. Now, an excellent idea has occurred to me, Señor Don José; you should be a lawyer."

"The law is a profession I detest," replied Pepe Rey. "I am acquainted with very respectable lawyers, my father among others, and he is one of the best of men. In spite of such a good example, I could not submit to exercise a profession which consists in defending the *pro* and *contra* of questions. I know no error, no preoccupation, no greater blindness, than that which families labor under who devote the majority of their young men to the law. The first and most terrible plague which afflicts Spain is the crowd of youthful advocates, to whose existence a fabulous number of lawsuits is necessary. Questions multiply in proportion to the demand. Even then, very many have no employment, and as a jurisconsult can not guide a plow or attend to the loom, this brilliant squadron of loungers is formed, full of pretensions, which foment quarrels, perturb politics, agitate dissensions, and engender revolutions. They must be fed. A great misfortune would it be were there lawsuits for all."

"Pepe, for God's sake, take care what you say," said Doña Perfecta, with marked severity. "But excuse him, Señor Don Inocencio—for he did not know that you have a nephew, who, although he has only recently left the university, is a prodigy of a lawyer."

"I spoke in general terms," declared Pepe firmly. "Being, as I am, the son of an illustrious advocate, I can not be totally ignorant that there are some who exercise that noble profession with great honor."

"No—my nephew is but a child yet," replied the priest, affecting humility. "Far be it from my thoughts to affirm that he is wonderfully learned, like Señor de Rey. Time will show— His talent is neither brilliant nor seductive. But I suppose that Jacintito's ideas are solid, his criticism healthy; that which he knows, he knows thoroughly— He understands neither sophistry nor hollow words—"

Pepe Rey became each time more uneasy. The idea of being, unintentionally, at variance with the ideas of his aunt's friends mortified him, and he resolved to maintain silence, fearing that Don Inocencio might ultimately throw the dishes at his head. Fortunately the small bell of the cathedral summoned the priest to the important duties pertaining to the choir, and relieved him from so painful a position. The venerable gentleman rose and took leave of all, behaving so courteously, so amiably, toward Pepe that the most intimate, ancient friendship might have united them. The cleric, after offering to serve him in any way, promised to introduce him to his nephew, that he might accompany him to see the town sights; expressing himself most kindly, he even deigned to slap the young fellow on the shoulder on his way out. Pepe Rey, delighted to accept these advances toward reconciliation, undoubtedly saw the heavens open when the priest quitted the dining-room and house.

CHAPTER VIII

IN ALL HASTE

A FEW moments after, the scene had changed.
Don Cayetano, seeking rest from his sublime labors
in a sweet dream that he was indulging in, stretched
himself out on a chair in the dining-room. Doña
Perfecta retired to attend to her household affairs.
Rosarito, seating herself near one of the glass doors
which gave on to the orchard, looked at her cousin,
saying, with the mute language of the eyes:

"Cousin, sit down near me, and tell me all that
you have to tell me."

This is how the mathematician interpreted it.

"Dear cousin," said Pepe, "how we must have
wearied you to-day with our disputes. God knows
that it gave me no pleasure to play the pedant as
I did; but it was the priest's fault— Do you know
that I find this priest peculiar?"

"He is an excellent person," replied Rosarito,
demonstrating the pleasure she derived from being
able to give her cousin all the data and news
needful.

"Oh, yes, an excellent person. Well he knows
it!"

"When you become better acquainted, you will know—"

"That I shall esteem him. But the fact of his being your mother's and your friend makes him mine—" affirmed the young man. "Does he come here often?"

"Every day. He often joins us," replied Rosarito ingenuously. "How good and amiable he is! and how fond he is of me!"

"Come, this gentleman already pleases me."

"He comes in the evening also to play at *ombre*," added the young girl. "In the early part of the evening several persons assemble here—the judge in the first place, the attorney-general, the dean, the bishop's secretary, the justice of the peace, the tax-gatherer, Don Inocencio's nephew—"

"Ah! Jacintito, the lawyer?"

"Yes. He is a poor young fellow, but as good as bread. Since he left the university, with his degree of doctor—for he is a doctor, and obtained marks for excellence— What do you think of that? Well, since his return, his uncle often brings him here. Mama is very fond of him— He is a very precise young man. He withdraws early with his uncle; he never frequents the Casino at night, neither gambles, nor is he at all dissipated; and he works in Don Lorenzo Ruiz's office, that of the best lawyer in Orbajosa. It is said that Jacintito will be a great lawyer some day."

"His uncle did not praise him to exaggeration," said Pepe. "I feel sorry I uttered so much nonsense about lawyers. Dear cousin, did I not cause you to feel uncomfortable?"

"Be quiet; I thought that you were right."

"But wasn't I a trifle—"

"Not at all, not at all."

"What a weight you have taken off my mind! The fact is, I found myself, without knowing how, in constant, painful opposition with the venerable priest. I felt it deeply."

"I believe you," replied Rosarito, raising her eyes to his, brimful of most loving expression, "but you are not like us."

"What does that mean?"

"I know I do not explain myself properly, cousin. I mean that it is not easy to you to accustom yourself to the ideas and conversation of people in Orbajosa. At least I fancy so—it is a mere supposition."

"Oh, no. I believe that you are equivocating."

"You come from another part, another world, where people are more active, wiser, are more refined in their manners, and have a habit of speaking ingeniously and in phrases that are the fashion— Maybe I do not explain myself clearly. I wish to say that you are accustomed to live in select society; you know so much. Here, you have not what is necessary to you; here, there are no learned men, no refinement. All is simplicity, Pepe. I fancy that you will become weary, that you will weary much, and, at last, will go away and leave us."

The sadness, which was Rosarito's normal expression, was so intensified that Pepe was deeply moved.

"You are mistaken, dear cousin. Neither do I bring those ideas you attribute to me here, nor are my character and judgment in discord with those around me. But let us suppose for a moment that they were."

"Let us suppose it—"

"In such a case, I have a firm conviction that between you and me, between us, dear Rosarito, a perfect harmony would be established. I can not be mistaken on this point. My heart tells me that it is no delusion."

Rosarito blushed; but she tried to conceal the blush by smiling and glancing about her, and said:

"Do not put me off with these artifices, now. If you say so, meaning that I shall always consider whatever you may say to be right, then I agree with you."

"Rosarito!" exclaimed the young man, "from seeing you my soul has been filled with the greatest joy— I have, at the same time, regretted that I had not come to Orbajosa sooner."

"I am not going to believe that," answered she.

Doña Perfecta

affecting joviality to cover her confusion. "Already?— Let us have no more nonsense— See, Pepe, I am a village maiden; I only speak vulgarly; I do not know French; I do not dress elegantly; I can only play the piano a little; I—"

"Oh, Rosarito!" replied her cousin, ardently, "had I doubted that you were perfect, I am now convinced that you are."

The mother entered suddenly. Rosarito, who had no response to make to her cousin's last words, knew, doubtless, the necessity of saying something, and looking at her mother she observed:

"Ah! I had forgotten to feed the parrot."

"Do not trouble yourself about that now. Why are you here? Take your cousin for a walk in the orchard."

The señora smiled with maternal suavity, pointing out to her nephew the leafy woodland beyond the crystal doors.

"Let us go," said Pepe, rising.

Rosarito darted out, like a bird set at liberty, through the door.

"Pepe, who is so wise, and must understand trees," declared Doña Perfecta, "will teach you how to ingraft them. See what his opinion is as regards those pear trees, which are to be transplanted."

"Come, come," said Rosarito from without.

She called impatiently to her cousin. Both dis-

appeared among the foliage. Doña Perfecta
watched them until they were out of view, and
then attended to the parrot. While the remains
of dinner were being removed she said in a low
tone, with pensive accent:

"How sullen he is! He might at least have
caressed the poor animal." Then, in a higher tone,
she added, believing in the possibility of being
heard by her brother-in-law:

"Cayetano, what do you think of the nephew?—
Cayetano!"

A low grunt indicated that the antiquarian
had returned to the knowledge of this miserable
world.

"Cayetano!"

"I am here—I am here—" murmured the
savant, drowsily. "This gentleman will maintain
the same erroneous opinion as do all, that the statues at Mundogrande date from the first Phenician
invasion. I will convince him."

"But, Cayetano—"

"But, Perfecta— Bah! You will likewise declare that I was asleep."

"No, man, why should I declare anything so
absurd? But you do not tell me what you think
of this young man?"

Don Cayetano placed his hand before his mouth
to hide a yawn, and then entered into conversation
with the señora. They who transmitted the facts

necessary to the composition of this history passed over the details of this dialogue; undoubtedly, because it was very confidential. As to what passed between the engineer and Rosarito that afternoon in the orchard, it has evidently not deserved mention.

On the afternoon of the following day events occurred which can not go unrecorded, as they were of greater importance. The two cousins were alone together at a somewhat advanced hour in the afternoon, after having rambled about the orchard; so wrapped up in each other that they had neither eyes nor ears for anything else.

"Pepe," said Rosarito, "all that you have told me is fantasy, a repetition of that which men of the world get off by heart. You think that because I am only a village maiden I shall believe all I hear?"

"If you knew me, as I think I know you, you would understand that I always say what I feel. But let us leave foolish subtlety and lovers' arguments, which only tend to falsify the sentiments. I shall only address you in the language of truth. Are you, perchance, a young lady whom I have met in a walk, or in society, with whom I amuse myself to pass the time? No. You are my cousin. You are even more— Rosarito, let us consider things in their proper light— Let us avoid subterfuge. I have come here to marry you."

Rosarito felt her face burn, and her heart beat violently in her breast.

"See, dear cousin," continued the young fellow, "I swear that, did I not love you, I should have already been far from here. Although courtesy and delicacy would have obliged me to make an effort, I should have had great difficulty in concealing my distaste to the match. It is my character."

"Cousin, you have not been here long," said Rosarito, laconically, trying to laugh.

"I have not been here long, and I already know all that I wish to know; I know that I love you; that you are the woman my heart is set upon, telling me day and night; I have come, I am conquered; that I have won you—"

This sentence served as a pretext to Rosarito to give way to the smile which had risen to her lips. Her spirit was surrounded by an atmosphere of joy.

"You will not bind yourself because you imagine you are valueless," continued Pepe, "and you are exquisite. You possess the admirable quality of shedding, at all hours, on those who surround you, the divine light of your soul. From first seeing you, from first looking on you, I perceived the noble sentiments and purity of your heart. Whoever beholds you sees a celestial life which God has, through oversight, left on this earth; you are an angel, and I adore you as such."

On expressing himself thus he seemed to be discharging a grave mission. Rosarito felt suddenly overcome by such profound sensibility that her spare bodily energy could not bear up against the excitement of her mind; and half fainting, she fell on a stone, which, sometimes, in those remote villages, serves as a seat. Pepe leaned over her. He remarked that her eyes were closed, her forehead supported by his hand.

Presently the girl recovered, and directing at her cousin, as she gently wept, a loving glance, said:

"I loved you before I knew you."

The young man assisted her to rise, and they were soon lost to view under the leafy branches of some bay trees. The afternoon waned, and a gentle shadow fell over the lower part of the orchard, while the last rays of the setting sun crowned with varied splendor the tops of the trees. The noisy republic of little birds twittered in the upper branches of the trees. It was the hour when, after joyfully careering through the immensity of the heavens, all were going to rest, and were disputing one with the other in the choice of an alcove. The chatter at times resembled recrimination and dispute, at others it was gracious and jesting. Those rogues, in their chirping idiom, uttered the most insolent things, biting and flapping their wings, as orators agitate their arms when they wish to make others believe the falsehoods that they utter. But here words of love, also, were heard, encouraged by the peaceful hour and beautiful spot. A quick ear might have caught the following words:

"Before knowing you, I loved you, and had you not come I should have died of grief. Mama gave me your father's letters to read, and, as they were always full of your praises, I said: 'Ah, if he were to be my husband.' For a long time your father did not suggest that we should marry, which I considered a great mistake. I did not know what to think of such negligence— My uncle Cayetano always, in mentioning you, said: 'There are few like him. The woman whom he marries will be a happy one—' "

"Ultimately, your father wrote, as you know— Yes, he could not have said less. I had expected it every day—"

Soon after the same voice added uneasily:

"Some one is coming after us."

Quitting the bay trees, Pepe saw two persons approaching, and, touching the leaves of a tender young tree, which grew where they were standing, he said in a loud tone to his companion:

"It is not wise to prune such young trees as this until they have attained more growth. Trees recently planted have not enough strength to undergo such an operation. You know that the roots can not grow except by the influence of the leaves; and it is for that reason that these are taken off—"

"Ah! Señor Don José," exclaimed the Penitentiary, laughing aloud, approaching the two young people, and bowing, "are you giving lessons in horticulture? '*Insere nunc Meliœe pyros, pone ordene, vites,*' as says the great singer. 'Ingraft the pear trees, dear Melibeus, train the vines—' And how are you, Señor Don José?"

The engineer and the priest shook hands. The latter, then turning round and beckoning to a young man who had followed him, said, smiling:

"I have the pleasure of presenting my dear Jacintito to you—a good piece—a giddy boy, Señor Don José."

CHAPTER IX

DISAGREEMENT INCREASES AND THREATENS
TO END IN DISLIKE

A SMILING, fresh countenance looked forth from behind the black cassock. Jacintito bowed to our young friend in a slightly embarrassed manner.

He was one of those precocious lads whom the indulgent university launches out before the proper time, to encounter the arduous struggles of the world, making them believe that they are men because they are doctors. Jacintito was full-faced, with an agreeable expression, with red cheeks like a girl; of plump figure, small stature, one might almost say very small, and without the least sign of a beard on his smooth chin. His age slightly exceeded twenty years. He had been educated from his infancy under his excellent, discreet uncle's direction, who saw, with pleasure, that the tender shrub was not distorted in its growth. A severe morality kept him straight; and in completing his scholastic course he rarely committed a fault. He terminated his university studies with marvelous rapidity; there was no class in which he did not excel; and when he began to work he promised, by his assiduity and skill as a lawyer, to win the laurels in the courts of justice as he had done at the university.

At times he was as wayward as a child, at others grave as a man. And, truly, though Jacintito was no favorite with pretty young girls, his worthy uncle found him perfect. He did not neglect to lecture him at all times, taking care to keep his bold wings clipped; but no mundane inclination of the youth could cool the good priest's great love for the charming sprout of his dear niece, Maria Remedios. All ceded before the little lawyer. Even the worthy priest's grave, methodical habits were put aside in any matter relating to his precious pupil. Every fixed, rigorous rule, arranged like a planetary system, lost its equilibrium only when Jacintito was ill or was about to take a journey. Useless celibacy of the clergy! If the Council of Trent prohibits their having children, God, not the devil, gives them nephews that they may participate in the sweet solicitude of paternity.

Examining impartially the qualities of this clever young man, it was impossible not to recognize that he was not deficient in merit. He was naturally inclined to be honorable, and noble actions called forth open admiration from him. In respect to his intellectual gifts and social knowledge, he possessed all that was necessary to become, in time, a celebrated man, such as there are so many of in Spain; he might become one of those we are pleased to term, hyperbolically, "a distinguished patrician, or an eminent public man," a species which is so abundant that they are scarcely appreciated at their true worth. At that tender age when the university grade serves for solder between puberty and manhood, few young men, and especially if they are flattered by their masters, are free from a fastidious pedantry, which, if it gives great prestige when near their mothers, is very amusing when seen in grave, grown-up men. Jacintito possessed this defect, excusable, not only on account of his youth, but also because his good uncle fomented that puerile vanity by imprudent applause.

When the four rejoined each other they continued to walk about. Jacintito preserved silence. The priest, reverting to the interrupted theme of the pear trees which were to be ingrafted, and of the vines which should be trained, quietly remarked:

"I am sure that Señor Don José is a great agriculturist."

"Not at all; I do not understand a word about it," replied our young friend, perceiving, with much disgust, that mania for supposing him to be instructed in all the sciences.

"Oh, yes; a great agriculturist," added the confessor. "But on agricultural affairs do not quote

me any innovations. For me, Señor de Rey, all that
science is contained in what is called the 'Bible of
the Country,' in the immortal Latin 'Georgics.'
All is admirable, from that grand sentence, '*Nec
cero terræ ferre omnes omnia possunt*'—which
means that all lands do not suit all trees, Señor
Don José—even to the superfluously exact treatise
on the bees, in which the poet explains the con-
cerns of those learned insects, and defines the drone,
saying:

> ' 'Ille horridus alter
> Desidia, latamque trahens inglorius alvum,'

of horrible and idle shape, crawling along on its
ignoble, weighted belly."

"You do well to translate it for me," said Pepe,
"for I understand but little Latin."

"Oh! the men of the day, what amusement can
they find in studying the ancients!" said the priest
sarcastically. "For it is only silly fellows like Virgil, Cicero, and Titus Livius, who have written
in Latin. I, doubtless, think differently, as my
nephew can bear witness, for I taught him that
sublime tongue. The vagabond knew it better
than I. Unfortunately, modern lectures have
caused him to forget it; and I am afraid he is an
ignorant fellow without suspecting it. For, Señor
Don José, my nephew has been given the latest
books, containing extravagant theories, to divert

himself with; and all is in flames both above and below, unless the stars be inhabited. See, I fancy you two will be good friends. Jacintito, you will beg of this gentleman to instruct you in sublime mathematics and in the knowledge of German philosophy, and you will become a man."

The good priest laughed at his own conceit, while Jacintito, pleased to see the conversation so much to his taste, addressed Pepe Rey, asking as his first question:

"Tell me, Señor Don José, what you think of Darwinism?"

Our young friend smiled on remarking his pedantry, and he was much inclined to punish Jacintito for his infantile vanity; but, thinking it more prudent to take no notice of either the nephew's or uncle's manner, he answered simply:

"I can not give any opinion on Darwin's works, for I have but a slight acquaintance with them. The labors of my profession have not allowed me to devote myself to those studies."

"Ah!" said the priest, laughing, "it is all comprised in this—that we are descended from apes. If it related only to certain persons of my acquaintance, it would be true."

"The theory of natural selection," added Jacintito emphatically, "is said to have many partizans in Germany."

"I do not doubt it," replied the priest. "They

should believe this theory to be a true one, as it affects Bismarck."

Doña Perfecta and Don Cayetano now joined the other four.

"What a beautiful afternoon!" exclaimed the señora; "but, all the same, nephew, you are much wearied."

"Not at all!" replied Pepe.

"Do not deny it. Cayetano and I have just been talking about it. You are wearied, and you try to hide it. It is not all the young fellows of this period who can be content to pass their youth, like Jacintito, in a town where there are no theatres, no comic opera, no ballets, no philosophers, no congresses, nor other diversions and pastimes."

"I am very content," answered Pepe. "It was only a short time since that I was telling Rosarito that this town and house suited me so well that I should like to live and die here."

Rosarito blushed, and the rest became silent. They all sat down in an arbor which was close by. Jacintito took a seat near the younger lady.

"See, nephew, I wish to speak to you about something," said Doña Perfecta, with the usual kind expression which emanated from her soul, as the aroma from the flower. "But do not think I wish to reprehend or to lecture you. You are not a child, and will easily understand me."

"Scold me, dear aunt; no doubt I deserve it,"

replied Pepe, who was already accustomed to the goodness of his father's sister.

"No, it is nothing more than advice. These gentlemen will decide if I am right."

Rosarito listened attentively.

"It is only this," added the señora, "that when you visit our beautiful cathedral you should behave with greater reverence."

"But what did I do?"

"It is not astonishing that you do not know your fault," said the señora, with feigned gaiety. "It is natural; you are accustomed to enter the clubs, academies, and congresses boldly, and you think you may enter the temple where dwells the Divine Godhead in the same manner."

"But, señora, pardon me," observed Pepe, seriously. "I entered the cathedral with the greatest composure."

"Do not dispute, man; do not dispute. If you take it thus I shall hold my tongue. Gentlemen, excuse my nephew. He was guilty of negligence —of distraction. How many years is it since he put foot in a sacred place?"

"Señora, I swear to you, although my religious ideas are not what you would wish, I am accustomed to behave in the most respectful manner in church."

"I assure you—see, if you are not guilty— I assure you that many people noticed you this

morning. The Señores de Gonzalez, Doña Robus-
tiana, Serafinita, and lastly, you even attracted the
bishop's notice. His lordship complained to me
about it this afternoon at my cousin's house. He
said there was no mistake, for he had been told
you were my nephew, and said that I should turn
you out."

Rosarito gazed with anguish at her cousin, foreseeing his replies before he uttered them.

"No doubt they have mistaken some one else for
me."

"No—no—it was you. But do not be offended;
we are all friends here, and are speaking confiden-
tially. It was you; I saw you myself."

"You!"

"Yes, I. You can not deny you were examining
the paintings, passing a group of the faithful, who
were hearing Mass? I assure you, you distracted
me in such a way with your comings and goings,
that—but—that is not exactly what I wished to
mention. You then went into the little chapel of
St. Gregory, ascended the steps to the high altar,
and made no genuflexion. After going all round
the church, you approached the sepulchre, put
your hands on the altar, and a second time passed
the worshipers, attracting attention. All the young
girls stared at you, and you appeared satisfied at
having so neatly disturbed the devotions and exemplary conduct of these good people."

"My God! I did all that!" exclaimed Pepe, half angrily, half smiling. "I am a monster, and did not at all suspect it."

"No, I know you are a good boy," said Doña Perfecta, observing the affectedly serious and immutable countenance of the priest, which resembled a cardboard mask. "But, my son, to have opinions, and to manifest them in this ostentatious manner, are very different; and a prudent and polite man would avoid such a danger. I know well your ideas are—no, do not get angry; if you become angry, I shall be silent. I say that it is one thing to be religious, and another to manifest it. I abstain from blaming you, as you do not believe that God created us in His image and likeness, but that we are descended from monkeys; you do not deny the soul's existence, but value it no more than the drugs sold in the shops—such as magnesia, or rhubarb pills."

"Señora, by God!" exclaimed Pepe in great disgust, "I see I have a very bad reputation in Orbajosa."

The others maintained silence.

"But I say you are not to blame for these ideas. But you are not right. If I begin to dispute with you, you, with your uncommon talents, will confound me a thousand times—no, none of that. I say these poor, foolish inhabitants of Orbajosa are pious and good Christians, even if none of them understands German philosophy; and you should not publicly depreciate their faith."

"Dear aunt," replied the engineer, gravely, "I have depreciated no one's faith, and I do not hold the opinions which you attribute to me. If I have not behaved as respectfully as I should in church, I was absent-minded. My judgment and attention were taken by the architectural work, and, frankly, I did not remark; but that was no reason why the bishop should say I should be turned out into the street, and that you should suppose me to be capable of comparing the functions of my soul to a pill from a shop. But I will tolerate this only as a jest, and no more than a jest."

Pepe Rey felt so greatly excited that his great prudence and moderation could scarcely prevent him from showing it.

"Now, see, I have made you angry," said Doña Perfecta, lowering her eyes and crossing her hands. "It is all for God! Had I known you would have taken it thus, I would have said nothing about it to you. Pepe, I beg you will forgive me?"

Hearing this, and seeing the submissive manner of his good aunt, Pepe felt ashamed of the harshness of his previous words, and tried to calm himself. The venerable confessor relieved him from his embarrassment by smiling with his habitual benevolence, and speaking thus:

"Doña Perfecta, one must allow artists some indulgence. Oh! I know them well. These gentlemen, when they see before them a statue, some musty armor, a ruined house, or an old wall, forget all else. Señor Don José is an artist, and has visited our cathedral, as the English visit it, who would carry off with the greatest delight the last tile of it to their museums. What matter the faithful? or that the priest is elevating the Sacred Host? that it is the moment for the greatest piety and reverence? that it—nothing makes any difference to the artist. It is true I do not understand the value of art when it disagrees with the sentiments I have expressed; however, it is the custom of the day to adore the shape, not the idea. God save me from entering into a discussion with Señor Don José on this theme; he who knows so much, and argues with the fine subtlety of modern times, would confound me directly in all that does not concern faith."

"The perseverance in considering me the most learned man in the world is extremely mortifying to me," said Pepe, regaining his harsh tone. "I would rather you looked upon me as a fool; I would prefer to be considered ignorant than to possess this Satanic science which all here attribute to me."

Rosarito began to laugh, and Jacintito thought he had found an opportune moment to display his personal erudition to advantage.

"Pantheism and panentheism were condemned by the Church, as were also the doctrines of Schopenhauer and the modern Hartmann."

"Gentlemen and señora," said the priest, seriously, "men who dedicate themselves so ardently to the culture of art, even although it be only that of form, merit the greatest respect. It is much better to be a lover of art and delight in the beautiful, even though it be but nude nymphs, than to be indifferent and to disbelieve in all. The mind that consecrates itself to the contemplation of the beautiful can never be entirely bad. It follows, then, that Señor Don José was admiring the marvels of our church; for my own part, I can pardon him with good grace all his irreverences; saving the opinion of the prelate."

"Thanks, Señor Don Inocencio," said Pepe, feeling his hostility revive toward the astute cleric, and being unable to withstand the desire to mortify him; "but do not believe that my attention was absorbed by the artistic beauties of which you suppose the temple to be full. Those beauties, beyond the imposing architecture of a part of the edifice, the three sepulchres in the chapels of ease, and some carving in the choir, I did not see. What occupied me was the consideration of the deplorable decadence in religious art, and I felt astonished, if not angry, at the innumerable artistic monstrosities with which the cathedral is filled."

All around him were dumb with surprise.

"I could not resist," added Pepe, "those varnished vermilion images, all so much like—God pardon me the comparison—the dolls that growing girls play with. And what can one say of those theatrical vestments with which they are clothed? I saw a St. Joseph in a mantle whose appearance did not tend to inculcate respect for the Holy Patriarch, whom the Church venerates. On the altars are accumulated images in the most deplorable artistic taste, and the multitude of crowns, branches, stars, moons, and similar metal or gold paper adornments, present a fantastical appearance, which is repulsive to religious sentiment, and dispirits one. Far from assisting religious contemplation, it hinders it, and the idea of the comic disturbs it. Grand works of art supply sensible thoughts, and elevate one's ideas in regard to dogmas, faith, mysterious exaltation, and the most noble mission. Ill-drawn figures and aberration in taste, grotesque works with which an imprudent piety fills the churches, accomplish their object also; but it is a sad one. It foments superstition, cools enthusiasm, obliges the eyes of the believer to be withdrawn from the altar, and with the eyes the souls of those whose faith is neither deep nor firm."

"The doctrine of the Iconoclasts," said Jacintito; "it seems it is widely spread in Germany."

"I am no Iconoclast, although I should prefer the destruction of all images to this exhibition of buffoonery which attracted me," replied the young fellow. "Seeing this is enough to make one wish that the august simplicity of ancient times would return; but, no, I do not renounce the admirable auxiliary that all arts, beginning with poetry and ending with music, lend to the relations between God and man. Long life to the arts, let them be displayed in the great ceremonies of religious rites! I am a partizan for ceremony."

"Artist, artist, and no more than an artist!" exclaimed the priest, moving his head with an expression of compassion. "Good paintings, good statues, good music. Glory in those sentiments, and the devil will carry off the soul."

"In regard to music," said Pepe Rey, taking no heed of the evil effect his words were producing in the mother and daughter, "do you imagine that my mind could be inclined for religious contemplation on visiting the cathedral, when, for the preludes and offertory at High Mass, the organist played passages from *La Traviata?*"

"In that you are right, Señor de Rey," said the lawyer, emphatically. "The other day the organist played all the waltzes of that same opera, and afterward a rondo from *The Grand Duchess.*"

"But how disgusted I felt," continued the engineer implacably, "when I saw a statue of the Virgin, which seemed to command great veneration, for many people were praying before it, and a great number of candles were burning there. The dress was an azure gown, with three golden borders, and was of such extraordinary shape that it even surpassed the most extravagant fashions of the day. Her face was almost hidden, surrounded as it was with all sorts of frills and laces, with a crown over them, encompassed by rays of gold, and a monstrous funeral canopy fitted up over the top. From the same loom, and embroidered in the same manner, were the trousers of the Child Jesus. I will not continue, for the description of the mother and child might cause me to be irreverent. I will only add that I could not avoid smiling; and, contemplating the profaned image for a few moments, I exclaimed, "Mother and Lady mine, how they have concealed you!"

Concluding with these words, Pepe observed with his hearing, for the twilight did not permit him to distinguish the countenances around him; but he believed they expressed bitter consternation.

"Then, Señor Don José!" exclaimed the priest quickly, smiling with an air of triumph, "that statue, which to your philosophy and pantheism appeared so ridiculous, is our Lady of Succor, patroness and advocate of Orbajosa, whose inhabitants venerate it in such a manner that they would be capable of stoning any one in the streets who spoke badly of it. Chronicles and history, sir, are full of the miracles performed by it, and even to-day are seen undeniable proofs of its protection. I would have you to know that her ladyship, your aunt, Doña Perfecta, is chief waiting-maid to the Holy Virgin of Succor, and that the gown which you thought so grotesque—yes, this dress which to your impious eyes looked so grotesque—went from this house, as did also the trousers of the Holy Child; and were the result of the marvelous needlework and piety of your cousin Rosarito, who now hears us."

Pepe Rey felt disconcerted. At the same instant, Doña Perfecta got up bruskly, and, without speaking a word, went in the direction of the house, followed by the confessor. Then all the rest rose. The foolish young fellow was going to beg pardon of Rosarito for his irreverence when he observed that she was weeping. Gazing at her cousin with a friendly look and one of gentle reprehension, she exclaimed:

"But what ideas you have!"

Then Doña Perfecta's voice was heard in a changed tone shouting:

"Rosarito! Rosarito!"

She ran into the house.

CHAPTER X

THE EXISTENCE OF DISLIKE IS EVIDENT

PEPE REY felt troubled and confused. Furious with those around him, and with himself, he tried to find out the cause of the repugnance existing between him and his aunt's friends. He was pensive and sad, foreseeing quarrels, and he remained sitting in the arbor for a short time, his chin sunk on his breast, frowning, and with his hands crossed. He thought himself alone.

Presently he heard a gay voice humming a song of the period. Looking up he saw Jacintito on the opposite side of the arbor.

"Ah! Señor de Rey," said the boy unexpectedly, "you can not attack the religious sentiments of the majority of the people with impunity. If you will do so, consider what happened during the first French Revolution."

When Pepe heard the buzzing of this insect his irritation increased. Nevertheless, he had in his soul no dislike to the young doctor. He, however, vexed him, as flies do, but nothing more. Rey felt the molestation which all importune in-

terference inspires, and, wishing to put the drone
to flight, said:

"What has the French Revolution to do with the
Virgin Mary's dress?"

He then rose to go into the house, but had not
proceeded four steps when he heard the buzz of
the mosquito, saying:

"Señor Don José, I wish to speak with you on a
very interesting subject; one which will cause a
conflict."

"A subject?" answered our young friend, returning. "Let us see what it is."

"You will have suspected it some time," said
Jacintito, drawing near to Pepe, and smiling with
that expression peculiar to business men, when
they are busied with anything serious. "What
have you to say about this lawsuit of yours?"

"What lawsuit? My friend, I have no lawsuits.
You, like a good lawyer, dream of litigants and
see sealed paper everywhere."

"But how? Have you had no notice of this lawsuit?" exclaimed the boy with astonishment.

"Of my suit! Exactly, I have none, nor ever
had one."

"But if you know nothing of this, I am very
pleased to have been able to warn you, that you
may put yourself on your guard. Yes, sir, there
is litigation."

"And with whom?"

"With Lycurgus and other proprietors of the estate named los Alamillos, the Poplars."

Pepe Rey felt stupefied.

"Yes, sir," added the little lawyer, "Lycurgus and I had a long conference to-day. As I am so friendly at this house, I had not expected to have the pleasure of warning you, but of begging you to bring all to an early settlement."

"But I, what have I to settle? What does this rabble say about me?"

"It seems that some streams which rise in this estate of yours have varied their course and fall over some of Lycurgus's tile-works, and the mill of another, occasioning considerable damage. My client—for he has employed me in this difficulty—my client, I say, pretends that you should reestablish the ancient drains for the streams, to avoid new defects, and to indemnify the damage, which the indolence of the principal proprietor has caused."

"I am the principal proprietor! If there is litigation, it will be the first fruit these celebrated Alamillos have ever yielded me, which were mine, and are so now; which, according to report, are everybody's, for this same Lycurgus, with his fellow-laborers, has encroached on it little by little, year by year, bit by bit, and it will cost much to reestablish the boundaries of my property."

"That is a separate question."

"It is no separate question. Understand," exclaimed the engineer, unable to restrain his anger, "that the veritable lawsuit will be the one I shall sustain against such people, who, doubtless, wish to vex and disgust me, so that I shall abandon all and leave them in possession of their plunder. We will see if there are lawyers and judges who will favor the stupid administration of those village justices, who live by lawsuits and prey like the moths on the produce of the mustard-field. Young gentleman, I owe you thanks for having told me the ruinous proposals of these clowns, who are worse than pickpockets. Well, I assure you that these same tile-works and the mill, which Lycurgus claims as his, are mine."

"You should make a revision of the deeds of the estate and see if they are inscribed therein," said Jacintito.

"What inscription is necessary? These villains shall not amuse themselves with me. I suppose that the administration of justice is honorable and loyal in the town of Orbajosa?"

"Oh, yes!" exclaimed the learned little lawyer eagerly. "The judge is an excellent man. He comes here every evening— But I am astonished that you should have received no intimation of Lycurgus's pretensions. Can not I act as mediator?"

"No."

"It will come on to-morrow— I am sorry that Uncle Lycurgus's haste should have deprived me of the pleasure and honor of defending you; but how was I to know— Lycurgus has engaged me to draw him out of his difficulties. I shall study the matter carefully. These servile rogues are the support of jurisprudence."

Pepe entered the dining-room in a very lamentable mental state. He saw Doña Perfecta speaking with the confessor; and Rosarito stood alone, her eyes fixed on the door, waiting, no doubt, for her cousin.

"Come here, good child," said the señora, smiling with little spontaneity. "You have insulted us, but we will forgive you. I know that my daughter and I are two rustics, who are incapable of ascending into mathematical regions, where you live, but, however—all is possible if you will only humble yourself to us some day, and entreat us to instruct you in the Faith."

Pepe replied with vague, formal expressions of courtesy and repentance.

"For my part," said Don Inocencio, looking at him sweetly and modestly, "if I have, in the course of these vain disputes, said anything that could offend Señor Don José, I beg that he will forgive me. Thus we are all friends again."

"Thanks. It is not worth the trouble."

"In spite of all," exclaimed Doña Perfecta, smiling more naturally, "I shall always feel the same toward my dear nephew, notwithstanding his extravagant and antireligious opinion. What do you imagine I have been thinking of to-night? To force Uncle Lycurgus to withdraw the suit he intends to annoy you with. I have sent for him to come, and he will be in the gallery awaiting me. Relieve your mind, I will settle him, although I know he has good reason for complaint."

"Thanks, dear aunt," replied the young fellow, feeling overcome by the wave of generosity so easily generated in her soul.

Pepe Rey glanced over to the spot where his cousin was standing, with the intention of joining her, but some sagacious questions from the priest recalled him to Doña Perfecta's side. Rosarito looked sad, listening with melancholy indifference to the little lawyer, who had just installed himself near her, and had begun a series of troublesome conceptions, with importunate, foolish jokes, which were in the worst taste.

"The most unfortunate thing for you," said Doña Perfecta to her nephew, when she surprised him observing the palpable variance there was between Rosarito and Jacintito, "is that you have offended poor Rosarito. You should do all you can to appease her. The poor little girl is so good!"

"Oh, yes, so good," added the priest, "that she will no doubt pardon her cousin."

"I believe Rosarito has already forgiven me," affirmed Rey.

"And if not, angelic hearts never hold much resentment," said Don Inocencio mellifluously. "I have great influence over this young girl, and will engage to drive from her generous soul all anger against you. I can do it in two words—"

Pepe Rey felt as though a cloud had passed over him, and said with intention:

"No time like the present."

"I will not speak to her now," added the capitular, "for she is listening with astonishment to Jacintito's fooleries— He is like a child. When he is in the vein, nothing will stop him."

The judge of the lower court, the alcalde's wife, and the dean of the cathedral, now entered the room. All saluted the engineer, displaying by their words and actions, on seeing him, the most intense curiosity.

The alcalde, or justice of the peace, was an active man, one of those who appear every day at some eminent person's house, aspiring to be received into the brood of those who are first in the administration and in politics. He gave himself important airs, and, in speaking of his juvenile toga, manifested great anger that he had not been ordained from the first President of the Supreme Tribunal. Into such inexpert hands, to a brain filled with wind, to such a conceited fellow had the State confided the most delicate and difficult functions of human justice. His manners were those of a perfect courtier, and revealed scrupulous and minute attention to all concerning his person. He had the silly habit of continually taking off and putting on his gold eyeglasses; and in his conversation frequently indicated the obligation he was under to go to Madrid, to lend his invaluable services to the Secretary of Gracia and Justicia.

The alcalde's lady was a good-natured woman, whose only failing was in supposing that she was related to the Court. She asked Pepe Rey several questions as to the fashions, naming establishments where she had had a mantle or a dress made on her last journey, contemporary with her visit to Muley-Abbas, and mentioning a dozen duchesses and marchionesses with great familiarity as having been her schoolfellows. She said that the Countess of M. (famous for her assemblies) was her friend, and that when, in '60, she was visiting her, the Countess had taken her to her opera-box in the Real, and afterward to Muley-Abbas, dressed in Moorish fashion, and accompanied by all her Moorish attendants. The alcalde's wife spoke (as it is expressed) with her elbows, and was not lacking in wit.

The dean was an old man, corpulent and choleric, plethoric and apoplectic; a man who had no thoughts for anything but his own fat body. He spoke only on religious subjects, and, from the first, behaved toward Pepe with the greatest contempt. The latter became more inept to accommodate himself to a society so little to his taste. His character, though not perverse, was hard, and but slightly flexible, and repelled the perfidy and accommodations of language to simulate concord when he did not feel it. He then maintained silence during the course of this fastidious assembly, obliged to listen to the impetuous oratory of the alcalde's wife, who, according to report, was capable of harassing the human ear as though she were possessed of a hundred tongues. If, during the brief respite the lady allowed his ears, Pepe Rey wished to join his cousin, the confessor held him down as fast as a mussel to a rock; and, drawing him apart with mysterious gesture, proposed to him a walk to Mundogrande with Don Cayetano, or a fishing party to the clear streams of Nahara.

At last it was ended, as all ends in this world. The dean retired, leaving a void in the house; and soon after the chatter of the alcalde's lady was but an echo, like the rumbling the recent passing over of a tempest leaves in the human ear. The alcalde then deprived the assembly of his presence, and, finally, Don Inocencio gave his nephew the signal for departure.

"Come, child, are we going to-day?" he said, smiling. "How you have teased poor Rosarito!

Is it not true, my daughter? Walk off, sir, at once."

"It is bed-time," said Doña Perfecta.

"It is work-time," replied the little lawyer.

"But you have finished business for the day," said the priest, "as usual. There is so much business—so much! Trouble no more about this ridiculous affair into which they have led you— I do not wish to praise him, Señor Don José; but do you know he has written a work on 'The Influence of Woman on Christian Society,' and another, a 'Little Work on the Catholic Movement in—' I do not know where. What should you understand about 'influences,' and 'little works.' These young fellows of the day dare all— Umph!—what children! But we must get home— Good-night, Doña Perfecta—good-night, Señor Don José—Rosarito—"

"I am waiting for Don Cayetano," said Jacintito, "he is going to give me 'Augustus Nicholas.'"

"Always burdening yourself with books—man! Sometimes when you enter the house, you look like a donkey. Well, well, we will wait."

"Señor Don Jacintito," said Pepe Rey, "does not write lightly; he prepares himself well for his works, that they may be a treasure of erudition."

"But he will get the headache, Señor Don Inocencio," said Doña Perfecta. "Take care, for

God's sake. I shall be much interested in his works."

"As we are waiting," said the little doctor, in a very conceited tone, "I will also take the third volume of 'Counsel.' What do you think, uncle?"

"Yes, man, do not let that leave your hand. You will then make no mistakes."

Happily Don Cayetano (who generally joined the circle at D. Lorenzo Ruiz's house) came in then, and, taking the books, uncle and nephew made their exit. Rey read in his cousin's sad countenance a great wish to speak with him. Doña Perfecta and Don Cayetano spoke only of domestic matters, while Pepe approached Rosarito, who said:

"You have offended mama."

Her eyes had in them a kind of terror.

"It is true," replied the young fellow. "I have offended your mama; I have also offended you."

"No, not me, I had already fancied the Child Jesus would not like the trousers."

"But I hope you both forgive me? Your mama has shown me great kindness."

Doña Perfecta's voice sounded through the dining-room with such a discordant accent that her nephew trembled with alarm when he heard it. She said imperiously:

"Rosarito, get to bed."

Troubled and full of anguish, the young girl

gave several glances round the room, as though she had been looking for something. As she passed her cousin, she said quietly these vague words:

"Mama is angry."

"But—"

"She is angry—do not defy her, do not defy her."

And she went out. Doña Perfecta afterward followed her, as Lycurgus was awaiting her ladyship; and, for a time, her voice and the peasant's could be heard in friendly conference. Pepe and Don Cayetano were thus left together, when the latter spoke thus, taking a light:

"Good-night, Pepe. Do not think I am going to sleep, I am going to work— But why are you so meditative? What is the matter with you?— Well, yes, to work. I am looking up information for some 'Memoirs on the Lineage of Orbajosa'— I have discovered some precious dates and notes. I shall turn them to account. In all the periods of our history the Orbajosians have been distinguished for their nobility, valor, and knowledge. It is said that but for the conquest of Mexico, the wars of the Emperor, those of Philip against heretics— But are you ill?— What has happened to you?— Well, eminent clergymen, brave warriors, saints, bishops, poets, politicians, all sorts of enlightened men, flourished in this humble land of the garlic— No, there has never been a Christian town that was more illustrious than ours. Its virtues and glories fill the history of the country, and even then overflow— Come, see you are dreaming; good-night— Well, then, I would not exchange the honor of being a son of this noble land for all the gold in the world. 'Augusta'—the ancients termed it 'Augustisima'—I call it now, for even now, as formerly, nobility, generosity, valor, are her patrimony— Then, good-night, dear Pepe— I am afraid you will not have a good one. What, has supper upset you?— Alonso Gonzalezde Bustamento is right in his 'Floresta Amena' when he says 'that the inhabitants of Orbajosa suffice, if only to minister to the greatness and honor of the kingdom.' Do not you believe thus?"

"Oh! yes, señor, I do not doubt it," replied Pepe Rey, taking his way to his room bruskly.

CHAPTER XI

DISLIKE INCREASES

DURING the days that succeeded Rey made acquaintance. with various people in the town, and visited the casino, forming friendships with some individuals who passed nearly all their time at that place.

But the young folks of Orbajosa did not live constantly there, as evil-disposed people said. In the afternoon one met with several gentlemen, who were wrapped in cloaks, standing in a corner near the cathedral, or in the square formed by the crossing of the Calle de Condestable and Calle de la Triperia, like sentries, watching the inhabitants pass. If the weather were fine these eminent luminaries of the urbsaugustense culture directed their steps, always wearing the inevitable mantle, to the walk named "Paseo Descalzas," which was lined by two rows of phthisical elm trees, and some discolored chestnut trees. Here the brilliant gentlemen watched the daughters of D. Fulano or D. Perencejo, who walked there regularly every afternoon, and addressed them in their walk. Toward night

the casino filled again, and, while a portion of the
associates abandoned their high understandings to
the delights of play, the other portion read peri-
odicals, or discussed in the café there divers subjects, such as politics, horses, bulls, or local reports.
The upshot of all these debates was the supremacy
of Orbajosa and its inhabitants over all other towns
and people on the face of the earth.

Among these remarkable and important men
of the illustrious city some were rich proprietors,
others were poor, but all were full of high aspira-
tions. Some possessed the imperturbable serenity
of the beggar, to whom nothing seems wanting as
long as he has an alms to preserve him from
famine, and the sun to keep him warm. The principal distinguishing feature in the Orbajosians was
a sentiment of lively hostility to all strangers who
went there; and whenever such a stranger presented himself in their august rooms, they believed
he had come to cast a doubt on the superiority of
the garlic country, or to dispute, through envy, the
incontrovertible preeminence that Nature had
conceded to it.

When Pepe Rey first went there he was received
with undeniable reserve, and, as in the casino there
were very many benevolent men, for the quarter
of an hour their new companion remained with
them they rendered him happy by all kinds of jokes
at his expense. When, to the reiterated questions

of the associates, he replied that he had come to Orbajosa with a commission to explore the earth tracks of the Nahara, and to study the country, all were convinced that Don José was a coxcomb, and wished to take upon himself the invention of charcoal plantations and iron roads. Some one said:

"But why should he interfere? These wise gentlemen believe that we are all fools here, and are to be deceived by silly jests— He has come to marry Doña Perfecta's daughter, and what he says about these earth tracks is simply to present an imposing appearance."

"And this morning," said another, who was a small trader, "I was told in the Dominquez's house that this gentleman does not possess a dollar, and has come to fish for Rosarito."

"It seems he is neither an engineer nor anything reputable," added an olive merchant, who had pawned his estate for double its value. "However, we shall see— These hungry people from Madrid believe themselves authorities in deceiving poor provincials, and think they can walk over us here, friend—"

"I know well he is famished."

"But half-laughing, half in earnest, he told us to-night we were barbarous vagabonds."

"That we live like Bedouins, gazing up at the sun."

"That we live by imagination."

"Just so; that we live by imagination."

"And that this town is like those in Morocco."

"Man, I have no patience to listen. Where would he see (unless in Paris) a street like the Calle de Condestable, where there are seven houses in a line, all magnificent, from Doña Perfecta's to that of Nicholas Hermandez's?— These rabble imagine that one has seen nothing, nor has been to Paris—"

"And he said with much delicacy that Orbajosa was a beggars' town, and also that he had heard we lived in the greatest possible misery here."

"We will see if he dare say as much to me. There will be a scandal in the casino!" exclaimed the taxgatherer. "Why did you not tell him the number of measures of oil that Orbajosa produced last year? Does not this stupid fellow know that in good years Orbajosa gives bread to all Spain, and even to every part of Europe? It is true that many years we have had a bad harvest, but that is not the rule; and then the garlic harvest. Does not this gentleman know that the garlic of Orbajosa caused the gentlemen of the jury at the London Exposition to become squint-eyed?"

These and other dialogues were heard in the rooms of the casino for some days. But in spite of this common talk among the young people, who were proud of even their dwarfish stature, Rey did not fail to meet with some sincere friends among the learned corporation, who were not all slanderers or wanting in good feeling. But our young man disgraced himself, if disgrace it can be called, by manifesting his impressions with his usual frankness, and thus drawing antipathy on himself.

The days went by. Besides the natural disgust that the customs of Episcopal society caused him, divers disagreeable things began to fill his soul with sadness. He felt particularly, among other matters, the trouble entailed by the lawsuits which almost overwhelmed him. It was not Lycurgus alone, but many others, who claimed damages and injury; and he was likely to lose the lands administered by his grandfather. He was always having some demand presented to him, some contract of which he knew nothing, and which he was told his mother had formed, but which he had not fulfilled; and they even went so far as to insist on the recognition of a mortgage on the estate of Alamillos, evidenced by a singular document drawn by his uncle. There was a crowd, a whole load of lawsuits. He had proposed to renounce the income from his property, but his pride would not allow him to give way to the claims of these sagacious clowns, and, as the magistracy claimed also for its supposed confusion of his land with the immediate Mount of Propois, the disgraced young fellow pictured himself in the house of detention until the debts which accumulated round him on all sides were paid. His honor was compromised, and he had no remedy; he must either plead or die.

He had been promised magnanimously by Doña Perfecta that she would help him to break his bonds by means of a friendly arrangement; but days passed by, and the good offices of the exemplary lady had no effect. Lawsuits poured in with the speed of a culminating sickness. Pepe Rey passed long hours in the daytime in the tribunal, making declarations, answering questions and cross-questions, and when he returned to the house, fatigued and choleric, he saw the sharp, grotesque countenance of the notary who brought him a daily portion of sealed papers, full of horrible formulas —that he might study the question.

He was not a man to suffer such reverses could they have been avoided by absence. He looked upon his mother's noble town as a horrible beast which dug its ferocious claws into him and sucked his blood. To free himself from it he would have taken his departure, but a deep interest, an affair of the heart, detained him, holding him fast bound, notwithstanding the pains of his martyrdom. Although he felt so much out of place, indeed a stranger, one might say, in that dark city of pleas, antiquities, envy, and calumny, he, on proposing to leave it without delay, still persisted, at the same time, in the project which had led him thither. One morning, finding a suitable opportunity, he disclosed his plans to Doña Perfecta.

"My nephew," replied the señora with her usual sweetness, "do not be too precipitate. Why should you think of flight? But you are like your father; why, man, you are like a spark— I have already told you that it gives me great pleasure to be able to call you my son. You have many good qualities, and are distinguished by your talents (saving defects, which we all have) ; you are an excellent young man, and this union was proposed by your father (to whom my daughter and I owe so much) for our acceptance. Rosarito will not oppose it, and I am willing. What is wanting then? Nothing; nothing but a little time. The marriage can not take place with the speed you desire, and which would cause dishonorable conclusions to be drawn about my daughter— If you take no notice of these quarrels they will vanish in the air. Wait, man, wait—why should you be in such a hurry? This hatred you feel toward our poor Orbajosa is a caprice. Ah! I see; you can not live but in the midst of counts, marquises, orators, and diplomatists— You wish to marry my daughter and to separate me from her forever," added she, sobbing. "So it is, inconsiderate young man; at least, have enough charity to wait a little longer for these nuptials you so ardently desire.

What impatience! What great love! I did not think that a poor village maiden could have inspired such volcanic passions!"

The reasonings of his aunt did not convince Pepe Rey, but he did not wish to contradict her. He resolved then to wait until she deemed it possible. A new cause for disgust soon arose to embitter his existence. He had been at Orbajosa for a fortnight, and during that time had received no letter from his father. It could not be the fault of the administration of the post-office at Orbajosa, for the functionary who held that post there was the friend and *protégé* of Doña Perfecta; she every day urged upon him the greatest care, so that no letters addressed to her nephew should go astray. Also, when the courier, who was charged with the correspondence, named Cristobal Ramos, whose nickname was Caballuco the Centaur, a person whom we already know, went to the house Doña Perfecta energetically admonished and reprimanded him in the following terms:

"Good service you couriers render!— How is it that my nephew has not received a single letter since he came to Orbajosa? When letters are entrusted to such giddy persons how are things to go on? I shall remonstrate with the governor of the province as to the class of men that are in the administration."

Caballuco shrugged his shoulders, looking at

Rey with an expression of the greatest indifference.

One day he came in with a note in his hand.

"Thank God!" said Doña Perfecta to her nephew. "Here is a letter for you from your father. Rejoice, man. My brother has been too lazy to write before— What does he say? Good news, no doubt," added she, seeing Pepe open the note with feverish impatience.

The engineer turned pale on perusing the first lines.

"Jesus! Pepe! What is the matter?" exclaimed her ladyship, rising in great affliction. "Is your papa ill?"

"It is no letter from my father," replied Pepe, revealing the greatest consternation in his countenance.

"Then what is it?"

"An order from the minister relieving me of the commission which he confided to me."

"How?— Is it possible?"

"A deprivation pure and simple, and terminating in a manner anything but flattering to me."

"There must be some great roguery!" exclaimed the señora, recovering from her astonishment.

"What humiliation!" murmured the young fellow. "It is the first time in my life I have ever received such treatment."

"But this governor will not be pardoned by God!

That he should treat you so! Would you like me to write to Madrid? I have many good friends there who would obtain reparation from this minister for his brutal treatment, and would force him to make you satisfaction."

"Thanks, señora. I require no recommendations," replied Pepe, with displeasure.

"But it is unjust, and too hasty, to thus destroy a young man of so much merit—an eminent scientific man— See! I can not restrain my anger!"

"I shall inquire," said Pepe, energetically, "who it is that has injured me thus—"

"It is that minister— But what can you expect from those infamous politicians?"

"There is some one here who wishes me to die of despair," affirmed the young fellow, visibly changed. "It is not the work of the minister; this and other oppositions are the result of some plan of revenge, of an unknown calculator, of an irreconcilable enemy, and this plan, this calculator, this enemy, do not doubt it, dear aunt, is here, in Orbajosa."

"You are becoming mad," replied Doña Perfecta, seemingly compassionate. "Why should you have enemies in Orbajosa? Why should any one wish to be revenged on you? Come, little Pepe, you have lost your judgment. The reading of those books, where it is said that our forefathers were either monkeys or parrots, has turned your brain."

She smiled sweetly in uttering the last sentence; and then, taking a tone of familiar and gentle remonstrance, she continued:

"My son, the inhabitants of Orbajosa are clowns and clumsy laborers, uninstructed, with no refinement, no *bon ton*. But, for loyalty and good faith, no one beats us—no one—no one."

"Do not think," said the young man, "that I accuse any one in this house. But I repeat that my implacable and cruel enemy is in this town."

"I wish you would instruct me in melodrama," replied the señora, again smiling. "I suppose you do not accuse Lycurgus, nor any of those who have lawsuits against you, for the poor fellows only protect their rights. And, in parenthesis, they do not want for reasons in the present instance. And, besides, Lucas loves you much; at least he told me so. Since he has known you he would lose his right eye for you, and the poor fellow is so affectionate to you."

"Yes—very affectionate!" murmured Pepe.

"Do not be foolish," added the señora, putting her hand on his shoulder, and looking at him earnestly. "Do you not think it is more likely that your enemy, if he exists, is in Madrid—in that centre of corruption, of envy, and of rivalry, and not in this pacific, quiet spot, where all is good-will and concord— It is doubtless some one who envies your talents— I warn you of one thing, and that is, that if you wish to investigate into the cause of this disgrace, and to seek explanations of the governor, we shall not fail to do it on our side."

Pepe Rey fixed his eyes on his aunt's face as though he would penetrate the inmost recesses of her soul.

"And I tell you if you wish to go, do not fail to do so," proceeded the señora calmly, perplexing him by her seeming candor and honor.

"No, señora. I do not think of leaving."

"Better! That is also my opinion. Here you are quieter, notwithstanding these cavilings with which you are tormented. Poor, dear Pepe! your knowledge, your uncommon knowledge, is the cause of your disgrace. We, of Orbajosa, poor vil-lagers, live happily in our ignorance. I feel it much that you are not content. But is it my fault that you weary yourself, and despair without rea-son? Do I not treat you as a son? Have I not received you as the hope of my house? What can I do more for you, if, in spite of all this, you do not like us, if you disparage us, if you scoff at our religion, if you despise our friends, does it follow that we should not treat you well?"

Doña Perfecta's eyes were full of tears.

"Dear aunt," said Pepe, feeling his rancor melt,

"so I have committed all these faults while I have been a guest of this house?"

"Do not be silly— Faults or no faults, between persons of the same family all is forgiven."

"But Rosarito, where is she?" asked our young friend, rising. "Am I not to see her to-day?"

"She is better. She can not yet come down."

"I can go up."

"No, man. She is very stubborn— I have forbidden her to leave her room to-day. I have locked her in."

"What a strange thing!"

"It will pass off. It is certain it will pass. We will see if her melancholy ideas have left her to-night. We will organize an assembly to amuse her. You might go to Don Inocencio's house and ask him to come to-night and bring Jacintito."

"Jacintito!"

"Yes, when Rosarito has these attacks, that young fellow is the only one who can distract her."

"But I will go up."

"No, man."

"Do you stand on ceremony in this house?"

"You are making fun of us. You will do as I tell you."

"But I wish to see her."

"No. How badly you understand the girl!"

"I believe I understand her well. Well, I will wait. But this solitude is horrible."

"Ah! there is the notary."

"Curse him a thousand times."

"And it seems to me that I also heard the proctor—he is an excellent man."

"May he be hanged!"

"Man, subjects of interest, when they are one's own, serve for distraction. Some one comes. I think it is the clever agriculturist. He is like a rat."

"Like a rat from hell!"

"Hullo! hullo! If I am not mistaken, Lycurgus and Pasolargo have just come in. Perhaps they have come to propose a settlement."

"I will throw myself in the tank."

"How ungrateful you are! when they all like you so much! See! that no one may be missing, here is also a constable. He is coming to summon you."

"To crucify me."

All the persons mentioned had entered the room.

"Good-day, Pepe, may you be amused," said Doña Perfecta.

"Swallow me, earth!" exclaimed the young man, desperately.

"Señor Don José!"

"My dear Señor Don José."

"Estimable Señor Don José."

"Señor Don José of my soul."

Doña Perfecta

"My respectable friend Señor Don José."

On hearing these conciliating words, Pepe Rey drew a deep breath, and delivered himself up. He abandoned his body and soul to these ill-bred fellows, who displayed horrible piles of sealed paper, while the victim, raising his eyes to Heaven, uttered the Christian prayer:

"My Father, why have you forsaken me?"

CHAPTER XII

THE TROYAS

Love, friendship, good air for moral respiration, light for his soul, sympathy, easy exchange of opinions and feelings were to Pepe Rey most necessary. Not having them, the shadows which fell over his spirit increased, and interior darkness brought with it dislike and bitterness. On the day succeeding the scenes referred to in the last chapter, he felt more than ever annoyed at the long and mysterious seclusion of his cousin; accounted for, in the first place, by some unimportant illness, and then as a caprice and the result of inexplicable nervous attacks. Rey was surprised by such contrary conduct to that he should have expected from Rosarito. Four days had passed without his having seen her, not certainly that he was not wishful to do so; and such a situation began to strike him as disrespectful and ridiculous, if, by a determined effort on her part, she might have overcome it.

"May I not see my cousin to-day?" he asked his aunt, crossly, when they had finished their dinner.

"No; God alone knows how I feel it! I had at least thought to-day. We will see this afternoon."

The suspicion that his adorable cousin was a victim of an unjustifiable confinement, and that she could not defend herself by her own firmness, and by taking the initiative, induced him to restrain himself and wait. Had it not been for this suspicion, he would have left that very day. He did not at all doubt Rosarito's love for him, but it was evident that a disavowed pressure was used to separate them; and it seemed to this honorable man that he ought to find out from whom such malignity proceeded, and to oppose it with the whole strength of his human will.

"I hope Rosarito's stubbornness will not last much longer," he said to Doña Perfecta, dissimulating his real sentiments.

That day he received a letter from his father, in which he said that he had had none from his son while he had been at Orbajosa, a circumstance which increased the young man's inquietude, and astonished him still more. At last, after having roamed about for some time in the orchard alone, he went out to the casino. He entered it like a despairing man, who thought of pitching himself into the sea.

He met several people in the principal rooms, who prattled and disputed. One group discussed

logically the subtle, difficult problem of bulls;
another argued as to which were the best bred don-
keys between Orbajosa and Villahorrenda. With
the greatest loathing Pepe Rey forsook these debates and went to the newspaper room, where,
turning over various reviews without finding any
pleasure in reading, he passed shortly after from
one room to the other, until he stopped, almost
without knowing it, in the one devoted to play.
For about two hours he gave himself up to the
horrible yellow devil, whose resplendent golden
eyes produced both torment and fascination.
Neither of these emotions caused the slightest
change in the darksome state of his soul; and the
disgust which had sent him to the green cloth drew
him away from it.

Leaving the tumult, he adjourned to a room
set apart for assemblies, in which at this hour
was not to be found a living creature; and he
indolently seated himself near the window and
looked out on to the street. Here were the nar-
rowest, most angular overhanging houses, overshadowed by the formidable cathedral, which at
the extremity reared its black worm-eaten wall.
Pepe Rey glanced round on all sides, above and below, and remarked on the peaceful, sepulchral
silence; not a footstep, nor a voice, nor a gaze.
Presently some singular noise struck his ears like
the whispers from some women's lips, and then the

sound of curtains being drawn, some words, and, finally, a sweet verse of a song, the bark of a little dog, and other signs of social existence which seemed very strange in such a situation. Observing well, Pepe Rey found that such noises proceeded from a large balcony with blinds, which ran from window to window, and displayed its monstrous fabric. He had not finished his observations, when a frequenter of the casino appeared suddenly at his side, and laughingly addressed him in this manner:

"Ah, Señor Don Pepe, rogue! have you shut yourself up here to cast sheep's eyes at young girls?"

He who thus spoke was Don Juan Tafetán, an amiable person, and one who had behaved toward Pepe, at the casino, with cordial friendliness and true admiration. With his small red face, his black whiskers, his vivacious eyes, his small stature, his hair carefully combed to conceal his baldness, Don Juan Tafetán presented a very different appearance to Anthony; but he was very sympathetic and gracious, and had a happy talent for relating pleasing adventures. He laughed much, and when he did so, it was all over his face, and from his forehead to his beard grotesque wrinkles formed. In spite of these qualities, and the applause which stimulated in him the disposition for piquant jokes, he was not malevolent. He wished well to all, and Pepe Rey always found his company agreeable. Poor Tafetán, anciently employed in the civil administration in the provincial capital, lived modestly on his salary from the Secretary of Benefices, and passed his time playing the clarinet gaily in the procession, in the ceremonies at the cathedral, as also at the theatre when some company of despairing comedians came to these countries with the idea of giving performances at Orbajosa.

But Don Juan Tafetán's greatest peculiarity was his affection for sprightly young girls. He even, when he could no longer hide his baldness with his six pomaded hairs, when he no longer wore whiskers, when he was bent and feeble under his weight of years, was still known as a formidable gallant. To hear him relate his conquests was enough to make one die with laughter, for of all the gallants of gallants, he was the most original.

"What young girls?" I see no young girls anywhere," replied Pepe Rey.

"Do you profess to be a hermit?"

One of the blinds in the balcony was opened, and a youthful face was seen, fresh and smiling, which was immediately withdrawn, like a light extinguished by the wind.

"Ah, I see!"

"Do you not know them?"

"Upon my word, no."

"They are the Troyas, the girls of Troy— But you know nothing good— Three precious little girls, daughters of a colonel of Estado Mayor de Plazas, who died in the streets of Madrid in '54."

The blind was again drawn, and two faces appeared.

"They are making fun of us," said Tafetán, making a friendly movement to the young girls.

"Do you know them?"

"Do I not know them? The poor girls are in misery. I do not know how they live. When Don Francisco Troya died, a subscription was raised to maintain them, but that did not last very long."

"Poor girls! I should fancy they are not models of probity."

"Why not? I do not believe the town says that of them."

Again the blind was moved.

"Good-afternoon, girls!" shouted Don Juan Tafetán, addressing himself to the three, who formed an artistic group. "This gentleman says it is no use your hiding yourselves—that you are to draw up all the blind."

But it was pulled down, and a peal of happy laughter enlivened the sad street. One would have thought a covey of birds had passed.

"Do you wish to go there?" said the subtle Tafetán.

His eyes shone, and a roguish smile played round his amorous lips.

"But what sort of people are they?"

"Get away with you, Señor de Rey— The poor girls are honorable. Bah! as though they could live on air, like chameleons. You would say, 'He who eats not, does he not sin?' These unhappy girls are, however, virtuous, and if they fall they can relieve their conscience, because it is great want that causes it."

"Then let us go."

A moment after, Don Juan Tafetán and Don Rey entered the room. The appearance of misery, with its horrible accompaniments, which could not be disguised, afflicted the young man.

The three girls were very neat, especially the two shorter ones; they were of dark complexion, with black eyes and slim figure. Well dressed and well shod, they would have looked like the offspring of a duchess, and worthy to associate with princes.

When their visitors entered, the three were very stately, but soon their natural disposition, genial, frivolous, and happy, showed itself. They lived in misery, like birds in prison, singing as blithely behind the iron bars as they would in a wealth of forest. They passed the day in sewing, which, at least, indicated a sense of probity; but in Orbajosa no one of their position associated with them. They were thus, in a certain measure, proscribed, degraded, hemmed in, and this gave rise to some scandal. But the truth was, that the Troyas' bad reputation really consisted in, more than in anything else, their fame for tale-bearing, freedom from prejudice, and restlessness. They wrote anonymous letters to grave people; gave nicknames to all residing in Orbajosa, from the bishop to the last upstart; threw small stones at the passers-by; whispered jokes behind the windows, to the confusion and alarm of pedestrians; knew all the events of the neighborhood, for they made constant use of all the skylights and openings in the different parts of the house; sang at night in the balcony; dressed themselves as masqueraders at the Carnival, that they might enter the great houses; with other absurdities and liberties only proper to small towns. But whatever might be the reason, it was true that the graceful Troyas were under the ban of their susceptible neighbors, and would remain so till the tomb closed over them.

"Is that the gentleman who, 'tis said, has come to seek for gold mines?" asked one.

"And to demolish the cathedral, that he may erect a shoe manufactory with the stones?" added another.

"And to do away with the sowing of garlic, to grow in its place the cotton plant and cinnamon tree?"

Pepe could not refrain from laughing at such absurdities.

"No; he has come here to make a collection of good girls to take back to Madrid," said Tafetán.

"Ah! there is a good chance for me to go," exclaimed one.

"All three—I will take all three," affirmed Pepe. "But I want to know one thing: why were you laughing at me when I was seated at the casino window?"

These words were the signal for another burst of laughter.

"It was only our nonsense," said the eldest.

"It was because we said you were worth more than Doña Perfecta's daughter."

"It was because she said that you were wasting your time, for Rosarito will have nothing to do with any one but church people."

"What things you say! I did not affirm anything of the sort. It was you who told us that this gentleman was a Lutheran atheist, and entered the cathedral, smoking, and with his hat on."

"But I did not invent it," replied the youngest. "Suspiritos told it me yesterday."

"And who is this Suspiritos who spreads such idle tales?"

"Suspiritos is—Suspiritos."

"My daughters," said Tafetán, sweetly, "here goes the orange seller. Call him, as we wish to buy some oranges."

One of the three called the orange merchant.

The conversation held by the young girls was sufficiently displeasing to Pepe Rey, dissipating the slight feeling of content which he had experienced on meeting with such happy, talkative companions. He could not, however, restrain a smile on seeing Don Juan Tafetán bring down a small guitar and flourish his hand over it with the grace and dexterity of a younger man.

"I have been told that you sing ravishingly," proffered Rey.

"That Don Juan Tafetán sings?"

"I do not sing."

"Nor I," said the second eldest, offering the engineer a portion of an orange she had just peeled.

"Maria Juana, do not leave off sewing," said the eldest Troya. "It is afternoon, and the cassock must be finished to-night."

"Do not work to-day. To the devil with the needles!" exclaimed Tafetán.

The second girl intoned a song.

"People are appearing in the street," said one

of the Troyas, looking over the balcony. Don Juan Tafetán's shouts have been heard in the square— Juana! Juana!"

"Well?"

"Suspiritos is in the street."

The youngest girl came to the balcony.

"Throw her a piece of orange."

Pepe Rey looked out also; he saw a lady passing, and that the youngest of the Troyas cleverly threw some orange-peel on to her hair. Then they shut the windows precipitately, and all three were nearly suffocated by their laughter, which no doubt could be heard below in the public thoroughfare.

"To-day do not work!" shouted one, kicking the work-basket with her foot.

"That is the same as saying that to-morrow we do not eat," added the eldest, picking up the scattered work.

Pepe Rey put his hand up instinctively for his purse. He would have willingly given them alms. The sight of these unfortunate orphans, condemned by the world on account of their frivolity, made him feel very sorrowful. If the only sin of the Troyas, if the only alleviation that could compensate them in their solitude, consisted in throwing orange-peel on to the passers-by, they might easily have been forgiven. Thanks to the austere manners of the town in which they dwelt, they had been preserved from vice; but the poor girls required food and raiment, and it might well be expected that they would throw more than orange-skins out of the window. Pepe Rey felt the greatest compassion for them. He noticed their wretched attire—composed, arranged, and mended in a thousand fashions, that it might look new; he observed their broken shoes—and again he put his hand up for his purse.

"Vice might well reign here," he thought; "but their physiognomies, furniture, all indicate that they are the remains of an honorable family. If these poor girls were as bad as 'tis reported, they would neither live so poorly nor work. There are rich men in Orbajosa!"

The three young girls approached him successively. Going from him to the balcony, from the balcony to him, they carried on a piquant and light conversation, which showed, so he read it, a species of innocence in the midst of so much giddiness.

"Señor Don José, what an excellent lady is Doña Perfecta."

"She is the only person in Orbajosa who is not nicknamed, the only person in Orbajosa of whom no evil is spoken."

"Every one respects her."

"Every one adores her."

To these sentences the young man replied with

praises in his aunt's honor; but he greatly desired to take money from his purse and say: "Maria Juana, take this for a pair of boots; Pepa, take this to buy a dress with; Florentina, take this that you may have enough to eat for a week." He was on the point of doing so. For a moment all three had run to the balcony to see some one pass, and Don Juan Tafetán came up to him and whispered:

"What monkeys they are! Is it not true?— Poor creatures! It seems like deception to see them so light-hearted, when—I feel sure they have had nothing to eat to-day."

"Don Juan! Don Juan!" called Pepilla, "here comes your friend Nicholas Hermandez, or rather Paschal Candle, with his large three-cornered hat. He is praying in an undertone, no doubt for the souls of those he has sent to the pit with his usury."

"It is well said that you are mockers."

"Ah, yes."

"Juana, draw the blinds. Let him pass, and when he reaches the corner I will shout: 'Candle, Paschal Candle!'"

Don Juan Tafetán ran to the balcony.

"Come, Don José, that you may know this model."

Pepe Rey took advantage of the moment that the three girls and Don Juan were amusing themselves in the balcony calling Nicholas Hermandez by the nickname which enraged him, and, approaching one of the work-tables, which was in the room, very cautiously, he put down the money he had won at play.

He then hurried to the balcony, where the two younger girls were shouting, amid peals of laughter: "Paschal Candle! Paschal Candle!"

CHAPTER XIII

A CAUSE FOR WAR

AFTER this roguery, the three commenced a conversation with the two gentlemen relating to all the affairs and people in the town. The engineer, fearing that his gift might be discovered while he was present, wished to be off, which greatly displeased the Troyas; one of them, who had left the room, returned, saying:

"Suspiritos is ringing the bell."

"Don José wishes to see her," added another.

"She is a very gay dame, and now she dresses her hair in the Madrid fashion."

"Come."

They rose and led the way to the dining-room (a place very little used), which looked out on to a terrace where there were some pots of flowers and some old furniture. From here might be seen the courtyard of an adjoining house, with a gallery full of green climbing plants and beautiful flowers in pots, carefully tended. All demonstrated the abode of modest, chaste, and well-to-do people.

The Troyas, approaching the edge of the terrace,

gazed fixedly at the neighboring house, and, imposing silence on the gallants, retired to a distant part of the walk, whence no one could perceive them.

"Now she is going out of the kitchen with some chickpea in a pan," said Maria Juana, stretching out her neck to look.

"Flap!" exclaimed one, throwing a small stone.

The noise of the projectile falling on the glass gallery was heard, and then an angry voice shouted:

"If you dare throw again! You have broken the glass."

The three hid in a corner of the terrace, and were joined by the two gentlemen, who found them convulsed with laughter.

"Madam Suspiritos is very much put out," said Rey. "Why do you call her so?"

"Because, when speaking, she sighs between each word; and, although wanting for nothing, she is always complaining."

There was a moment's silence in the other house. Pepita Troya peeped cautiously.

"Let us throw again," she whispered, telling the others to keep quiet. "Maria, give me a stone. Now then—flap!—there it goes."

"You managed badly. It fell on the ground."

"Once more to see if I can hit it— We will wait until she comes out of the kitchen again."

"Now, now she comes. On guard, Florentina.'
"One, two, three!— Paf!—"
They heard an exclamation of sorrow, an execration, a manly voice, since it issued from a man. Pepe Rey could distinctly hear these words:

"Demons! They have struck my head!— Jacintito! Jacintito! But what a neighborhood this is!"

"Jesus! Marie! Joseph! what have I done?" exclaimed Florentina, full of consternation. "I have thrown it at Don Inocencio's head."

"The confessor?" demanded Pepe Rey.

"Yes."

"Does he live there?"

"Where should he live?"

"This lady of sighs—"

"Is his niece, his mistress, I know not what. We amuse ourselves by attacking her, but with the confessor we never dare jest."

While this dialogue passed quickly, Pepe Rey saw that, facing the terrace, and not far from it, the panes of a window belonging to the bombarded house were open; he saw a rosy face, a face he knew, a face which stupefied and alarmed him, and rendered him pale and trembling. It belonged to Jacintito, who, interrupted in his grave studies, opened the window hastily, and showed himself with his pen in his ear. His modest countenance, fresh and smiling, gave to his appearance a resemblance to the dawn of day.

"Good-afternoon, Señor Don José," he said gaily.

The other voice was again heard.

"Jacintito, Jacintito!"

"Here I am. I was saluting a friend—"

"Let us go, let us go," said Florentina with anxiety. "The confessor is going up to Don Nominativo's room, and will give us a lecture."

"Yes, let us go; we will shut the dining-room door."

And they all forsook the terrace.

"You should have remembered that Jacintito could see you from his temple of wisdom," said Tafetán.

"Don Nominativo is our friend," replied one of the girls. "From his temple of science he tells us a thousand sweet things, and throws us kisses."

"Jacintito?" questioned the engineer. "What a diabolical name you have given him!"

"Don Nominativo—"

The three began to laugh.

"We named him so because he is very learned."

"No; because when we were little, he was little also; then—yes. We went out on to the terrace to play, and could hear him studying his lessons aloud."

"Yes, and all the blessed day he was singing."

"Declining, woman. That is, he proceeded in this manner: nominative, genitive, dative, accusative."

"I suppose you have already found a nickname for me," said Pepe Rey.

"Let Maria Juana tell you it," replied Florentina, quietly.

"I?—you tell him."

"You have no name yet, Señor Don José."

"But I shall have. Promise that you will let me know it, that I may receive confirmation," said the young fellow, with the intention of withdrawing.

"But are you leaving?"

"Yes. I have caused you to lose a lot of time. Girls, to work. Throwing stones at neighbors and pedestrians is not the most suitable employment for such pretty, deserving young girls— Do not be vexed—"

And without listening to the reasonings and compliments of the young people he hurriedly left the house, leaving them to Don Juan Tafetán.

The scene he had witnessed, the priest's vexation, the inopportune appearance of the little doctor, added to his confusion, and to the disagreeable presentiments which tormented the poor engineer's soul. He heartily regretted having been drawn to the Troyas' house, and to fill up his time in a better manner, he, while his hypochondria lasted, walked through the town streets.

He visited the market, the streets of Triperia, where stood the principal shops; he observed the divers aspects presented by the industry and commerce of great Orbajosa; and as he met with no fresh cause of annoyance he took the road to the promenade of Descalzas, but there he only found a few stray dogs, for, as a strong wind blew, cavaliers and ladies had remained at home. He went to the apothecary's, where there was an assembly of ruminating advocates of progression, who were perpetually discussing an endless theme, but who never wearied of it. He at last went to the cathedral, where the organ could be heard and the beautiful canticles of the choir. He entered, kneeling before the high altar, as he recalled to mind the warnings his aunt had given him about want of reverence in church. He then visited a side chapel, and was about to enter another, when an acolyte, or beadle, approached, and in a very uncivil, insolent manner addressed him thus:

"His lordship says that you are to go out."

The engineer felt a rush of blood to his head. Without speaking a word he obeyed. Ejected on all sides either on account of his valor or by his own disgust, he had no choice but to return to his aunt's house, where awaited him:

First, Lycurgus, to announce another lawsuit.

Secondly, Don Cayetano, to read him a new treatise on the lineage of Orbajosa. Thirdly, Caballuco, for a reason he had not made the others acquainted with. Fourthly, Doña Perfecta with a good-natured smile, the reason of which we shall see in the following chapter.

CHAPTER XIV

DISLIKE IS STILL ON THE INCREASE

A FRESH attempt to see his cousin had resulted in his downfall that afternoon. Pepe Rey shut himself up in his room to write various letters, and could not rid himself of a certain idea.

"To-night or to-morrow," he said, "I will accomplish it by some means or another."

When he was called to supper, Doña Perfecta, approaching him, said, with her usual smile:

"Dear Pepe, do not feel worried, I will appease Don Inocencio— I know all— Maria Remedios, who has just left here, has informed me."

Her ladyship's face expressed the greatest satisfaction, resembling an artist who was proud of his work.

"What?"

"I excuse you, man. You had good luck at the casino, did you not? Behold the result of bad companions! Don Juan Tafetán, the Troyas. It is horrible, dreadful! Have you thought well on it?"

"I have thought well about all, señora," replied Pepe, determined not to dispute with his aunt.

"I am much inclined to write and tell your father what you have done."

"You may write what you please."

"We will see. You would exculpate yourself by equivocation."

"I do not equivocate."

"Then confess you were in the house—"

"I was."

"And that you left them some money, for Maria Remedios told me that this afternoon. Florentina went to a shop to ask them to change it. They could not earn it by their sewing. You were in their house? Then—"

"Then I gave it to them. Assuredly."

"You do not deny it?"

"Why should I? I suppose I may do as I please with my money."

"But surely you did not throw stones at the confessor?"

"I did not."

"You mean to say that they, in your presence—"

"That is another thing."

"And insulted poor Maria Remedios."

"That I also deny."

"And how do you justify your conduct? Pepe— for God's sake! You say nothing, you are not sorry, you do not protest—no—"

"Nothing, absolutely nothing."

"Are you trying to aggravate me?"

"I have not aggravated you—"

"We shall see, do not make your fault graver. Man, take this stick and beat me."

"I do not beat people."

"What, wanting in respect! What! and are you going to eat no supper?"

"I intend to sup."

Then there was about a quarter of an hour's silence. Don Cayetano, Doña Perfecta, and Pepe ate without a word. But presently Don Inocencio interrupted them by entering the dining-room.

"How do you feel, Señor Don José, my cherished one? Did you think I should really resent it," said he, extending his hand to the young man, and looking at him in a compassionate manner.

The engineer felt so confused that he did not reply.

"I refer to what happened this afternoon."

"Ah! Indeed!"

"And to your expulsion from the sacred precincts of the cathedral."

"His lordship the bishop," said Pepe Rey, "should reflect well before ejecting a Christian from the church."

"That is true; I can not imagine who can have put it into his lordship's head that you are a man of evil reputation; I do not know who can have told him that you boast everywhere of your atheism; that you mock at holy persons and things, and even project demolishing the cathedral to erect with its stones a grand edifice of pitch and tar. I had tried to dissuade him from doing so; but his lordship is a little obstinate."

"Thanks for so much kindness."

"And especially as the confessor has no reason for such consideration toward you. Particularly after your behavior this afternoon."

"Bah!—that!" said the priest laughing. "That I should take notice of that roguery! I wager that Maria Remedios has related that affair to you. And I forbade her, forbade her in a very decided manner. It was not worth the trouble; was it, Señor de Rey?"

"You should be the judge of that—"

"It seemed to me like this. Young people's jests— Youth, so says modern times, are inclined to vice and to vicious actions. Señor Don José, who is a talented man, can not be expected to be perfect—who knows but that the graceful girls seduced him and then relieved him of his money, making him an accomplice to their insolent behavior and criminal insults to their neighbors! My dear friend, for the dolorous part I have played in this afternoon's jests," he added, raising his hands with compassionate air, "I can not but be offended and mortified at your having been the witness of such a disgraceful incident. I felt truly grieved when Maria Remedios came and related all to me— My niece is such a gossip— For she related to me all about the money, your playing the fool with the young girls on the terrace, running about and pinching, and Don Juan Tafetán dancing. Bah! these things should be done secretly."

Pepe Rey did not know which confused him most, his aunt's severity or the hypocritical condescension of the priest.

"He has nothing to say for himself," continued his aunt. "And he does not even seem ashamed of his conduct. All will hear about it. We must only try to keep it from my dear daughter, for in her nervous state we are afraid of attacks of anger."

"Well, it is not much, señora," added the confessor. "My opinion is that we need not talk about this, but if any one says he threw the stone, we can satisfy them— And it was not the fun I was annoyed at, Señor Don José, but I thought they had broken the skin of my head and made the brains come out."

"I was sorry for that accident," murmured Pepe Rey. "It caused me much regret; but I had no part in it."

"Your visit to these Señoritas Troya has created a talk in the town," said the priest. "This is not Madrid, sir; here we are not living in that centre of corruption, of scandal—"

"There one may visit the most obscene places," proffered Doña Perfecta, "and no one knows it."

"Here every one is watched," proceeded the confessor. "We take notice of all that is done by our neighbors, and, with such a system of vigilance, public morality attains a high degree— Believe me, believe me, my friend, I do not say this to mortify you; you are, I know, the first enlightened gentleman of the day—the first, yes, señor— '*Trojæ qui primus ad oris.*'"

Then he began to laugh, slapping the engineer on his shoulder several times, in token of friendship and benevolence.

"How grateful I am," said the young man, covering his anger by the words he thought most suitable for replying to the cunning irony of his interlocutors, "to find so much generosity and tolerance, when I merited the contrary by my criminal proceedings!—"

"But why? An individual who is of our own race and who bears our name," said Doña Perfecta, "how can we treat him as we should another? You are my nephew, you are the son of the best and most saintly of men, my dear brother Juan, and it is enough. Yesterday afternoon the bishop's secretary was here to tell me that his lordship felt much displeased that I retained you in my house."

"Is it so?" murmured the priest.

"It is so. I said that, with all due respect to the bishop, whom I love and reverence, my nephew is my nephew, and I could not eject him from my house."

"This is a new peculiarity that I have noticed in this country," said Pepe Rey, pale with anger. "It seems that here the bishop rules the household affairs."

"He is a holy man. He likes me so much that he fancies—he is afraid that you will imbue us with your atheism, your prejudice, your strange opinions— I have repeatedly told him that you are really good."

"One must concede something to a superior and talented man," said Don Inocencio.

"And this morning, when I was at the house of the Cirujedas, ah! you can not imagine how they made my heart ache. I was told you had come to raze the cathedral; that you were commissioned by the English Protestants to preach heresy in Spain; that you passed the whole night gambling at the casino; and went out, drunk—

" 'But, señoras,' said I, 'do you wish me to deny my nephew a lodging?' Besides, they were wrong about your being intoxicated, and, as to play, I did not know you gambled until to-day."

Pepe Rey would have spoken in this situation with the boldness that the most prudent man feels inwardly, from violent love and a blind brutal strength, which generally leads to blows, breaking of heads and crushing of bones. But his aunt was a woman, and Don Inocencio was old and a priest. And, also, such violence is improper, and avoided by Christian and well-educated people. He wished to give expression to his restrained anger by means of manifestly decorous but pointed words, although that seemed a premature moment for uttering them, and he finally determined not to employ that resource until he should be really leaving the house and Orbajosa. Resisting, then, his fury, he kept silence.

Jacintito arrived when supper was finished.

"Good-evening, Señor Don José," he said, holding out his hand to the young man. "You and your friends prevented me from working this afternoon. I could not write a line, and I had so much to do!"

"I am sorry, Jacintito, but they told me that you sometimes joined them in their games and gaiety."

"I!" exclaimed he quickly, becoming red. "Bah! you well know that Tafetán does not speak a word of truth— That is certain, Señor de Rey; and are you leaving?"

"Do they say so here?"

"Yes; I heard it in the casino, at Don Lorenzo Ruiz's."

Rey looked at Don Nominativo's fresh features for a minute, and then replied:

"It is not so. My aunt is very well satisfied with me, despite the calumnies related of me by the Orbajosians—and she will not turn me from her house, even to please the bishop."

"I turn you out—never! What would your father say?"

"In spite of your goodness, my dear aunt, in spite of the priest's cordial friendship, I have decided to leave—"

"You leave!"

"Doña Perfecta's eyes shone with a peculiar light. The priest, although a very expert man in dissimulation, could not hide his joy.

"Yes, and this very night—"

"But, man, how hasty you are! Can not you even wait until to-morrow morning?— Here— Juan, go and tell Lycurgus to prepare the pony— I suppose you will take something cold— Nicholasa!—that piece of cold veal from the larder— Librada! this young gentleman's clothes."

"I did not think you would have taken such a peevish resolution," said Don Cayetano, thinking ' he ought to express some opinion.

"But you are going—are you not?" questioned the priest.

"At what hour does the morning train leave?" asked Doña Perfecta, whose eyes expressed a feverish impatience.

"Yes, I am going to-night."

"But, man, there is no moon."

In Doña Perfecta's soul, in the confessor's, and

in the young doctor's, resounded with celestial harmony those words, "This very night."

"I suppose, dear Pepe, you will go— I wrote to-day to your father—your excellent father!" exclaimed Doña Perfecta, with all the facial symptoms of one who was on the verge of tears.

"Can I trouble you with a few commissions?" asked the savant.

"It is a good opportunity to secure an edition of Abbé Gaume's works, which I am short of," said the lawyer.

"See, Pepe, what is the result of these attacks of violence," said the señora, smiling, with her eyes fixed on the dining-room door. "For I had forgotten to tell you that Caballuco awaits you."

CHAPTER XV

DISLIKE INCREASES UNTIL IT ENDS IN A DECLARATION OF WAR

ALL glanced toward the door, where the imposing Caballuco stood, looking serious, clouded, perplexed, wishing to salute with amiability, but disfigured by the exertion done by trying to smile urbanely, and to fold his herculean arms in a proper position.

"Forward, Señor de Ramos," said Pepe Rey.

"No," objected Doña Perfecta. "It may be some nonsense he wishes to say to you."

"Let him say it."

"I will not allow foolish questions to be ventilated in my house—"

"What do you want of me, Señor de Ramos?" asked Pepe Rey.

Caballuco muttered something.

"Enough, enough!—" exclaimed Doña Perfecta, smiling. "Do not vex my nephew more. Pepe, take no notice of this clown— Shall I tell you what Caballuco's complaint is?"

"Complaint? I can guess it," said the confessor,

throwing himself back in the armchair, and laughing long and loudly.

"I wish to tell Señor Don José it—" grunted the formidable horseman.

"Silence, man, silence; for God's sake, do not deafen us."

"Señor Caballuco," said the priest, "does not know that gentlemen from Court are shocked by the rude customs of these savage lands—"

"In two words, Pepe, the question is this: Caballuco does not know why—"

She could not continue for laughter.

"Does not know why!" added Don Inocencio, "one of the young Troyas, Maraquita Juana, if I am not mistaken— He is jealous! After his horse, the principal object in creation is Maraquilla Troya."

"A good aim!" exclaimed the señora. "Poor Christobel! You thought that a person like my nephew— Let us see, what were you going to say? Speak!"

"Señor Don José and I will talk presently," replied the local brave man, retiring abruptly.

A short time after Pepe Rey left the dining-room, and repaired to his room. In the gallery he encountered his Trojan antagonist face to face, and could not repress a smile on seeing the serious, stern countenance of the offended courier.

"A word," said the latter, placing himself impudently in the engineer's way. "Do you know me?"

Expressing himself thus, he laid his hand heavily on the young man's shoulder with such insolent familiarity that Pepe repulsed him energetically.

"There is no need to crush me in that style."

The braggadocio, slightly taken aback, hesitated for an instant, and then, looking at Pepe Rey in an audaciously provoking way, repeated his song:

"Do you know me?"

"Yes; I know you are an animal."

And pushing him unceremoniously aside, he went to his room. Although his brain was in such a fermented state, our disgraced friend speedily settled his brief and decisive plans; to break Caballuco's head without loss of time; to take leave of his aunt, and reason severely, though courteously, with her; to bid the priest, coldly, good-by; to embrace the inoffensive Cayetano; to administer, by way of rejoicing, a cudgeling to Lycurgus; to quit Orbajosa that same night, and to shake the dust of that town off his shoes. But these thoughts of the persecuted young man did not prevent him, in the midst of such bitterness, from remembering another disgraced person, whom he supposed to be in a more afflicted and sorrowful position than his own. A servant hereupon entered the engineer's room.

"Did you give her my message?" he promptly asked.

"Yes, sir; and she gave me this."

Rey took from the girl's hand a page of a newspaper, on the margin of which he read these words:

"They tell me you are going. I shall die—"

When he returned to the dining-room Lycurgus met him at the door and said:

"At what time do you require the pony?"

"No time," replied Rey, quickly.

"Then you are not going to-night?" said Doña Perfecta. "It is better that you should not leave until to-morrow?"

"Nor to-morrow."

"When?"

"We shall see," said the young man, coldly, looking at his aunt with imperturbable calmness. "At present I do not intend leaving."

He assumed a menacing appearance. Doña Perfecta became first red-hot, and then pale. She looked at the priest, who had taken off his gold spectacles to see clearer, and then successively at all who were in the room, including Caballuco, who had just entered and had seated himself on the edge of a chair. Doña Perfecta looked around like a general reviewing his army. She then studied the meditative, calm face of her nephew as though he were an enemy who had suddenly presented himself when she had believed him to have taken refuge in a shameful flight.

Ah! Blood, ruin, and desolation!—A great battle was beginning.

CHAPTER XVI

NIGHT

ORBAJOSA slept. The musty lanterns, which illuminated the streets, glimmering at the crossways and narrow pathways, looked like eyes that could not overcome sleep. By their feeble light could be distinguished vagabonds, watchmen, and gamblers enveloped in their cloaks. The only sounds that disturbed the peace of the historical city, were the serenade of some lover, and the wild uproar of the drunkard. The Ave Maria Purisima of the night-watch rose like a sickly complaint from the sleeping population.

In Doña Perfecta's house silence reigned. It was only broken by a dialogue which was taking place between Don Cayetano and Pepe Rey in the library. The savant *was* sitting calmly in an armchair before his table, which was covered with divers piles of papers, containing notes, annotations, and references, in a slightly disordered state, on account of the variety and abundance. Rey had his eyes fixed on the copious mass of papers; but his thoughts had flown to a spot very remote from the temple of knowledge.

"Perfecta," said the old man, "although an excellent woman, has the defect of being scandalized by every frivolous insignificant action. My friend, in these provincial towns, the least slip is dearly paid for. You can not have committed any grave fault by going to the Troyas' house. I think that Don Inocencio, beneath his pretense of being a good man, is a mischief-maker. What difference could it make to him?"

"We have arrived at a time, Señor Don Cayetano, when it is necessary to act in a determined and energetic manner. I must see and speak with Rosarito."

"But you can see her."

"I am not allowed to do so," replied the engineer, giving the table a blow with his fist. "Rosarito is shut up."

"Shut up!" exclaimed the savant, incredulously. "The truth is, that I do not like her facial appearance, nor her general aspect, nor the stupid expression that is in her beautiful eyes. She is sad, speaks little, weeps. Friend José, I am much afraid that this child is likely to be attacked by the terrible infirmity to which many of my family have been victims."

"A terrible infirmity! What?"

"Madness—or, rather, monomania. In my family there has only been one person free from it, I—I am the only one who has escaped."

"You!— Putting aside the monomania," said Rey, impatiently, "I wish to see Rosarito."

"Nothing more natural. But the isolation in which her mother keeps her is a hygienic system, dear Pepe; the only system that has been successfully employed by the members of my family. Remember that the person whose presence and voice would make the greatest impression on Rosarito's delicate nervous system is her heart's choice."

"Notwithstanding all," said Pepe, "I wish to see her."

"Perhaps Perfecta will not oppose it," said the savant, fixing his attention on his notes and papers. "I do not wish to take the responsibility."

The engineer, seeing that he could obtain no assistance from the good Polentinos, rose up to leave the room.

"You are going to work, and I do not wish to hinder you."

"No, it is still early. Look at the heap of precious dates that I have put together to-day! Listen! In 1537, an inhabitant of Orbajosa, named Bartholomew of the Hoyo, went to Civita Vecchia in the galleys of the Marquis de Castel Rodrigo. Another; in the same year, two brothers—sons, likewise, of Orbajosa—named Juan and Roderigo Gonzalez del Arco, embarked in the six ships that sailed for Maestrique on the 20th of February; which, near to Calais, gave battle to an English

Doña Perfecta

ship, and the fleet commanded by Van-Owen.
Finally, here is an important exploit by our navy.
I have found out that an Orbajosian, one Mateo
Diaz, colonel in the Guards, was he who, in 1709,
wrote and printed in Valencia the 'metrical praise,
funeral song, lyrical eulogy, numerical description, ·
glorious toils and glorious sorrows of the Queen
of the Angels.' I possess a precious copy of this
work, which is worth all the gold in Peru. Another Orbajosian is the author of that famous
'Treatise on the various species of the weasel,' in
which I was instructing you yesterday; and in the
summing up I gave a passing glance at the labyrinth of the unpublished history of this illustrious
peasant. I am anxious to rescue all these names
from the unjust obscurity and oblivion in which
they are at present. What purer enjoyment, dear
Pepe, than to revive all the lustre of the works of
praise, epic prayers, and literary works of the country in which one is born? No better employment
could devolve on a man, in return for the little
knowledge and hereditary fortune Heaven has
blessed him with, during the short time that even
the longest lived pass in this world. Thanks to me,
Orbajosa will be regarded as the cradle of Spanish genius. But what do I say? Is not her illustrious race well known for its nobility—the nobility
of the real generation urbsaugustana? Few places
are known where the plants and shrubs of all vir-

tues have grown more vigorously, free from the malevolent weeds of vice. Here all is peace, mutual respect, Christian humility. Charity is practised here as it was in the apostles' time; here envy is not known; here are not known criminal passions; and, if one hears robbers and assassins spoken of, one may rest assured that they are not the children of this noble land, but belong to the number of those unhappy ones perverted by the preachings of demagogues. Here is seen the national character in all its purity and rectitude—noble, incorruptible, simple, patriarchal, hospitable, generous. It is so pleasant to live in this peaceful solitude, far from the labyrinth of cities, where reign, ay! falsehood and vice! For these reasons I can not often go to see my many friends in Madrid; for these reasons I live in the sweet companionship of my loyal peasants and my books, breathing continually this salubrious atmosphere of honor that is little by little becoming unknown in our Spain, and only exists in those humble and Christian towns which, by their emanations of virtue, know how to preserve it. And do you not think, dear Pepe, that this peaceful asylum has greatly helped to free me from the terrible hereditary infirmity of my family? In my youth, I, even as my brothers and father, manifested a lamentable propensity for the most absurd frenzy; but here you behold me perfectly cured, and I know noth-

ing of that infirmity but what I see in others. It
is for this reason that my little niece causes me
anxiety."

"Praise to the air of Orbajosa, which has preserved you," said Rey, unable to repress a sense of
the ridiculous that such an extraordinary argument
caused, even in the midst of his sorrow. "To me
it has proved so unhealthful that I believe I should
become a maniac did I remain here much longer.
I wish you good-night, and plenty of work."

"Good-night."

He went to his room, but felt no desire either
for sleep or physical repose. On the contrary, he
was so greatly excited that he felt he must be doing
something. He walked backward and forward
across his room. He then threw up the window
which opened on to the orchard, and, leaning his
elbows on the sill, gazed out into the blackness of
the night. He could see nothing; but the sleepless
man sees all, and Rey, his eyes staring into the
obscurity, saw pass before him all the various in-
cidents of his disgrace. The darkness did not permit him to distinguish either the flowers of the
earth nor those of the sky, which are the stars. The
entire absence of light produced the effect of an
illusory movement in the masses of trees, which
seemingly extended themselves, turning and twist-
ing about like the flow of a sea of shadows. Formidable flux and reflux, an unequal struggle of

strength, agitated the silent globe. The mathematician contemplated this extraordinary projection of his soul over the night, and said:

"The battle will be terrible. We shall see who will conquer."

The insects of the night whispered mysterious words in his ear. Here, a harsh chirping of birds; there, a clack such as the tongue makes; on this side, murmurs of compassion; yonder, a vibrating sound like to the bell hung round the neck of cattle. Presently Rey heard a singular noise—a rapid remark which could only come from a human tongue and lips. This exhalation crossed the young man's brain like a flash of lightning. It seemed to buzz like a fugitive S, which, being repeated, increases in intensity. He looked on all sides, he searched the higher part of the house, and then, in one of the windows, fancied he could distinguish an object resembling a white bird moving its wing. In his state of mental excitement Pepe Rey thought for a moment it was a ghostly pigeon—but this bird was nothing more than a handkerchief.

The engineer jumped through the window into the orchard. Observing well, he saw his cousin's hand and face. He fancied he could distinguish her imposing silence by putting her finger to her lips. Presently the sympathetic shadow waved its arm and disappeared. Pepe Rey entered his room again quickly, and, taking care to make no noise, passed to the gallery, and then along it slowly. He felt his heart beat, as though it would burst from his bosom. He waited a moment—and at last heard some sounds on the staircase. One, two, three—it was made by shoes.

He directed his steps in the midst of the great darkness, and held out his arms to assist the person who was descending. In his soul reigned a gentle exaltation; but, why deny it? with this sweet sentiment suddenly mingled another, like an infernal inspiration, the desire for revenge. The footsteps approached nearer. Pepe Rey advanced, and another pair of hands clung united with his.

CHAPTER XVII

LIGHT IN DARKNESS

THE gallery was long and wide. At the extremity was the door of the engineer's room; in the centre, that of the dining-room, and at the other end the staircase and a large closed door, with a flight of steps. This door opened into the little chapel where the family kept the images of their domestic devotion. Sometimes the holy sacrifice of Mass was celebrated there.

Rosarito led her cousin to the chapel door, and drew him down on to a step.

"Here?" murmured Pepe Rey.

By the gestures of her right hand Rosarito gave him to understand that this was a sanctified spot.

"Dear cousin Rosarito—thanks for having allowed me to see you!" he exclaimed, clasping her fervently in his arms.

He felt his cousin's cold fingers on his lips, imposing silence. He kissed them frantically.

"Are you cold—Rosarito—why do you tremble?"

Her teeth chattered, and her whole body shook with feverish convulsion. Rey felt his cousin's red-hot face against his own, and exclaimed in alarm:

"Your face is like a volcano. Are you ill?"

"Very."

"Are you really ill?"

"Yes."

"And you have come out—"

"As you see."

The engineer stretched out his arms to shelter her; but she moved.

"Await me," she said, rising hastily. "I am going to my room to put on my traveling cloak. Extinguish the light, Pepe." Rey had omitted to put out the light in his room, and by the door issued a brightness, illuminating all the gallery. He returned in an instant. The darkness was profound. He had to feel his way by the wall to reach the place where his cousin stood. He rejoined her, and wrapped her up carefully from head to foot.

"Are you all right now, my darling?"

"Yes, quite right!— With you."

"With me—and forever!" exclaimed the young man, joyfully.

She drew herself away from his arms, and rose up.

"What are you going to do?"

He heard the noise of a door being unlocked. Rosarito had inserted the key in the invisible lock, and cautiously opened the door on the steps of which they had been sitting. There arose a smell of dampness (caused by the place having been shut up for some time) from these obscure precincts as from a tomb. Pepe Rey felt his hand touched, and heard the voice of his cousin faintly saying:

"Come in."

They proceeded several paces. He likened himself to Elias conducted to unknown places by the angel of the night. She was groping about. At last her sweet voice murmured:

"Sit down."

And they both sat down on a wooden bench; Pepe Rey again embraced her. At the same instant he received a blow on the head from a very hard object.

"What is it?"

"The feet."

"Rosarito— What are you saying?"

"The feet of the Divine Jesus, the image of Christ Crucified, Whom we adore here."

Pepe Rey felt as though a cold lance had pierced his heart.

"Kiss them," said the young girl imperiously.

The mathematician kissed the nailed feet of the holy image.

"Pepe," then exclaimed the young lady, clasping her cousin's hand fervently, "do you believe in God?"

"Rosarito!—what are you saying? What silly thing is in your thoughts?" replied her cousin in astonishment.

"Answer me."

Pepe Rey felt some moisture on his hands.

"Why do you weep?" he asked anxiously. "Rosarito, you kill me with your absurd doubts. Yes, I believe in God. Did you doubt it?"

"I, no; but every one says that you are an atheist."

"You would not have been deserving in my eyes, you would have been despoiled of your aureola of purity and prestige, could I have believed you would credit such a thing."

"I have heard you called atheist, and, although I had no reason to be convinced differently, I have protested from the bottom of my soul against such calumny. You could not be an atheist. From the moment I saw you, I believed in your having religious sentiments, as I have myself."

"You have spoken well. Then, why do you now question me as to whether I believe in God?"

"Because I wished to hear it from your own mouth, and to rejoice in hearing you affirm it. It is so long since I heard your voice!— What greater pleasure than to hear it afresh, and after so long a silence, exclaiming, 'I believe in God!' "

"Rosarito, even malefactors believe in Him. If

there are atheists, and I doubt it, they are the calumniators, the intriguers who infest the world. For my part, I care little for intrigues and calumnies, and if you surmount them, and shut your heart to those sentiments of discord, which a perfidious hand has tried to introduce there, nothing will be wanting to our happiness."

"But let us pass on, Pepe, dear Pepe—do you believe in the Devil?"

The engineer preserved silence. The obscurity of the chapel did not allow Rosarito to see the smile with which her cousin received such a singular question.

"Certainly I believe in him," he said at last.

"What are we to do? Mama has forbidden me to see you, but, with the exception of your atheism, she has said nothing ill of you. She tells me to wait; that you will decide; that you are going; that you will return— Tell me frankly— do you think badly of my mother?"

"Not at all," replied Rey, appreciating her delicacy.

"Do you not think with me, that she loves me much; that she loves us both; that she only desires our good, and, at last, will grant us the permission we desire?"

"If you believe this, so do I— Your mama adores us both— But, dear Rosarito, I must confess that the 'Devil' has entered this house."

"Do not jest," replied she tenderly— "Ah, mama is very good. Not once has she told me that you were not worthy to be my husband. No, she only insists on your atheism. Besides, she says I have manias, and that one of them is loving you with all my soul. In our family it is a law not to openly contradict the hereditary frenzy we suffer from, as it only increases it."

"I think you have on your side good physicians who have proposed to cure you, and that, at last, my adorable girl, they will succeed."

"No, no, a thousand times!" exclaimed Rosarito, burying her face on her cousin's bosom. "That I should wish to become mad with you! For you I am patient; for you I am ill; for you I despise life, and expose myself to die— I already foresee it; to-morrow I shall be worse, it will oppress me— I shall die. What does it matter?"

"You are not ill," replied he, energetically. "You have only the slightest moral disturbance, which naturally causes slight nervous affections; you suffer from nothing more than an occasional trouble, arising from the horrible violence used toward you. Your pure and generous soul does not understand it. Granted; pardon those who injure you; you are grieved, attributing your misfortune to dismal, supernatural influences; you suffer in silence, delivering your innocent neck to the hangman; you allow yourself to be killed, and even the knife placed to your throat appears to you like the thorn of a flower pricking you in your walk. Rosarito, rid yourself of these ideas; realize our true position, which is a serious one; seek the cause of it where it really is, and do not be intimidated; do not submit to the mortifications which are imposed upon you, destroying your soul and body. The valor you are wanting in will restore your health, for you are not really ill, my dear girl, you are—do you wish me to tell you? You are frightened, terrified. What you are truly suffering from is what the ancients did not know how to define, and so termed it withcraft. Rosarito, love, confide in me! Rise and follow me! I say no more."

"Ah! Pepe—my cousin! I believe you are right!" exclaimed Rosarito, in a flood of tears. "Your words resound in my heart like violent blows, which, awakening me, give me new life. Here, in this obscurity, where we can not see each other's face, an ineffable light goes out from you and irradiates my soul. What gift do you possess that you can thus transform me? When I knew you no other sufficed. On those days that I did not see you I returned to my old insignificant existence, to my first timidity. It would be like a Limbo without you, my Pepe— It is sufficient that you should tell me; I rise and follow you. We will go together wherever you will. Do you know that I feel well? I am no longer feverish; I have recovered my strength; I wish to run and shout, that my whole being may be renewed, that it may be augmented and centuplicated, in order that I may worship you. Pepe, you are right. I am not ill, I am only frightened, or rather fascinated."

"That is it, fascinated."

"Fascinated. Terrible eyes watch me, and render me mute and tremulous. I am afraid; but of what? You alone have the singular power to restore me to life. I listen to you; I become better. I believe if I were to die, and you passed near my tomb, that even in the ground I should feel you. Oh! if I could but see you now! But you are here by my side, and I do not doubt that it is really you— It is so long since I saw you! I was becoming mad. Each day of solitude seemed to me a century— I told myself to-morrow, that to-morrow, and yet again to-morrow. I passed the nights by my window, and the glimmer of the light from your room consoled me. To see your shadow on the window was for me a divine apparition. I extended my arms out, in thought, shedding tears and shouting, without being able to do so aloud. When I received your message by the servant; when I received your letter saying that you were going, I became very sad. I thought my soul would leave my body, and that I should gradually die. I fell

—feel like the bird shot when on the wing, which falls and dies in the same moment— To-night, when I saw you retire so late, I could not resist the desire to speak with you, and so came down. I believe that all the audacity that may be contained in my life has been consumed and employed in one single act, in this, and that I shall hereafter continue timid— But you will give me courage; you will give me strength; you will help me; am I not right? Pepe, my dear cousin, tell me that it is so; tell me I shall become strong, and I shall do so; tell me that I am not ill and I am no longer so— I am better already. I feel so well that I laugh at my imaginary malady."

So saying, Rosarito threw herself frantically into her cousin's arms. He would have kissed her. Ah! but their lips did not meet, for, having inclined his head, he came violently into contact with the feet of the crucifix. It caused him to see stars. In the state of his mind, and the natural hallucination which dark places cause, it seemed to Rey that it was not his head that had knocked against the holy feet, but that the image had moved, admonishing him in a very brief and eloquent manner. Partly laughing and partly serious, he raised his head, and said:

"Lord, do not punish me, I have done no wrong."

At the same instant Rosarito seized the young

man's hand, pressing it against her heart. He heard a pure, grave, angelic, feeling voice speaking in this manner:

"Lord, whom I adore, Lord God of the world and Guardian of my house and family; Lord, whom also Pepe worships; Holy Christ who died on the Cross for our sins; before Thee, before Thy wounded body, before Thy head crowned with thorns, I say that this is my spouse; and that, after Thee, he it is whom my soul loves most; I say that I declare him to be my spouse, and that I will rather die than belong to another. My heart and my soul are his. Grant that the world may not oppose our happiness, and concede me the favor of this union, that I may swear to be his before the world as I do in my conscience."

"Rosarito, you are mine!" exclaimed Pepe joyfully. "Neither your mother nor any one else shall prevent it."

His cousin rested on his breast. She trembled in his loving young arms, as the dove in the eagle's claw.

Through the engineer's mind passed a thought only befitting the devil; but then he was in this case the devil. Rosarito made a slight movement of fear; it was like the trembling of surprise, as though she foresaw danger.

"Swear to me that you will not draw back," said Pepe, confusedly, intercepting this movement.

"I swear it to you by the ashes of my father who is—".

"Where?"

"Below our feet."

The mathematician thought the flags moved under his feet—but no, they did not, although he fancied it in spite of his being a mathematician.

"I swear it," repeated Rosarito, "by the ashes of my father, and by the God who sees us— May our bodies, united as they are, repose under these stones when God shall call us from this world."

"Yes," replied Pepe Rey, with deep emotion, feeling his soul full of inexplicable perturbation.

They both remained silent for a few minutes. Rosarito then rose.

"Already?"

She sat down again.

"You tremble again," said Pepe Rey. "Rosarito, you are ill; your face burns."

"I feel as though I were dying," murmured the young girl, with dismay. "I do not know what is the matter with me."

She fell fainting into her cousin's arms. Feeling her face, he found it was covered with cold perspiration.

"She is really ill," he said. "This is the result of a really foolish action."

He raised her in his arms, trying to reanimate

her, but as she did not cease trembling, nor did she recover from her swoon, he resolved to carry her out of the chapel to see if the fresh air would revive her. And it did so. On coming round, Rosarito manifested much inquietude at finding herself out of her room at such an hour. The cathedral clock struck four.

"How late!" exclaimed the young girl. "Liberate me, cousin. I think I can walk. Truly I am very ill."

"I will go up with you."

"On no account. I can creep up to my room. Did you not hear a noise?"

Both kept silence. The anxiety depicted on her countenance made them both quiet.

"Did you hear nothing, Pepe?"

"Absolutely nothing."

"Listen attentively— Now, now it sounds. It is a murmur at some distance, a great distance, and is now near, very near. It might be either my mother's heavy breathing, or the creaking of the weathercock on the cathedral. Ah! I have a very sensitive ear."

"Excessively sensitive— And now, my dear cousin, I will carry you up in my arms."

"Good, carry me to the top of the staircase, and then I can go alone, and when I have rested a little I shall be all right— But do you not hear anything?"

They were on the first step.

"It is a metallic sound."

"Your mother's breathing."

"No, no, it is not. It now sounds in the distance. Perhaps it is a cock crowing."

"It may be."

"I could fancy I hear two words. 'I see there; I see there.'"

"Now, now I hear it," murmured Pepe Rey.

"It is a scream."

"It is a bugle."

"A bugle?"

"Yes. We must go up quickly— Orbajosa will be aroused— I hear it clearly. There is a bugle if not a trumpet. The troop has arrived."

"Troop?"

"I fancy this military invasion will be propitious to me— I am happy. Rosarito, we are already up."

"I am likewise happy— We are up."

As they were at the top of the stair, the two lovers took leave of each other, talking in such low tones that they could scarcely hear each other.

"I will sit down near the window looking on to the orchard, so that you may know that I have reached my room all right. Good-by."

"Good-by, Rosarito. Take care not to fall against the furniture."

"I know my way well, cousin. We will see each other again. Sit by your window if you wish to receive my telegraphic signs."

Pepe Rey did as she commanded him; but, after watching for some time, did not see Rosarito. He thought that he heard agitated voices on the top floor.

CHAPTER XVIII

THE TROOP

THE inhabitants of Orbajosa heard the sound of the bugle in the vague twilight of their late dreams, and opened their eyes, saying:

"The troop."

Some said, half-asleep, half-awake:

"At last they have sent us this rabble."

Others rose hastily, shouting thus:

"Let us see those confounded fellows."

Some one else apostrophized in this manner:

"We have necessarily anticipated this— They will ask for tithes and contributions, we shall reply with blows and more blows."

In another house these words, pronounced joyfully, could be heard:

"If they should have sent my son! If they should have sent my brother!"

All rose from their beds, dressed quickly, opened the windows to see the noisy regiment that entered with the dawn of day. The town was sad, silent, old; the army, gay, bustling and young. The one entering the other gave the appearance of a mummy imbued with the marvelous gift of life, noisily leaping vigorously from the damp sarcophagus, to dance around it. What motion, what huzzas, what laughter, what mirth! There is nothing so interesting as an army. It is the country in its youthful, vigorous aspect. Whatever the conceited individuality of the same country has, or can possibly have, of inability, of insurrection, of superstition at times, of blasphemy at others, all disappear under the iron rod of discipline, of the prodigious body formed by so many insignificant little figures. The soldier, or rather the corpuscle, on separating himself, after breaking away from the line, from the mass which observe a regular and even at times sublime life, generally preserves some of the qualities peculiar to the army. But it is not always so. Separation is often accompanied by a sudden check, with the result that though an army be glorious and honorable, a reunion of soldiers may be an insupportable calamity; and those towns that weep with joy and enthusiasm on seeing enter their precincts a victorious battalion, shake with fright when they see soldiers free and separate.

This last took place in Orbajosa, for in those days there were no praises to sing, nor any motive to weave crowns, or work triumphant inscriptions, nor to mention the exploits of our brave men—for which reason fear and suspicion reigned in the

Episcopal city, which, though very poor, was not wanting in treasures of birds, fruits, money, and gifts, which ran great risks since the before-mentioned disciples of Mars had arrived. Besides this, the Polentinos country, being cut off from the movement and bustle consequent on traffic, newspapers, railroad, and other agents, which it is not necessary to enumerate now, did not at all approve of the turmoil thus created in its peaceful existence.

Whenever a propitious juncture had been offered it had displayed in the same manner a lively dislike to submit to the central authority that either for good or evil governs us; and again calling to mind its last year's privileges, and ruminating over them, as does the camel over the grass it has eaten on the preceding day, there often arose from this independence the most deplorable results, which at times caused the governor of the province no little trouble. In the history of Orbajosa there had always been such a precedent, or, to put it more clearly, turbulent ancestry. No doubt it retained some energetic fibres from those remote periods in its bosom, which, according to Don Cayetano's enthusiastic opinion, had been commemorated by unheard-of epic battles; and, although in visible decline, it still showed its violent anxiety to perform great exploits, even should they be savage and extravagant. Having given to the world so many eminent sons, it, doubtless, wished that its actual vassals, the Caballucos, Merengues, and Pelosmalos, should revive the glorious deeds of former years.

Whenever there were revolts in Spain, this town wished to prove that it did not exist in vain on the face of the earth, by becoming the theatre of real war. Its genius, its situation, its history, had caused it to be chosen as a secondary place for raising recruits. This country had supplied this national fruit in 1827, during the Seven Years' War, in 1848, and at other periods of our history. Parties and partizans were always popular, a dismal circumstance arising from the War of Independence, one of a number of good things which have had their origin in infinite detestable matters. *Corruptio oplimi pessima.* And as the popularity of parties and partizans coincide, and is always on the increase, so grew hatred for all who entered Orbajosa with pretexts of delegation, or as instruments of the central power. Soldiers were always received badly there, and whenever an old inhabitant gave a narration in which there was crime, theft, assassination, violation, or any other dreadful event, he added, "This happened when the troop came!"

And having said so much, I may add that the battalions which arrived there on the day we have already referred to did not pass through the streets until it was sufficiently light for them to see clearly.

As the date of this event is of no importance, I need only say that it happened at no very distant period, nor at a very near one, as might have been said of Orbajosa (in romances, "Urbs Augusta," some modern savants, who have examined the garlic fields, declare that it is the best growing garlic country in the world), that it is neither very near to nor distant from Madrid; neither can I assure you that its glorious foundations are laid either to north, east, south, or west (they may be in any of these directions), that those Spaniards who may so desire may cast round their eyes and smell the flavor of the garlic. He who wishes to discover its exact situation must search among the municipal schedules.

The regiments were received with very poor grace, and accommodated in the worst rooms in the houses. The young girls of the town were truly not so displeased, but such a vigilance was kept over them, and they could not decently show their joy at the arrival of such a mob. The few soldiers who were sons of the district were the only ones who were welcomed. The rest were looked upon as intruders.

At eight o'clock in the morning a lieutenant-colonel of cavalry entered with his billet Doña Perfecta Polentinos's house. The servants received him, by the señora's orders, for she was in a deplorable condition of mind, and did not wish to go down to meet the soldiery, and had given orders that the colonel should be quartered in the only available room in the house, the one occupied by Pepe Rey.

"They must manage as well as they can," said Doña Perfecta with a sour expression, "and if they think they are not suited they may turn into the street."

Was it her intention to vex her infamous nephew, or had she really no other available room in her house? We do not know, neither have the chroniclers of this true story said a word enlightening us on this important question. What we do know is, that far from the two comrades being annoyed that they were to lodge together, they were greatly delighted, for they were old friends. They experienced a great and joyous surprise on meeting each other, and did not cease asking questions and uttering exclamations, pondering on the singular accident which had united them in such a situation, and on such an occasion.

"Pinzon—you here! But how is this? I did not expect you were coming—"

"I heard it said that you had set out for these lands, Pepe Rey, but did not expect to meet with you in horrible, savage Orbajosa."

"But what a happy occurrence; indeed it is a

most happy one, providential in fact. Pinzon, between you and me, we will do something startling here."

"And we shall have plenty of time to meditate on it," replied the other, sitting down on the bed where the engineer was resting, "for it seems we are to lodge together here. Who the devil's house is this?"

"Man, it is my aunt's. Speak more respectfully. Do you not know my aunt?— But see! I will get up."

"Very well, and I will get to bed, for I need rest very much— What a road, friend Pepe, what a road, and what people."

"Tell me, have you come to fight in Orbajosa?"

"Fight?"

"I say it because perhaps I may help you."

"What a town; but what a town!" exclaimed the military man, taking off his helmet, laying to one side his sword and shoulder-belt, his traveling pouch, and cloak. "This is the second time that we have been sent here. I swear to you that the third time I shall take French leave."

"Do not speak badly of these good people. But at what a time you have come! I could believe that God has sent you to my assistance, Pinzon— I have a terrible project in view, an adventure, if one might so term it, a plan, my friend—and I should scarcely have known how to proceed without you. A moment ago I was full of anxiety, thinking if I could only find a friend here, a good friend—"

"Project, plan, adventure—one of these, Sir Mathematician; do you wish to direct the globe, or perhaps it is a love affair—"

"It is serious, very serious. Get to bed, sleep a little, and then we can talk."

"I shall get to bed, but not to sleep. You can tell me anything you wish. Only I beg of you that you will talk as little as you can of Orbajosa."

"It is precisely of Orbajosa that I wish to speak to you. So you also have an antipathy to this corner of notable clowns?"

"These garlic people— We call them garlic-growers—well, they may be notable if you like, but to me they stink like the fruit of their country. It is a town ruled by men who inspire distrust, who teach superstition and hatred of mankind. When you have related all you wish I will tell you something—a quarrel, half playful, half-earnest, which took place here last year when I was here. When you hear it you will laugh, and I shall rid myself of my anger— But what is past is past."

"What has happened to me is not at all funny."

"But the reasons for my abhorrence of these people are various. I must inform you that it was here that, in '48, some cruel partizans assassinated

my father. He was a brigadier and had left the
service. The governor had sent for him, and he
was on his way to Villahorrenda to set out for
Madrid, when he was set upon by half a dozen
villains— There are several races of warriors here.
The Aceros, Caballucos, Pelosmalos—an expedition periodical, as they are termed by those who
know well what they are talking about."

"I suppose that the arrival of two regiments and
some cavalry will not be to the taste of these
delightful people?"

"I know that well enough. We have come to
overrun the country. We have plenty of ammuni-
tion. The Government dares not dismiss the
greater part of the bodies of magistrates without
despatching some troops to these towns. As this
land is so turbulent; as two neighboring provinces
are similarly affected; and as, besides, this municipal district of Orbajosa has such a brilliant history
in all the civil wars, we were afraid that the savages here would occupy the roads and destroy
all that they could lay their hands on."

"Wise precaution! But for my part, I should
think that as long as these people continue to increase, as long as there remains a stone, there will
be no peace in Orbajosa."

"Exactly my opinion," said the military man,
lighting a cigar. "It seems to me that the partizans
are flattered in this country. All those who devas-

tated the territory in 1848, and at other periods, or if not they, their sons, are employed in the offices, the magistracy, as couriers; they are constables, sacristans, judicial commissioners. Some of them are timid noblemen, and are they who arrange the elections, and have influence in Madrid, pronouncing doom—in fact, it is terrible."

"Tell me, may I hope that these partizans will perform such deeds in these days? If it is so, you will demolish the town, and I will help you."

"If I am right—they will," said Pinzon, "for the revolts of the two neighboring provinces spread like a curse from God. And, between us, friend Rey, I believe it will last long. Some laugh and assure themselves that there can not be another civil war like the last. They do not know the country, they do not know Orbajosa and its inhabitants. I insist that things are now so strained, that we shall have a new, cruel, and bloody struggle, which will last God only knows how long. What do you think?"

"Friend, when in Madrid, I laughed at all that was said about the possibility of a civil war, that would be as long and terrible as the Seven Years' War; but now, that I am here—"

"That is exactly the case in these enchanted countries; one only has to look around at these men and to listen to two words, to know the footing they are on."

"Well, yes— I am scarcely able to explain my ideas very clearly, or on what I have founded them; but here I have looked at things in a different light, and believe in the possibility of long, fierce wars."

"Exactly."

"But now, something other than a general war engages my attention, a private matter in which I am interested, which I mentioned to you a short time since."

"You tell me that this is your aunt's house. What is her name?"

"Doña Perfecta Rey, of Polentinos."

"Ah! I know the name. She is an excellent person, and the only one that I have not heard the garlic-growers speak badly of. When I was here last time I heard her kindness, charity, and virtues mentioned everywhere."

"Yes, my aunt is very good, very amiable," said Rey.

Then there was a short silence.

"Ah! now I remember—" exclaimed Pinzon suddenly. "How things go out of one's head. Yes, they told me in Madrid that you were about to marry a cousin. All was known. Is it to the pretty, heavenly Rosarito?"

"Pinzon, we will talk about it quietly."

"I suppose that there is opposition?"

"More. Terrible strife. I require powerful friends, active, of great experience in difficult affairs, very cunning and bold."

"Man, this is more serious than a combat."

"Much more serious. I could easily fight with a man. With women, with invisible enemies who work in the dark, it is impossible."

"We shall see. I am listening attentively."

Lieutenant-Colonel Pinzon stretched himself out full length on the bed to rest. Pepe Rey drew a chair up, and, leaning his elbow on the bed and his head on his hand, began his conference, consultation, explanation of his plan, or whatever it might be, and spoke for a long time. Pinzon listened to him with deep attention, saying nothing, with the exception of a few questions as to events, and in order to enlighten himself on any particular point. When Rey had finished Pinzon looked serious. He stretched himself and yawned slightly, for he had not slept for three nights, and finally remarked:

"Your plan is dangerous and difficult."

"But not impossible."

"Oh, no! nothing is impossible in this world. I will think well about it."

"I have meditated on it well."

"And you are resolved to carry it out? See! these things are not the custom. It might not succeed, and it would not promise well in that case for the perpetrator,"

"I have resolved."

"For my part, although it is a dangerous and serious affair—very serious—I am disposed to help you, come what may."

"I can rely on you?"

"To the death."

CHAPTER XIX

TERRIBLE COMBAT—STRATAGEM

THE first shots were soon fired. At dinner-time after acquainting Pinzon with his plan, the first condition of which was for the two friends to feign non-acquaintance with each other, Pepe Rey went to the dining-room. There he met his aunt, who had just returned from the cathedral, where she had been, as was her custom, all the morning. She was alone, and seemed to be in deep thought. The engineer remarked that under that pale, marble countenance there was a certain beauty; it was like the clouds originating from the reflection of the sun's rays. She immediately recovered her sinister clearness on seeing him; but again, on rapidly glancing at her nephew's face, her usual kind expression was imprinted on her studious features.

There was silence during the meal. They did not wait for Don Cayetano, for he had gone to Mundogrande. When they had nearly finished eating, Doña Perfecta said:

"And this military fellow, whom the governor has sent us to-day, is he not coming to dinner?"

"He seems more sleepy than hungry," replied the engineer, without looking at his aunt.

"Do you know him?"

"I have not seen him before."

"Then we shall be amused by the lodgers our governor has sent us. Here must we provide beds and food for these stray people from Madrid, to be ready at any hour they may be disposed for them."

"It is because they are afraid that parties will rise," said Pepe Rey, feeling as though a spark were kindled in his veins, "and the Government has decided to crush the Orbajosians, to crush them, to reduce them into dust."

"Man, pity, pity for God's sake, do not pulverize us!" exclaimed the señora, sarcastically. "What unfortunate creatures we are! Have mercy, man, and let these unhappy people live! And so, will you assist the troops in this great work of crushing us?"

"I am not military. I shall only applaud when I see the germs of civil war extirpated, with insubordination, discord, highway robbery, and barbarousness, which exist here to the shame of our epoch and country."

"All that!"

"Orbajosa, dear aunt, holds scarcely anything but garlic and banditti; for bandits are those who, in the name of a political or religious opinion, take

up arms and seek for adventures every four or
five years."

"Thanks, thanks, dear nephew," said Doña Perfecta, becoming paler. "Since Orbajosa consists
of these alone, then why have you come here to
seek more among us?"

Pepe felt the rebuff. His soul kindled. It was
very difficult for him to behave toward his aunt
with the consideration that her sex, state, and position merited. He spoke in an outburst of violence,
and with an irresistible impetuosity, and he
launched forth at his interlocutor:

"I came to Orbajosa," said he, "because you
sent for me; you concerted with my father—"

"Yes, yes, it is true," replied the señora, inter-
rupting him quickly and recovering her usual
sweetness, "I do not deny it. It is true that I was
culpable. I am guilty of your tediousness, of your
licentiousness, of all the unpleasant disagreements
that have taken place in my house since you
arrived."

"I am pleased you acknowledge it."

"Of course, you are a saint. I ought really to
go on my knees before your perfection, and beg
pardon, ought I not?"

"Señora," said Pepe Rey, seriously, forgetting
his dinner, "you should blush to jest with me in
such a despicable manner. I should never have
come here. No, I should have been far happier

had I never come to Orbajosa when you asked me."

"That is certain. Your father and I arranged that you should wed Rosarito. You came here to make her acquaintance. I then accepted you as my son. You seemed to love Rosarito."

"Pardon me," objected Pepe. "I loved, and was loved by Rosarito; you appeared to accept me as a son; you received me with false cordiality, employed all the arts of cunning, from the first moment, to annoy me, and hinder the fulfilment of my father's proposal; you tried, even from the first day, to make me despair, to weary me; and, with your lips wreathed with smiles and uttering tender words, you have martyred me, consuming me with a slow fire; you have worked against me secretly and raised up lawsuits; you deprived me of the official commission with which I was charged at Orbajosa; you have deprecated me in the town; you caused me to be ejected from the cathedral; you have kept me apart from my heart's desire; you have mortified your daughter by an inquisitorial seclusion, which has almost cost her her life, and which would have done, had not God helped her."

Doña Perfecta became scarlet. But this lively proof of her offended pride and her discovered thoughts passed rapidly away, leaving her pale, with a greenish tint. Her lips trembled. Throwing down her dinner, she suddenly rose. Her nephew also rose.

"My God! Holy Virgin of Help!" exclaimed the señora, raising both hands to her head and behaving as though she were in the last stage of despair. "Is it possible that I deserve such atrocious insults? Pepe, my son, is it you who speak so? If I have really done all that you have said, then truly I am very sinful."

She threw herself on a sofa and hid her face in her hands. Pepe, approaching her slowly, observed his aunt's anguish and the tears which she had shed abundantly. In spite of his conviction, he could not conquer the slight pity which she aroused in him, and, feeling timid, he experienced some little pain for having spoken so violently and so long.

"Dear aunt," he proceeded, putting his hand on her shoulder, "if you reply to me with tears and sighs, you will disturb, but not convince me. Reasons, not sentiments, are wanting. Speak to me, tell me that I am mistaken, prove it to me also, and I will acknowledge my error."

"Leave me. You are not my brother's son. If you were, you would not have insulted me as you have done. So I am a schemer, a comedian, a hypocritical harpy, a schemer for breaking off matches."

So saying, she uncovered her face, and contemplated her nephew with a beatific expression. Pepe was perplexed. The tears, as also his father's sister's sweet voice, could not be insignificant phenomena to the mathematician's soul. The words stuck in his throat as he begged pardon. A man of great energy as a rule, every accident of sensibility, every agent that acted on his heart, changed him suddenly into a child. A mathematical matter. It is said that Newton was the same.

"I should like to give you reasons that would suffice," said Doña Perfecta, motioning that he should sit down near her. "I should like to remove your displeasure. That you might see if I am good, if I am indulgent, if I am humble. I think you would withdraw, that you would deny absolutely, all that you have accused me of— No, no, I will not deny it."

The engineer was silent with astonishment.

"I do not deny it," continued the señora. "What I do deny is the injurious construction you have put upon it. And what right have you to judge me without knowing anything but what you guess and conjecture? Have you such supreme intelligence that you should judge those around you, and pass sentence on them? It is God alone who knows one's intentions."

Pepe felt still more astonishment.

"Is it not lawful to sometimes employ in this world indirect means for the fulfilment of a good and honorable end? What right have you to judge such actions of mine that you do not understand? I, dear nephew, treating you with a sincerity which you do not deserve, confess to you that if I have effectually made use of subterfuges to bring about a good end, that I have, at the same time, followed that which was beneficial to you and to my daughter. Do you not understand? You must be ignorant. Ah! your grand mathematical knowledge, as also that of German philosophy, is not capable of penetrating the subtleties of a prudent mother."

"You astonish me more and more," said the engineer.

"You may be as much astonished as you will, but confess your barbarity," said the soñora, gaining courage; "acknowledge your levity and your brutal treatment of myself in accusing me as you have done. You are an inexperienced boy, with no knowledge but what you have gained from books, which teach nothing of mundane matters, or of those of the heart. You have learned but to make roads and wharves. Ah! my young man, one does not enter the human heart by railway tunnels, nor reach its depths by boring as in mines. One does not read the conscience with naturalists' microscopes, nor decide the culpability of one's neighbors' opinions by the measure."

"For God's sake, dear aunt!"

"Why do you call on God if you do not believe in Him?" asked Doña Perfecta in a solemn tone. "If you believed in Him, if you were a good Christian, you would not venture perfidious judgment on my conduct. I am a pious woman; do you hear? I have a tranquil conscience; do you hear? I know what to do, and why I do it; do you hear?"

"I hear, I hear, I hear."

"God, in whom you do not believe, sees what you can not see—the intention. I say no more; I wish to enter into no longer explanation than is necessary. Perhaps you will understand me when I say that I wished to achieve my desire without causing scandal, without offending your father, without offending you, without having to give an explanation to people. I will say nothing of that, for you should understand, Pepe. You are a mathematician. You see what is before you, and no more; brutal nature, and no more; strokes, angles, weights, and no more. You see the effect, but not the cause. He who does not believe in God does not see the cause. God is the supreme intention of the world, and he who does not acknowledge Him judges as you judge, foolishly. For example, in the tempest you note but the destruction, the fiery ravages, the consequent misery, the earthquake's desolation; and yet, proud sir, in all these apparent calamities, one may seek for the goodness of the intention. Yes, sir, the intention of Him who is always good, and never commits evil."

This confusing, subtle, mysterious jargon did not convince Rey; but he did not wish to argue with his aunt by the rugged path of such arguments, and simply said:

"Good; I respect intentions."

"Now that you seem to recognize your error," continued the pious señora, becoming each time bolder, "I will confess something else, and that is that I see I was wrong to adopt such a system, although my object was a good one. Taking into consideration your violent character, taking into consideration your incapacity to understand me, I ought to have looked the question in the face, and said to you, 'My nephew, I do not wish you to marry my daughter.'"

"That is the language you should have used to-ward me from the first day," replied the engineer, breathing more freely, as though he felt relieved of a great weight. "I thank you much for those words. After the stabs I have received in the dark, this blow in full daylight is very agreeable to me."

"Then I repeat the blow," affirmed his aunt, with as much force as displeasure. "You know it now. I do not wish you to marry Rosarito."

Pepe kept silence. There was a long pause, during which each watched the other attentively, as though each found the other's face the most perfect work of art.

"Do you not understand what I said?" repeated she. "Let all rest, there will be no wedding."

"Permit me, dear aunt," said the young fellow firmly, "I am struck dumb with this declaration. In the state at which things have arrived, your negative is of little value to me."

"What do you say?" shouted Doña Perfecta loudly.

"What you hear. I shall marry Rosarito."

Doña Perfecta rose up indignantly, majestically, terribly. Her attitude was that of a mother pronouncing an anathema. Rey remained sitting, serene, courageous, with the passive courage of a profound persuasion and unquestionable resolution. All his aunt's rage had no effect on him; although she threatened him, he did not even move an eyelash.

"You are a madman. Marry you to my daughter! marry you to her! I will not!"

The señora's trembling lips articulated these words with a truly tragic accent.

"You do not wish it! She thinks otherwise."

"I do not wish it!" repeated the señora. "Yes, I say it and repeat it. I do not wish it, I do not wish it."

"She and I desire it."

"Fool! are you and she the only people in the

world? Are there no parents, no society, no conscience, no God?"

"Because there is society; because there is conscience; because there is God," affirmed Rey, seriously, rising and raising his arm, and pointing to heaven, "I say and repeat that I will marry her."

"Miserable, proud man! And if you will trample all down, do you think there are no laws to impede your violence?"

"Because there are laws, I say and repeat that I shall marry her."

"You respect nothing."

"Nothing that is unworthy of respect."

"And my authority, and my will, I—am I— nothing?"

"Your daughter is all to me; the rest nothing."

Pepe Rey's firmness was like the boast of an incomparable strength, with a perfect consciousness of the same. He dealt successive strokes and bruises, without the least attenuation. His words were like, if such a comparison be permitted, a fierce artillery.

Doña Perfecta fell again on the sofa, but not to weep, and a nervous convulsion shook her limbs.

"It seems that for this infamous atheist," she said, with great fury, "there exist no social customs, nothing more than a whim. He is an unworthy, avaricious man. My daughter is rich."

"If you think to wound me by this subtle artifice, pretending to wrongly interpret my sentiments, that you may injure my dignity, you make a mistake, dear aunt. You say I am avaricious. God knows I am not."

"You have no dignity."

"That is only an opinion like all else. The world may believe in your infallibility; I do not. I am far from believing that what you say has any weight before God."

"But are you sure of what you say? But do you still persist after my refusal? You trample on all. You are a monster, a bandit!"

"I am a man."

"A wretch! We will finish: I deny you my daughter; I deny her to you."

"Then I shall take her! I shall take no more than is mine."

"Leave my presence!" exclaimed the señora, rising hastily. "Fool, do you think my daughter will consent?"

"She loves me, as I do her."

"You lie, you lie!"

"She told me so herself. Allow me in this matter to believe her rather than her mother."

"When did she tell you, for you have not seen her for many days?"

"I saw her last night, and she swore to me before the Christ in the chapel that she would be my wife."

"Oh! scandalous and libertinous! What is this? My God! what dishonor!" exclaimed Doña Perfecta, again placing her hands to her head, and taking several steps through the room. "Did Rosarito leave her room last night?"

"She came out to see me. It was early."

"How vile your conduct is! You have behaved like a thief, like a common seducer."

"I have behaved according to your school. My intention was good."

"And she came down!— Ah! I suspected it. This morning at dawn I surprised her dressed in her room. She told me she had been for I know not what— You are the real criminal, you— She is a disgraceful girl. Pepe, I might have expected anything from you, even such an outrage— All is finished. March off! You no longer exist for me. I pardon you, as long as you go— I will not say a word of this to your father— What horrible egotism? No, there is no love in you. You do not love my daughter."

"God knows that I adore her, and that is sufficient for me."

"Do not name God with your lips, blasphemer; and hold your peace!" exclaimed Doña Perfecta. "In the name of God, whom I dare invoke, for I believe in Him, I tell you that my daughter shall never be your wife. My daughter shall be saved, Pepe. My daughter shall not be condemned to live in hell, for hell it would be in a union with you."

"Rosarito shall be my bride," repeated the mathematician, with pathetic calmness.

The pious lady was still more irritated by her nephew's serenity. With a catch in her voice she spoke thus:

"Do not think to frighten me with your threats. I know what I say. For, can you trample down a dwelling, a family? can you trample on human and divine authority?"

"I will trample down all," said the engineer, almost losing his calmness, and expressing himself with some agitation.

"You will trample on all! Ah! I saw well that you were a barbarian, a savage, a man who lives by violence."

"No, dear aunt, I am gentle, upright, honorable, and an enemy to violence; but, between you and me, between us, this is the law, and I am destined to observe it: to save this poor tormented creature, an angel of God, who is being martyred unjustly. It is this spectacle, this injustice, this unheard-of violence that converts my rectitude into barbarism, my reason into strength, my honor into violence like to that of assassins and thieves; it is this spectacle, señora, that induces me not to regard your law, and that induces me to take no notice of it, and to trample on all. This that appears an extravagance is an inevitable law. I shall act as does society when a brutality as illogical as irritating is opposed to its march. It passes over it and destroys it by a ferocious attack; such am I at this moment— I even do not recognize myself. I was reasonable and am a brute; I was respectful and am now insolent; I was cultured and have become savage. You have brought me to this extremity, irritating me and drawing me from the good road which I was tranquilly traveling. Whose fault is it, yours or mine?"

"Yours! yours!"

"Neither you nor I can decide. I believe that we both want to do right. You, with violence and injustice; I, with injustice and violence. We have each become as barbarous as the other, and we will fight and wound each other unmercifully. God permits it. My blood will fall on your conscience, yours will be on mine— I will finish there, señora; I do not wish to vex you with useless words. Now we shall begin our exploits."

"Our exploits, well," said Doña Perfecta, bellowing rather than speaking. "I believe Orbajosa is not deficient in a Civil Guard."

"Good-by, señora. I leave this house. I think we shall meet again."

"Go! go! go!" she shouted, pointing to the door with energetic gesture.

Pepe Rey went out. Doña Perfecta then muttered some incoherent words, which were clearly an expression of her anger, and fell on a chair with either a nervous attack or from fatigue. The servants came to her assistance.

"Go for Don Inocencio!" she shouted; "at once—quickly, and tell him to come."

And then she bit her handkerchief.

CHAPTER XX

RUMORS—FEARS

THE day following this lamentable dispute various rumors respecting Pepe Rey and his conduct ran all over Orbajosa, from house to house, district to district, from the casino to the apothecary's, and from the "Descalzas' Walk" to the "Puerta de Baidejos." All repeated them, and commentaries were so freely made that, had Don Cayetano gathered them up and compiled them, they would have formed a rich "memento" of Orbajosian benevolence. Among the divers kinds of reports spread, some had reached a culminating point, one of them being as follows:

"That the engineer had been so furious because Doña Perfecta had refused to allow Rosarito to marry an atheist, that he had raised his hand against his aunt."

The young man had taken lodgings in the widow Cusco's house, an establishment which was *montado*, as 'tis said. It was neither the highest nor the lowest of the most handsome in the country. He was frequently visited by Lieutenant-Colonel

Pinzon, to learn what each had done in respect to the web they were weaving, and for which the soldier possessed the most happy disposition to make it efficacious. He was constantly conceiving some new fancy, hastening to act upon what he had thought of with excellent spirits, and saying to his friend:

"The paper that I am doing, dear Pepe, can not be counted as one of the most graceful things; but to cause disgust to Orbajosa and its inhabitants I would go on all fours."

We do not know what subtle means the cunning military man, who was an adept in the world's ways, used; but it is certain that, after having lodged for three days in the house, he had gained the good-will of all. He greatly pleased Doña Perfecta, who could not hear his zealous praises as to the good order of the household unmoved, as also his remarks on the grandeur, piety, and august magnificence of the señora. He had stood on good terms with Don Inocencio from the first. Neither the mother nor the confessor prevented his talking to Rosarito (to whom they had allowed liberty since the ferocious cousin's absence); and by his sparing courtesy, his clever flattery and able address, he had acquired considerable power, and even familiarity, in the Polentinos house. But the object on which he centred his skill was a servant, by name Librada, whom he seduced (casually speaking) to carry messages and little notes to Rosarito, of whom he pretended to be enamored. The girl could not resist the briber, thereby realizing many kind words and much money; but she was ignorant as to who sent the notes, and, although she liked Don José much, had she known that this was a new trick of his, she would not have betrayed her mistress for all the money in the world.

One day Doña Perfecta, Don Inocencio, Jacintito, and Pinzon were all in the orchard. They were discussing the troop, and the mission that had brought it to Orbajosa; and the confessor had condemned the tyrannical conduct of the Government, and, almost without knowing it, Pepe Rey's name was mentioned.

"He is still at the lodging house," said the little lawyer. "I saw him yesterday, and he wished to be remembered to you, Doña Perfecta."

"He is very insolent— Ah! Señor Pinzon, you must be astonished to hear me use such language in mentioning a nephew—you know—that gentleman who occupied the room which you now have."

"Yes, I know! Not that I know him personally, but by sight and fame. He is our brigadier's intimate friend."

"The brigadier's friend?"

"Yes, señora, of him who commands the brigade

since it came to this country, and which he has distributed in different towns."

"And where is he?" questioned her ladyship.

"In Orbajosa."

"I believe he lodges in the Polaviejas' house," said Jacintito.

"Your nephew, señora," continued Pinzon, "and Brigadier Batalla are very intimate, very much so, and one sees them together at all times in the town streets."

"Then, my friend, I conceive a bad opinion of this chief," replied Doña Perfecta.

"He is—he is unfortunate," said Pinzon in a tone as though of commiseration for such a hard sentence.

"I do not include those present, Señor Pinzon, and believe in your honor," affirmed Doña Perfecta. "I can not deny that there are some models in the Spanish army—'"

"Our brigadier was an excellent military man before he gave himself up to spiritualism—"

"Spiritualism?"

"It is a sect that calls on spirits and hobgoblins by rapping on tables!" exclaimed the priest, laughing.

"For curiosity—only for curiosity," said Jacintito, emphatically, "I have sent for Allan Cardec's work from Madrid. It is well to be informed about everything."

"But is it possible that there can be such absurdities? Jesus! Tell me, Pinzon, is my nephew of this sect of rappers on benches?"

"I fancy that it was he who initiated our brave Brigadier Batalla."

"But, Jesus!"

"It is so; and then he fancies," said Don Inocencio, unable to resist laughing, "he shall speak with Socrates, St. Paul, Cervantes, and Descartes, as I can now speak to Librada, to beg her for a match. Poor Señor de Rey! Well said I, that such a head contained no good."

"For the rest," continued Pinzon, "our brigadier is a good soldier. If he sins somewhat, he is excessively hard. He takes all orders from the Government literally, and, if people here vex him much, he is capable of not leaving a stone standing of Orbajosa. Yes, I warn you, that you may be careful."

"But this monster will cut off all our heads. Ah! Señor Don Inocencio, these visits of the troops recall to my mind all that I have read of in the lives of martyrs, when a Roman proconsul was appointed over a Christian town—"

"That is not a very good comparison," said the confessor, looking at the soldier over his spectacles.

"It is a little sad; but I really felt I ought to tell you," declared Pinzon, benevolently. "Now, my friends, you are at our mercy."

"The country authorities," objected Jacintito, "still behave well, however."

"I believe you are mistaken," replied Pinzon, who was observing the señora and the confessor with deep interest.

"An hour ago the justice of the peace for Orbajosa was dismissed."

"Not by the authority of the provincial governor?"

"The governor has put in his place a delegate from the Government, who should arrive this morning. All the magistracy leave to-day. The minister has so commanded, fearing, I do not know why, that they were not favorable to the central authority."

"Well, well, we are—" murmured the priest, frowning and protruding his lower lip.

Doña Perfecta meditated.

"We have also to dismiss some of the judges of the principal causes, among others, him of Orbajosa."

"The judge! Periquito! Is not Periquito the judge?" exclaimed Doña Perfecta, with the voice and gesture of one who has had the misfortune to be stung by a viper.

"He who was judge in Orbajosa is no longer so,"

said Pinzon. "They will send the new one to-morrow."

"An unknown?"

"An unknown!"

"A rogue, perhaps— The other was so honorable—" said the señora, uneasily. "He never lost me a cause which I entrusted to him. Do you know who is to be the new justice of the peace?"

"Pray inform me who is to be the chief magistrate."

"See, I will tell you from whence comes the deluge, and then we will finish," said the priest, rising.

"Of course we must thank the brigadier; are we at his mercy?"

"For a few days, neither more nor less. Do not be angry with me. In spite of my uniform, I am an enemy to martial law; but we are commanded to fire—and we fire. There could not be a worse office than ours."

"Yes, it is so," said the señora, concealing her fury badly. "You have confessed it— What with neither justice of the peace nor judge—"

"Nor provincial governor."

"They may also take away our bishop, and send a monkey in his place."

"There is only that wanting— If they dare do it," murmured Don Inocencio, lowering his eyes, "they do not seem to stop at trifles."

"And it is all because they are afraid that parties may arise in Orbajosa!" exclaimed the señora, crossing her hands and trembling from head to foot. "Frankly, Pinzon, I do not know how it is that even the stones do not rise up. I wish no ill to you, but it is quite possible that they will convert even the water we drink into mire— You tell me that my nephew is an intimate friend of the brigadier?"

"So intimate that they are never separate all day long; they were companions at college. Batalla loves him like a brother, and does anything that he wishes. In your place, señora, I should feel uneasy."

"Oh! my God! I fear a trample-down!" exclaimed she, restlessly.

"Señora," said the priest, energetically, "before consenting to this honorable house being trampled down, before consenting to the least injury being done to this very noble family, I, my nephew— all the neighbors in Orbajosa—"

Don Inocencio did not conclude. His anger was so great that he could not speak. He took several martial steps, and then came and sat down.

"I think these fears are vain," said Pinzon. "In a case of necessity, I—"

"And I—" repeated Jacintito.

Doña Perfecta was staring at the glass door of the dining-room, where a graceful figure might be seen. As she gazed, the señora's face became darkly clouded with fear.

"Rosarito, come here, Rosarito," she said, recovering from her shock. "I fancy that you look better and happier to-day—yes. Do you not think that Rosarito looks better? As though she could be otherwise."

All agreed that she looked most happy.

CHAPTER XXI

FEAR IS EXCITED

AT this time the Madrid journals published the
following:

"It is not certain that any party will rise in Orbajosa and its neighborhood. They write to us from
that locality, saying that that country is little disposed for war, and that they consider Brigadier
Batalla's presence useless at that point.

"It is said that Brigadier Batalla will quit Orbajosa, where the army is not required to give proof
of its strength, and will go to Villajuan de Nahara,
where there are several parties.

"It is now certain that the Aceros are in league
with some horsemen near to Villajuan, the nearest
to the judicial district of Orbajosa. The governor
of the province of X—— has telegraphed to the
Government, saying that Francis Acero entered
the Roquetas, where he levied money and begged
food. Domingo Acero (Faltriquera) is roving in
the ridges of the mountain Jubileo, actively pursued by the Civil Guard, who have killed one man
and apprehended another. Bartholomew Acero is

he who set fire to the civil registry of Lugarnoble, retaining the justices of the peace and two principal inhabitants as hostages.

"In Orbajosa complete tranquillity reigns, according to the letter we have seen, and there they only think of field labors and of the near harvest of garlic, which promises to be magnificent. The immediate district is infested with factions; but Brigadier Batalla gives a good account of them."

In effect, Orbajosa was quiet. The Aceros were a fighting dynasty, which merited, according to some, to figure in a collection of romances, and had taken for their share the adjoining province, but the insurrection did not spread to the Episcopal town. It seemed as though modern education had at last overcome the desire for conquest, and that the delights of an enduring peace might be enjoyed. And it is certain that even Caballuco, one of the most prominent in the historical contumacy of Orbajosa, had distinctly given every one to understand that he had no wish to quarrel with the Government nor to enter into engagements which might cost him dear.

Whatever people may have said, the violent character of Ramos had become softened by time, and the fieriness which he had inherited from the Caballucos—fathers and grandfathers—had cooled down slightly, although his ancestors had been the

best race of warriors that had devastated the earth.
And besides, in these days, the new provincial governor had held a conference with this important
personage, receiving from his lips the greatest as-
surances that he would contribute to public peace,
and avoid all occasion of disturbance. He brought
forward trustworthy witnesses to prove that he was
living in love and companionship with the soldiers,
sharing a meal with one or another sergeant at the
tavern, and even said that he was destined to receive
a good position in the magistracy in the capital of
the province. Oh! how difficult it is for the historian, who aspires to impartiality, to truly portray
the opinions and thoughts of notable people, whose
names have been well known to the world. I do
not know one who has been able to do so, and
the want of certain dates gives rise to lamentable
equivocation. In presence of such finished works
as Brumario's military expedition, Rome sacked
by Borbon, the destruction of Jerusalem, what phi-
lologist or what historian is able to determine the
thoughts that preceded or followed in the heads
of Bonaparte, Charles V, and Titus? Our responsibility is immense! To partly relieve ourselves
from it, we relate words, sentences, and even conversations of this same Orbajosian emperor, and by
these means each may form the opinion which
seems to him most correct.

There can be no doubt whatever that Christobel

Ramos went out, and at night, from his house, and, traversing the Calle del Condestable, saw three laborers, who, mounted on mules, were coming in an opposite direction to him, and, on questioning them as to their destination, they replied that they were going to Doña Perfecta's house, to carry her the various first-fruits of their orchards, and some money due on the approaching rent-day. These men were Señor Pasolargo, a young man named Frasquito Gonzalez, and the third, who was of medium stature and coarse complexion, was called Vejarruco, although his real name was José Esteban Romerio. This occurred, according to authenticated dates, at night, and two days after the conversation which took place between Doña Perfecta and Pinzon, which was related in the last chapter, and which he who so desired has been able to read. Caballuco walked with the three companions, soliciting the good company of these men, and entered her ladyship's house with them. He then gave Librada some messages of little importance which a neighbor had confided to him, while the three laborers before mentioned, with Lycurgus, entered the dining-room (it was a strange coincidence that Lycurgus was present) and commenced a conversation relating to the harvest and their houses.

The señora was in an ugly humor, and harshly reproached them for the dryness of the heavens and the barrenness of the earth—phenomena for which the poor men were not to blame.

Don Inocencio made his appearance on the scene.

When Caballuco came in, the good priest saluted him affectionately, and signed to him to take a seat by his side.

"Here is this person," said the señora contemptuously. "It seems it is a falsehood all they say of this worthless man! Tell me, Caballuco, is it true that the soldiers dealt you some blows this morning?"

"Me! me!" said the Centaur, rising indignantly, as though he had received a great insult.

"So 'tis said," added the señora. "Is it not true? I believed it, for why should such a thing be said? They spat at you, and you thought yourself honored by the military men's saliva."

"Señora!" vociferated Ramos energetically, "saving the respect I owe you, who are my mother, more than my mother, my lady! my queen!—then I say, saving the respect I owe to the person who has given me all I possess —saving the respect—"

"What? it seems to me that you intend to say a great deal, and say nothing."

"Then I say, saving the respect, it is a calumny about the blow," he added, expressing himself with much difficulty. "All talk about me if I come in or if I go out, if I go or if I come—and all, what for? Because I wish to hold myself aloof from any revolt in the country. Petro is well in his house, ladies and gentlemen. Why has the troop come?—it is unfortunate; but what are we to do? Who has dismissed the justice of the peace, secretary, and judge?—it is unfortunate. I wish the stones of Orbajosa would rise against them, but I have passed my word to the governor, and even now I—"

He scratched his head, frowned gloomily, and, each time becoming more surly, proceeded:

"I am a brute, heavy, ignorant, ardent, obstinate, or anything you like, but I have no desire to be a cavalier."

"Pity on Cid Campeador," said Doña Perfecta, with the greatest scorn. "Do you not think as I do, Señor Don Confessor, that there is not now one man in Orbajosa who has any shame?"

"That is a grave opinion," replied the capitular, without looking at his friend, or raising his meditative face from his hand, on which he rested it. "It seems to me that this neighborhood has accepted the heavy military yoke with the greatest submission."

Lycurgus and the three laborers laughed heartily.

"When the soldiers and new authorities," said the señora, "have relieved us of our last dollar, as well as of the honor of the town, we will send all the valiant men in Orbajosa to Madrid in a glass urn, that they may be either placed in the museum or serve as a sign in the streets."

"Hurrah for the señora!" exclaimed he who was known as Vejarruco, gaily. "What she has just said is as good as gold. But do not tell me there are no brave men, for I am for the Aceros, and had I not three sons and a wife, and might be crippled, and if—"

"But you have not given your word to the governor?" questioned the señora.

"To the governor!" exclaimed Frasquito Gonzalez. "There is not a greater rogue in the country who deserves to be shot. Governor and Government are all the same. The priest foretold to us on Sunday all sorts of high-sounding things about the heresy and offenses against religion which are committed in Madrid— Oh! I heard him— And, finally, he wept in the pulpit, saying that religion has now no defenders."

"Here is the great Christobel Ramos," said the señora, bringing her hand down heavily on the Centaur's shoulder. "Mounted on horseback, he traverses the square and the field, to attract the soldiers' attention; they see him, shiver at the hero's fiery countenance, and run away dead with fear!"

The señora finished her sentence with an exaggerated laugh, which sounded more offensive from the profound silence the others observed. Caballuco turned pale.

"Señor Pasolargo," continued the señora, becoming serious, "when you came here to-night, I was about to send for your son Bartholomew, as I require him here. I must have some good men in my house; and even then the morning sun may behold my daughter and me murdered."

"Señora!" exclaimed all.

"Señora!" shouted Caballuco, rising, "are you in jest or earnest?"

"Señores Vejarruco and Pasolargo," continued the señora, taking no notice of the local braggadocio, "I am not safe in my house. No one in Orbajosa is, much less I. My soul is troubled. I can not close my eyes all night."

"But why? Who frightens you?"

"We shall see!" exclaimed Lycurgus, ardently, "if I, old and infirm, am not capable of fighting against all the Spanish army, if they touch the señora's skirt—"

"With Señor Caballuco," said Frasquito Gonzalez, "we are more than enough."

"Oh, no," said the señora, with cruel sarcasm. "Do you not see that Ramos has given his word to the governor?"

Caballuco sat down again, and, putting one knee over the other, crossed his hands on them.

"I steer clear of cowards," added their mistress implacably; "I have nothing to say to such. Perhaps I am in danger of seeing my house attacked, of having my dear daughter snatched from my arms to be trampled on and insulted in a most infamous manner!"

She could not continue. Her voice was smothered, and she began to weep disconsolately.

"Señora, for God's sake, be calm! Come—there is no reason yet—" said Don Inocencio, hastily, with an expression of great affliction. "One should always be resigned, and try to bear the calamities that God sends."

"But—who?—señora— Who has frightened you with such shameful tales?" questioned one of the four. "Orbajosa would rise up to defend the señora."

"But who, who?" repeated the others.

"Come, do not trouble her with importunate questions," said the confessor officiously. "You may retire."

"No, no; I may want them," said the señora, quickly, drying her tears. "The presence of good servants is a great consolation to me."

"Cursed be my race!" said Lucas, giving a blow on his knee, "if all these foolish reports are not the work of the señora's nephew!"

"Of Don Juan Rey's son?"

"From meeting him in the station at Villahorrenda, and his speaking to me with his mellifluous voice and courtly phrases," proffered Lycurgus, "I took him to be a gentleman—not that I wish to be wanting in respect to the señora— But I knew him— I stamped him from that very day, and I am not mistaken. I know very well, as 'tis said, that the clew is manufactured for the thread, that the cloth is known by the design, and the lion by its claws."

"Say nothing against this unfortunate youth in my presence," said she of the Polentinos, severely. "However great his faults, charity forbids us to talk about them and make them public."

"But charity," said Don Inocencio, energetically, "does not prevent us taking precautions against evil; and it is of this we are treating. Now that the chief characters and valor of Orbajosa are so much decayed; now that this town is disposed to offer its face for the soldiers to spit at, we must unite to defend ourselves."

"I will defend myself as well as I can," said Doña Perfecta, resignedly, crossing her hands. "The Lord's will be done!"

"What a noise about nothing!— For the life of!— How frightened all are in this house!—" exclaimed Cabullaco, half in fun, half in earnest. "One would imagine that Don Pepe is a region" [legion] "of devils. Do not be alarmed, señora. My little nephew, Juan, who is thirteen, will guard the house, and we will see, nephew for nephew, which can do the most."

"We already know what your courage and boasts are worth," replied the señora. "Poor Ramos! you wish to impose on us by your show of bravery, while I have found out that it is worthless."

Ramos grew slightly pale, fixing on the señora a singular look, in which were mingled fear and respect.

"Yes, man; do not look at me so. I now know that I must not rely on braggarts. Would you wish me to tell you plainly what I think of you? You are a coward!"

Ramos moved as though he felt an itching in different parts of his body, displaying great uneasiness. His nostrils expanded, and he sniffed the air like a horse. This corporeal combat was caused by torment, passion, savagery, which consumed and raged within his breast. After trying to utter some words, and chewing others, he rose and roared in this manner:

"I will cut off Señor de Rey's head!"

"What foolishness! You are a brute as well as a coward!" she said, paling. "Who spoke here of killing? Yes; I do not wish any one to be killed, much less my nephew, whom I love in spite of his wrongdoing!"

"Homicide! What atrocity!" exclaimed Don Inocencio, scandalized. "This man is mad!"

"To kill!— The very idea of a homicide horrifies me, Caballuco," said the señora, closing her gentle eyes. "Poor man! When you have desired to display courage you have howled like a carnivorous wolf. Get away from here, Ramos; you alarm me."

"Did not the señora say you were frightened? Did you not say they would destroy the house, and steal the girl?"

"Yes, I am afraid so."

"And it is the act of one man," said Ramos, scornfully, again sitting down. "It is the act of Don Pepe Poquita Cosa with his mathematics. I did wrong in saying I would slice his neck. With an effeminate man of his stamp he should have his ear taken off and thrown into the river."

"So, you laugh now, beast. It is not alone my nephew who will commit all these acts of injustice which I have mentioned, and which I fear; if it were he alone, I should not be alarmed. I should command Librada to guard the door with a broom—and that would suffice— No, it is not he alone; no."

"Then whom?"

"Are you a donkey? Do you not know that my nephew and the brigadier who commands this confounded troop confabulate?"

"Confabulate!" exclaimed Caballuco, pretending that he did not understand the words.

"They are cronies," said Lycurgus. "They talk together; that means they are cronies. I understood what the señora meant."

"It reduces itself to this: That the brigadier and officials are hand and glove with Don José; and whatever he desires the soldiers desire also; and that these soldiers are capable of violence and barbarity, since such is their office."

"And we have no justice of the peace to appeal to."

"Nor judge."

"Nor governor. That is to say, we are at the mercy of these infamous men."

"Some soldiers," said Vejarruco, "carried off the prettiest of Uncle Julian's daughters yesterday, and the poor man could not find her on returning to his house; but she was found crying and barefooted near to the old fountain with a broken pitcher."

"Poor Don Gregory Palomeque! the notary of Naharilla Alta," said Frasquito. "These rogues stole all the money he had in his house, but the brigadier, when questioned, said it was a lie."

"Tyrants! tyrants not born of women!" proffered another. "I say that I do not agree with the Aceros."

"And what is known of Francisco Acero?" questioned Doña Perfecta, quietly. "I should be sorry if he were unfortunate. Tell me, Señor

Don Inocencio, was not Francisco Acero born at Orbajosa?"

"No; he and his brothers are from Villajuan."

"I am sorry for Orbajosa," continued Doña Perfecta. "This poor city is disgraced. Do you know if Francisco Acero has passed his word to the governor that he will not annoy these poor soldiers in their attacks on maidens, in their acts of impiety, sacrilege, and infamous felony?"

Caballuco gave a start. He felt as though he were stung, as though wounded by a blow from a sabre. His face flushed and his eyes shone, while he shouted thus:

"I have passed my word to the governor, for the governor promised me that it would have a good result."

"Barbarian, do not shout. Speak like a man, and we will listen to you."

"I promised that neither I nor my friends would raise factions in the land of Orbajosa. To all those who have desired to sally out to play at war I have said: 'Go with the Aceros, that we may not be troubled here.' But there are many honorable men—yes, señora—and good—yes, señora—and valiant—yes, señora—who are scattered about in the villages, and commons, and mountains, each in his dwelling, eh? And I have but to say half a word, eh? and they will all take out their guns, eh? and will hasten either on horseback or on foot

where I will. I am not a grammarian, but I know
how to give my word, for I did give it, and if
I do not go out it is because I do not wish to do
so; and if I desire parties there will be parties, and
if I do not wish it, no; for I am whom I am, the
same man as ever, as you all know. And as I said
before, I am no grammarian, am I? and they do not
tell me things in my dreams, do they? and if they
wish me to go out they will declare it aloud, will
they? for why has God given us a tongue but for
to say this and that? The señora well knows who
I am, as well as she knows that I am indebted to
her for the shirt I wear, and for the bread I eat
to-day, and for the first chickpea that I sucked
when I was vexed, and for the coffin in which they
put my father when he died, and for the physicians and medicine that cured me when I was ill;
and the señora well knows that if she said to me:
'Caballuco, break your head,' I should go to a
corner and break it against the wall; the señora
knows well that if she told me it was day, although
I know it is night, that I should equivocate and
declare it was day; the señora knows well that I
love her more than anything else under the sun.
To a man of so much heart, if she says: 'Caballuco, stop, animal, do this or do the other; take
back your words and oaths, they are dreams,' I
should pinch here and strike there."

"Come, man, calm yourself," said Doña Perfecta

kindly. "You are choking like those Republican orators who come here to preach free religion, free love, and I know not what other free things. Let them bring you a glass of water."

Caballuco took a piece of rag and used it as a handkerchief, rolled it up into a ball, passed it over his broad forehead and over the back of his head to dry himself, for he was covered with perspiration. They brought him a glass of water, and the priest, with a meekness befitting his sacerdotal character, took it from the servant's hands, presented it to Ramos, and held the salver while he drank. The water, as it ran down Caballuco's throat, produced a gurgling sound.

"Now bring me another, Señora Librada," said Don Inocencio, "I feel a burning sensation within."

CHAPTER XXII

INDIGNATION

"As regards the factions," said Doña Perfecta, when the others had finished drinking, "I tell you to act as your conscience directs."

"I do not listen to its dictation," shouted Ramos. "I shall obey the señora's will."

"Then I will give you no advice on such a serious matter," replied she, with the circumspection and suavity which became her so well. "It is serious, very serious, and I can not advise you."

"But the señora's opinion—"

"My opinion is that you shall open your eyes and see, open your ears and hear— Consult your heart. I grant you that you have a large heart. Consult that judge; that counselor knows much, and do as it commands you."

Caballuco reflected, pondering on all that a sword might ponder on.

"We reckoned those in Naharilla Alta yesterday, said Vejarruco, "and there were thirteen fit for a great undertaking. But as we were afraid

236

the señora would be angry, we have done nothing. It is now time to clip."

"Do not you busy yourself with the clipping," said the señora. "There is time. That will not be neglected."

"My two boys," proffered Lycurgus, "were disputing together yesterday; one wished to go to Francisco Acero, and the other did not. I said to them: 'Patience, my sons, and all will go; I should hope that they make as good bread here as in France.'"

"I said this evening to Roque Pelosmalos," declared Señor Pasolargo, "that when Señor de Ramos would go so far as to say that, that he had already all his arms at hands. What a pity that the two brothers Burguillos have gone to work the estate of Lugarnoble!"

"You go and seek them," said Doña Perfecta quickly. "Señor Lucas, you prepare a horse for Uncle Pasolargo."

"I, if the señora wishes it, and Señor de Ramos likewise," said Frasquito Gonzalez, "will go to see if Robustiano, the mountain guard, and his brother Petro would also like—"

"It seems to me a good idea. Robustiano is not afraid to come to Orbajosa, although he owes me something. You may tell him that I forgive him the six and a half pesos. These poor fellows, who so generously sacrifice themselves for an opinion, are easily pleased. Is it not so, Señor Don Inocencio?"

"Here is our good Ramos," replied the priest, "tells me that his friends were displeased with him on account of his lukewarmness, but, when they saw he was determined, placed all their boxes of cartridges in their girdles."

"But what! are you determined to lend assistance?" asked Doña Perfecta. "I have not advised you to that, and if you do it, it is by your own desire. Neither has Don Inocencio recommended anything of the sort to you. Well, if you have so decided, you must have powerful reasons for so acting. Tell me, Christobel, would you like to sup? What will you have, then?—candidly?"

"As to my having advised Señor de Ramos to take the field," said Don Inocencio, looking over his spectacles, "the señora is right in that. I, as a priest, could advise no such thing. He knows what others are doing, and that they are even up in arms; but it seems to me improper—very improper—and I have no wish to imitate them. I would carry my scrupulosity to the extreme by not saying a word to Señor de Ramos on the difficult question of his rising in arms. I know that it is Orbajosa's wish; I know that all the inhabitants of this noble city would bless him; I know that deeds worthy to be transmitted to history will be done; but, nevertheless, allow me to observe a discreet silence."

"You have spoken well," added Doña Perfecta. "I do not like priests to meddle in such matters. A clergyman should so conduct himself. We well know that, in solemn, grave circumstances, for instance, when country and faith have been in peril, there have been priests who have incited men to fight, and have even done so themselves. Well, even God has taken part in celebrated battles, under the form of angels or saints, so that His ministers might well do it. During the war against the infidels how many bishops commanded the Castilian troops?"

"Many. And some were noted warriors. But these times are not like those, lady. It is true that, if we consider things seriously, faith is in greater danger now than formerly. For what do these armies that occupy our city and immediate towns represent? What do they represent? Are they other than the infamous instruments which use their perfidious conquests for the extermination of faith; of those atheists by which Madrid is infested? We know it well. There are in that centre of corruption, scandal, irreligion, and disbelief some malignant men who, having sold themselves to the stranger for gold, are employed to destroy the seed of faith in our Spain. Do you believe this? They allow us to say Mass, and you to hear it, as a consideration, through shame—but in better days. For my part, I am calm. I am a man

who does not trouble himself with any temporal
or mundane interest. Doña Perfecta knows it
well; all know it well who know me. I am peaceful, and the triumph of evil-doers does not frighten
me. I know well that we may expect terrible
times; that when we dress ourselves in our sacerdotal garb our life hangs by a thread; for Spain,
do not doubt it, will see scenes similar to those of
the French Revolution, when thousands of pious
priests perished in a day. But I do not worry.
When the headsman calls I will offer my neck;
I shall have lived long enough. For of what use
should I be? None—none."

"I will eat the dogs!" exclaimed Vejarruco,
showing his fist, as hard and strong as a hammer, "if we can not exterminate all this thievish
rabble."

"They said that next week they would commence
to destroy the cathedral," declared Frasquito.

"I suppose that they will destroy it with picks
and hammers," said the priest, laughing. "There
are artifices which these tools do not possess, and
which are more edifying. We well know that, according to pious tradition, our beautiful chapel of
Sagrario was destroyed by the Moors in a month,
and rebuilt by angels in a single night. Let them
—let them destroy it!"

"In Madrid, as the priest related to us the other
night," said Vejarruco, "there are so few churches

left that some priests say Mass in the streets; and
as they are molested, and people say injurious
things about them, and also spit at them, many do
not like to say it."

"Here, fortunately, my sons," declared Don Inocencio, "we have no such scenes. And why? Because they know what class of men you are; because they are acquainted with your ardent piety
and your courage. The first who laid hands on
our priests and worship would not gain much.
Poor Spain! so holy, so humble, and so good!
Who would have thought you would have been
brought to this extremity? But I maintain that
impiety will not triumph. No, sir. There are
still courageous men; still men like our ancestors.
Is it not true, Señor Ramos?"

"There are; yes, sir," replied Ramos.

"I have a blind faith in the triumph of God's
law. All will rally in its defense. Or, if not some,
there will be others. Each will gain the palm of
victory, and with it eternal glory. The evil-doers
will perish, if not to-day, to-morrow. He who
goes against God's law will fall; there is no remedy. It may be in this way, it may be in another;
but he will fall. Neither his subtlety, nor his hid-
ing-places, nor his artillery will save him. God's
hand is raised against him and his heresy. Let us
pity him, and hope for his repentance. And as to
you, my sons, do not hope that they will enlighten

you as to the steps they really intend to take. I know that you are good; I know that your generous determination, and the noble object you have in view, will wash away all stain of sin by the shedding of your blood, perhaps. I know that God will bless you; that your victory, even as your death, will render you sublime in the eyes of God and man. I know that you will deserve psalms and praises, and all kinds of honors; but, notwithstanding this, my sons, my lips shall not incite you to battle. I have done nothing yet, neither will I now.

"Try to regulate the impetuosity of your noble hearts. If you are ordered to remain in your houses, remain in them; if you are ordered to sally forth, sally forth in good time. I resign myself to become a martyr, and bow my neck to the headsman, if this wretched troop continues here. But if a noble, ardent, and pious impulse of Orbajosa's sons will contribute to the great work of the extirpation of the country's calamities, I shall hold myself to be the most happy of men, if only in being one of your countrymen; and all my life of study, of penance, of resignation, will not seem to me to be of as much merit in the sight of heaven, as one day alone of your noble heroism."

"You could not say more, nor could you say it better!" exclaimed Doña Perfecta, with great enthusiasm.

Caballuco had leaned down on his bench, with his elbows on his knees.

When the priest had finished speaking, he took hold of his hand and, bowing over it, kissed it fervently.

"No better man was ever born of woman," said Lycurgus, wiping, or pretending to wipe, away a tear.

"Long life to the confessor!" shouted Frasquito Gonzalez, throwing his cap up boldly to the ceiling.

"Silence," said Doña Perfecta. "Sit down, Frasquito. You are one of those who make a great noise and do little."

"Blessed be God, who has inspired you with these golden words!" exclaimed Christobel, excited to admiration. "What two persons I have before me? While these two live, what does the world wish for more? All the people in Spain should be thus. But how can they be so when there are but rogues left? In Madrid, where the Court is, whence come the laws and commands, all is robbery and deception. Poor religion, how you have been treated! We only see sinners. Doña Perfecta, Señor Don Inocencio, by my father's soul, by my grandfather's soul, by my soul's salvation, I swear that I wish to die."

"To die!"

"May these thievish dogs kill me. Let them say

they killed me, because I could not circumvent them! I am very small."

"Ramos, you are great," said Doña Perfecta, solemnly.

"Great! great!— My heart is very great. But have I strong fortified places? have I horses? have I artillery?"

"That is a thing, Ramos," said Doña Perfecta, smiling, "that I should not trouble about. Have not the enemy all these things that you are wanting in?"

"Yes."

"Then make them give it up."

"They are to give it up, yes, señora. When I say that they are to give it up."

"Dear Ramos!" exclaimed Don Inocencio, "yours is an enviable position. Detach yourself; elevate yourself above the vile multitude; behave as did the greatest heroes of the world. You are able to say that God's hand guides yours— Oh! what grandeur and honor! My friend, it is not flattery. What purpose! what activity! what valor! No, men of such temper must not die! The Lord is with them, and the enemy's bullet and steel are turned away from them— Do not be alarmed. Do not be frightened. Why should such men be frightened of the cannons and firearms of the heretics? Dear Caballuco, on seeing you, on seeing your valor and noble bearing, I am reminded of, without being able to help it, the verses in the romance on the conquest of the Empire of Trapisonda:

> " 'The valiant Roldan arrived,
>   With all the weapons, armed,
>   On stout Briardor,
>   His powerful horse,
>   And strong Durlindana
>   Well-girded at his side.
>   A lance like a lateen,
>   The strong shield buckled on . . .
>   By the visor of his helmet
>   Fire came darting out;
>   Smiting with the lance,
>   As with a fine rush,
>   He all the army meeting,
>   Fiercely threatened them.' "

"Very good!" exclaimed Lycurgus, clapping his hands. "And I say, like Don Renialdos:

> " No one in Don Renialdos' touch,
>   If he wishes to be free!
>   He who wishes otherwise
>   Will be well paid.
>   For all the rest of the world
>   Escapes not from my hands
>   Without some pieces staying to make,
>   Or being corrected severely.' "

"Ramos, you wish to sup; you wish to have something now; is it not so?" asked the señora.

"Nothing, nothing," replied the Centaur, "unless I happen to take a dish of gunpowder."

So saying, he gave a great horse-laugh, took several steps through the room, watching the others attentively, and, pausing before the group, fixed his eyes on Doña Perfecta, and, in a voice of thunder, uttered these words:

"I say that which I have always said, 'Life to Orbajosa; death to Madrid!'"

And he gave such a blow on the table that the house roof shook.

"What tremendous strength!" said Don Inocencio.

"What fists you have!"

All looked at the table, which had been broken asunder.

They then gazed on Renialdos or Caballuco, and could scarcely admire him sufficiently. Undoubtedly there was beauty in his countenance, in his green eyes, animated by a strange feline splendor, in his black hair, in his herculean body; there was a certain air, too, of greatness, a resemblance to those great races that governed the world. But in his general aspect there was a pitiful degeneration, and it was difficult to recognize nobility and heroism in his present brutality. In comparison with Don Cayetano's celebrated men, he was as the mule to the horse.

CHAPTER XXIII

MYSTERY

THE conference lasted some time after the event we last referred to; but we will dwell no longer on it, as it is not indispensably necessary to the good understanding of this history. They at last retired, Don Inocencio, as was his custom, being the last to do so. The priest and the señora had scarcely had time to interchange two words when an aged and very confidential servant entered, a woman who was Doña Perfecta's right hand; and the latter, on perceiving that she was anxious and troubled, suspected that some evil had happened in the house.

"I can not find the señorita anywhere," said the servant in reply to Doña Perfecta's question.

"Jesus! Rosarito!—where is my daughter?"

"Our Lady of Succor, protect me!" shouted the Penitentiary, taking up his hat, and preparing to follow the señora.

"Search for her well— But were you not with her in her room?"

"Yes, señora," replied the old servant tremulously, "but the devil tempted me, and I fell asleep."

"Cursed be your sleepiness!— Jesus, mine! What is the matter? Rosarito! Rosarito!— Librada!"

They went upstairs, they came down; and then they returned upstairs, taking a light, and searching everywhere. Presently they heard the Penitentiary calling from the staircase in a jubilant tone, "Here she is! here she is! She is coming."

An instant later mother and daughter met face to face in the gallery."

"Where were you?" questioned Doña Perfecta, in a severe tone, examining her daughter's face.

"In the orchard," replied the young girl, more dead than alive.

"In the orchard at this hour? Rosarito!—"

"I was warm; I sat down near the window, dropped my handkerchief out, and then went down to find it."

"Why did you not send Librada for it?— Librada! Where is that girl? Has she also slept?"

Librada presently came. Her pale countenance expressed consternation and guilt.

"How is this? Where were you?" demanded Doña Perfecta in terrible anger.

"Then, lady—I went to get the clothes that were in the room near the street—and I fell asleep."

"Every one has slept here to-night. It seems to

me that no one in my house will sleep to-morrow. Rosarito, you may retire."

Understanding that it was necessary to act promptly and energetically, Doña Perfecta and the priest began immediately to make investigations. Questions, threats, entreaties, promises were employed with consummate skill to inquire into the truth of the incident. Not a shadow of culpability rested on the old servant; but Librada confessed plainly, between tears and sighs, all her knavery, which may be comprised in the following: "That Señor Pinzon, shortly after he began to lodge in the house, had sent notes to Señorita Rosarito. He had given money to Librada, so she said, that he might employ her as a messenger to carry these love-letters and tender messages. The young lady showed no anger, rather pleasure, and thus several days had passed in this manner. Finally, the servant declared that Rosarito and Señor Pinzon had that night concerted that the young lady should see him, and talk with him outside of the window of his room, which looked out on to the orchard. They had confided in the maid-servant, who offered to warn them by means of a song, should any one be likely to discover them in the act. According to arrangement, Pinzon was to leave his room at his usual hour, and, returning at nine, was to reenter it, from which, as also from the house, he would sally clandestinely later, and would come back muffled up at a still more advanced hour. In this way he would not be suspected. Librada was on the watch for Pinzon, who entered, well wrapped up, and without speaking a word. He went into his room, just as the young lady descended into the orchard. Librada, while the interview lasted, established herself as sentry in the gallery, in order to advise Pinzon if any danger were at hand; and he, at the end of an hour, went out again, still well covered by his cloak, and without speaking."

When this confession was concluded, Don Inocencio asked the miserable girl:

"Are you sure that he who entered and went out was Señor Pinzon?"

The criminal did not reply, but she looked greatly perplexed.

Doña Perfecta inquired angrily:

"Did you see his face?"

"But who could it be, if it were not he?" replied the young woman. "I am certain it was he. He went straight to his room—he knew the way well."

" 'Tis strange," said the priest; "living in the house, he has no necessity to employ such means— He might have pretended to be ill, and remained away. Is it not so, señora?"

"Librada!" exclaimed the señora, with increased anger, "I swear by God that you shall go to the house of correction!"

She then crossed her hands, pressing the fingers of one with the other so fiercely that she drew blood.

"Señor Don Inocencio!" she exclaimed, "we shall die—there is no remedy but death."

She then began to weep disconsolately.

"Courage, señora," said the priest, pathetically. "Much courage— It is precisely now that you must have much. This requires serenity and a big heart.

"Mine is immense," said she between sobs.

"Mine is very small," said the priest; "but we shall see."

CHAPTER XXIV

THE CONFESSION

MEANWHILE Rosarito, her heart palpitating, unable to weep, unable to be calm, pierced with the cold steel of an immense sorrow, with her thoughts traveling swiftly from the world to God, and from God to the world, stupefied and half mad, was in her room late at night, on her knees, her hands crossed, with her nude feet on the floor, her burning temples resting on the side of the bed, in the dark, alone, and in silence. She was careful not to make the slightest noise, that she might not attract her mother's attention, the latter sleeping, or appearing to sleep, in the next room. She raised her thoughts to Heaven in this strain:

"Lord, my God, how is it that formerly I did not know how to lie, and now I know? How is it that formerly I did not know how to dissimulate and now I know? Am I an infamous woman?— This that I feel, and what has happened to me, is the fall of those who are never able to rise again— Have I ceased to be good and honored?— I do not recognize myself. Am I myself, or is it an-

other placed in this situation?— What terrible
things in so few days! How many divers sensa-
tions! My heart is consumed with so much feeling!— Lord, my God, do You hear my voice, or
am I condemned to pray eternally without being
heard?— I am good, no one will convince me
that I am not good. To love, to love very much;
is that wrong?— But no—this is no illusion, no
deception. I am worse than the worst women on
earth. A large snake within me kills me and en-
venoms my heart— What is this that I feel? Why
do You not kill me, my God? Why do You not
condemn me to hell for eternity?— It is dreadful,
but I confess it, I confess it to God alone, Who hears
me, and I will confess it to the priest. I abhor my
mother. And why is this? I can not understand
it. He has not said a word against my mother to
me. I do not know how I have come to this—
How wicked I am! The devils have taken possession of me. Lord, come to my aid, for I can not
conquer by myself— A terrible impulse draws
me from this house. I wish to fly, I wish to run
far from here. If he does not carry me off I shall
go and creep behind him through the streets—
What divine joy is this within my breast which is
mingled with such bitter pain?— Lord God, my
Father, enlighten me; I wish to love only. I do
not wish rancor, which is devouring me, to rise.
I do not wish dissimulation, falsehood, deceit to

take root. To-morrow I will go out into the street and will shout in the middle of it, and to all who pass will say: 'I love, I detest'— My heart will unbosom itself in this manner— How happy I should be could I conciliate all; love and respect every one! Holy Virgin, protect me!— Again that terrible idea! I do not wish to think it, but it comes. I do not wish to feel it, but I do feel it. Ah! I can not deceive myself in that particular. I can neither destroy it nor diminish it—but I can confess it, and I do confess it, saying: 'Lord, how I detest my mother!' "

At last she fell into a lethargy. In her uncertain sleep imagination reproduced all that had happened that night, deforming it, without altering its essence. She heard the cathedral clock chime nine; she saw, with joy, the old servant sleeping beatifically, and then she left the room quickly, noiselessly; she softly descended the staircase, not moving a step until she was certain of not making the slightest sound. She went out to the orchard, giving a glance at the servants' room and the kitchen; in the orchard she stopped a moment to look at the sky, which was dark and spangled with stars. The wind was hushed. Not a breath disturbed the profound calm of the night. It seemed as though it was silently and fixedly attentive, resembling eyes which gaze without moving an eyelash, and ears that lie in ambush, in the expectation of a great adventure— Night was observing. She then approached the glass door of the dining-room and cautiously looked through from a certain distance, fearing that those within might observe her. By the light from the dining-room lamp she could distinguish her mother's shoulders. The Penitentiary was seated to the right, and his profile was discomposed in an extraordinary manner; his nostrils were distended like the beak of some strange bird, and all his figure resembled a black, dense mass, with angles here and there, acute and risible. Caballuco faced him, more like a dragon than a man. Rosarito could see his green eyes, resembling two large lanterns of convex glass. Each movement, as also the powerful size of the animal, inspired her with fear. Lycurgus and the other three presented a grotesque appearance. She had seen elsewhere, no doubt in the clay puppets at the fair, a similar stupid smile, similar clumsy features and expressionless gaze. The dragon waved his arms, and, as they moved, they gave one the idea of the revolutions of a mill's sails, while the green globes turned round like the lanterns at a chemist's, from one side to the other. She felt blinded. The conversation seemed interesting. The confessor waved his wings. He was like a little bird who wished to fly, but was unable. His beak lengthened and twisted. He shook his feathers with symptoms of fury, and then, drawing in and becom-

ing calm, hid his plucked head under his wing.
Then the little clay figures acted as though they
wished to be taken for persons, and Frasquito
Gonzalez succeeded in passing for a man.

Rosarito felt an inexplicable awe in presence
of this friendly concourse. She withdrew from the
glass door, and, proceeding step by step, looked
around on all sides to see if she were observed.
Although she could see no one, she fancied that
a million eyes were fixed on her— But her fears
and confusion were dispersed unexpectedly. In
the window of the room occupied by Señor Pinzon
a blue man appeared, the buttons shining on his
dress like so many glowworms. She approached.
At the same moment she felt herself lifted up by
some strong arms, as though she were a feather,
and was placed rapidly in the middle of the cham-
ber. All changed. Suddenly a report sounded,
a heavy blow which shook the house even to its
foundations. Neither one nor the other suspected
the cause of the clamor. They trembled and were
silent.

It was the moment that the dragon had broken
the dining-room table.

CHAPTER XXV

UNFORESEEN SUCCESS—AN UNDISCOVERED FUGITIVE

THE scene changes. A beautiful, clean, humble, joyful room is seen, both commodious and of surprising neatness. A fine rush-mat covers the floor, and the white walls are adorned with fine prints of saints, and sculptures of dubious artistic value. The ancient mahogany furniture shines brilliantly from the Saturday polishing, and the altar, where a pompous Virgin, in blue and silver dress, is adored by the faithful, is covered by a thousand geegaws, half sacred, half profane. There are, besides missals, much holy water, a timepiece with *Agnus Dei,* a plaited palm from Palm Sunday, and not a few flower-pots of inodorous artificial flowers.

An enormous oak shelf holds a rich and choice library; here is Horace, the epicurean and sybarite, by the side of tender Virgil, in whose verses we see the inflammable Dido's heart palpitate and consume itself; Ovid, the long-nose, as sublime as obscene and flattering, near Martial, the cunning

257

linguist and wit; Tibulus, the impassioned, near Cicero, the great; severe Titus Livius near terrible Tacitus, shoot of the Cæsars; Lucretius, the pantheist; Juvenal stripped of his plumes; Plato, he who imagined that the best comedy of ancient times was giving turns to a mill's wheels; Seneca, the philosopher, of whom it is said that the best act of his life was death; Quintilian, the rhetorician; Sallustius, the rogue, who said so much about virtue; both Plinys, Suetonius, and Varro; in a word, all the Latin letters, from when one lisps his first word with Livius Andronicus, even to Rutilius, with whom one breathes his last sigh.

But while making this useless, though rapid enumeration, we have not observed that two women have entered the room. It is very early, but in Orbajosa they rise early. The birds are singing even though they are imprisoned; the bells are ringing for church; and even the goats, who are going to be milked at the house doors, are tinkling their little bells merrily.

The two ladies who have just entered the dwelling have come from hearing Mass. They are dressed in black, and each carries in her right hand her book of devotion, and her rosary wrapped round her fingers.

"Your uncle can not be long now," said one of them; "we left him beginning Mass; but he must have already finished, and will now be in the sacristy, taking off his vestments. I should have been glad could I have waited to hear the Mass, but to-day is a day of the greatest fatigue for me."

"I have only heard the prebend's to-day," said the other. "The prebend says his in a breath, and I think I have not profited by it, for I was so preoccupied I could not help thinking of the terrible things that are happening to us."

"What is to be done?— We must have patience— We will see what advice your uncle gives us."

"Ay!" exclaimed the second, heaving a deep pathetic sigh. "My blood boils."

"God will protect us."

"To think that a person like you, a lady like you, should be threatened!— Last night, Doña Perfecta, I did as you wished. I went to the widow Cuzco's lodging-house, and I begged for new information. Don Pepito and Brigadier Batalla are always conferring together— Ay, Jesus, my God and my Lord!—they confer about their infernal plans and despatch bottles of wine. They are two lost ones, two drunkards. Doubtless they discuss some great wickedness. When I was busying myself last night in your interests, when I was at the lodging-house, I saw Don Pepito go out, and I followed him—"

"And where did he go?"

"To the casino; yes, señora, to the casino," replied the other, slightly confused. "Then he returned to his house. Ay! how my uncle reprehended me for having remained so long in this spying business—but I could not help it— Divine Jesus, help me! I could not help it; seeing such a person as you in so much danger renders me mad— No, no, señora, I will do my best, that these rogues shall not assault the house and carry off Rosarito."

Doña Perfecta, for it was she, fixed her eyes on the floor, and meditated. She was pale and anxious. At last she exclaimed:

"But I do not see how it can be prevented."

"I see," replied the other, quickly (the confessor's niece and Jacintito's mother)—"I see a very simple way, the way that I have already proposed to you, and which you do not like. Ah! señora, you are too good. On occasions like this it is better not to be quite so good—to set aside one's scruples. For, will that offend God?"

"Maria Remedios," said Doña Perfecta haughtily, "do not talk nonsense."

"Nonsense!— You, with your wisdom, will not go to your nephew's rooms. What could be more simple than what I propose? Since there is no justice to protect us, we ourselves must be the great dispensers of justice. Have you not in your house

men who would serve you in anything? Then, call
them and say, 'See, Caballuco, Pasolargo, or whoever it may be, to-night you must muffle up well,
so that no one will recognize you; take a trustworthy friend with you and go to the corner of
Santa Fez Street. Wait a little, and when Don
José Rey passes the Calle de la Triperia to go to
the casino—for he is sure to go to the casino; do
you understand well?—when he passes, meet him
and give him a fright—' "

"Maria Remedios, do not be silly," replied Doña
Perfecta with magisterial dignity.

"Nothing more than a fright, señora: hearken
well to what I said, a fright. What is the matter,
have I counseled a crime?— Jesus, my Father and
Redeemer! The idea alone fills me with horror,
and I seem to see signs of blood and fire before my
eyes— Nothing like that, my lady— A fright,
and nothing more than a fright, by which that villain will understand that we are well defended.
He goes alone to the casino, quite alone, and there
he is joined by his friends, they of the sabre and
helmet. Fancy, he might receive a fright, and,
perhaps, some broken bones; no serious wounds,
understand—for in this case he might be intimidated and flee from Orbajosa, or keep his bed a
fortnight. That is it, recommend them to give him
a good fright. No killing— Caution them on that
point, but let him feel their hands well."

"Maria," said Doña Perfecta, haughtily, "you are incapable of an elevated idea, of a great and salutary resolution. That which you counsel me to is a cowardly indignity."

"Well, I shall hold my peace—"

"Oh, dear me, what a fool I am!" exclaimed the confessor's niece, humbly. "I shall keep my fooleries to console you when you have lost your daughter."

"My daughter!—lose my daughter!—" exclaimed Doña Perfecta, suddenly carried away by anger. "To hear it mentioned makes me furious. No, no, I will not lose her. If Rosarito does not detest this lost man, as I desire, she shall detest him. I shall use my authority as a mother— We will uproot her passion, or rather, her caprice, as the tender herb is uprooted before it has had time to make roots— No, that can not be, Remedios. Happen what may, it shall not be! That madman is not worthy of her, nor any such other infamous men— Before seeing her the spouse of my nephew, I will accept any evil that may come, even death."

"Rather death, rather buried and making food for the worms," affirmed Remedios, folding her hands as though she were praying, "than to see her in the power of— Ay! señora, do not be offended if I tell you something; it is that it would be great weakness to allow Rosarito to have any more secret interviews with this bold man. The case of last night, according to my uncle, appears to me to be an infamous trick of Don José's to accomplish his object by means of scandal— Many do so— Ay, Divine Jesus, I do not know how any one could look at the face of any man unless he were a priest!"

"Silence! silence!" said Doña Perfecta, vehemently, "do not talk to me about last night. What a horrible affair! Maria Remedios— I understand how anger may make one lose one's soul forever. I burn— Unhappy me, that I should see such things, and am not a man!— But if they told the truth about last night, then I have my doubts. Librada swore and swore again that it was Pinzon who entered. My daughter denied all. My daughter never lies!— I insisted in my suspicions. I think that Pinzon is a rascal, but nothing more—"

"We come back to the same point, that this prosperous mathematician is the author of all the evil— Ay! my heart did not deceive me the first time that I saw him— Then, señora, you may resign yourself to even more terrible doings if you do not decide to call Caballuco and say, 'Caballuco, I hope that—'"

"Coming back to the same? Well, you are simple!"

"Oh, yes; I am very simple, I know it; but if I

can not improve, what can I do? I say what I think, although I am not learned."

"What you think of; this vulgar nonsense about a beating and a fright, any one might think of. You have no brain, Remedios; when one wishes to resolve a great problem, you bring forward such absurdities. I have a resource more worthy of noble, well-born people— To thrash, what stupidity! Besides, I do not desire my nephew to receive a scratch by my orders: that, by no means. God will chastise him in the way He thinks best. We have only to work in such a way that God's designs may not be frustrated, Maria Remedios; in these affairs one must appeal directly to the cause of things. But you do not understand such language—you see nothing but the surface."

"Thus it is," said the curé's niece, humbly. "For God has denied me much; I understand none of these sublimities."

"You should go to the bottom—to the bottom of things, Remedios. Do you understand now?"

"Yes."

"My nephew is not my nephew, woman; he is the blasphemer, the sacrilegious man, the atheist, the demagogue— Do you know what a demagogue is?"

"One of those who burned Paris with petroleum, and devastated the churches and fired at the images— You see I know that well."

"Then my nephew is all that— Ah! if I were alone in Orbajosa! But, no, my daughter. My nephew, by a series of fatalities, which are so many proofs of the evils that God at times permits for our chastisement, represents the army, the Government authority, the justice of the peace, the judge; my nephew is not my nephew; he is the nation's official, Remedios; he is that second nation, comprised of those lost ones who govern in Madrid, and who do so by their material strength; of that apparent nation, for the real one is silent, and pays and suffers; of that fictitious nation which signs the decrees, pronounces discourses, and makes a farce of Government, a farce of authority, a farce of all. This is my nephew to-day; you must accustom yourself to see the inside of things. My nephew is the governor, the brigadier, the new justice of the peace, the new judge; for all favor him on account of the unanimity of his ideas; they are his flesh and blood, wolves of the same pack— Understand this well; we have to protect ourselves against all these, for all are one, and one is all; they must be attacked in common, and not with thrashings near a street corner, but as our grandfathers attacked the Moors—the Moors, Remedios!— My daughter, understand this well; open your mind, and let an idea that is not vulgar enter therein— Elevate yourself; raise your thoughts, Remedios—"

Don Inocencio's niece was struck with astonishment at so much grandeur.

She opened her mouth to say something consistent with such marvelous thought, but only breathed a sigh.

"As the Moors," repeated Doña Perfecta. "It is a question of Moors and Christians. And you fancy that, by frightening my nephew, all will be ended! How foolish you are! Do you not see that his friends support him? Do you not see that we are at the mercy of this rabble? Do you not see that that lieutenant is capable of setting fire to my house if he is annoyed?— Do you not understand that? Do you not comprehend that we must dive to the bottom? Do you not comprehend the immense grandeur, the terrible extension of my enemy, who is not a man, but a sect?— Do you not comprehend that my nephew, opposed to me as he is to-day, is not only a calamity but a plague?— Against it, dear Remedios, we have a battalion from God, who will annihilate the infernal militia from Madrid. I tell you it will be great and glorious—"

"If it ends so—"

"But you do not doubt it? We shall see terrible things here to-day!" said Doña Perfecta, very impatiently.

"To-day, to-day! What time is it? Seven. So late, and nothing happened?"

"Perhaps my uncle may know then, for here he is. He is coming upstairs."

"Thanks be to God!" said Doña Perfecta, rising to go out to meet the confessor. "He will tell us some good news."

Don Inocencio entered hurriedly. His expressive countenance indicated that his soul, consecrated to piety and Latin studies, was not as tranquil as usual.

"Bad news," he said, placing his hat on a chair and unfastening the strings of his mantle.

Doña Perfecta turned pale.

"They are seizing people," added Don Inocencio, lowering his voice, as though each chair hid a soldier. "They suspect, no doubt, that here their troublesome yoke will not be borne, and are going from house to house, laying hands on all those who have a reputation for courage."

Doña Perfecta flung herself despairingly on to a chair, and pressed her fingers tightly on the arms of it.

"Will there be many who will stay to be apprehended?" asked Remedios.

"Many of them—but very many," said Don Inocencio, in a patronizing manner, "have had time to get away, and have gone with arms and horses to Villahorrenda."

"And Ramos?"

"I was told at the cathedral that they are searching for him with the greatest perseverance— Oh, my God! to thus apprehend these unhappy people who, so far, have done nothing— See, I do not know how the good Spaniards can be patient. Señora Doña Perfecta, in reflecting on the prisoners, I have forgotten to tell you that you must immediately return to your house."

"Yes, at once. Are these bandits surveying my house?"

"Perhaps. Señora, we are at a woful period," said Don Inocencio, with solemn and anxious accent. "May God protect us!"

"In my house I have half a dozen well-armed men," replied Doña Perfecta, greatly changed. "What iniquity. Are they capable of also apprehending these?"

"It is certain that Señor Pinzon will have denounced them. Señora, I repeat that it is a woful time; but God will protect the innocent."

"I am going. Do not omit to come."

"Señora, when I have dismissed the class—for I think, as there is so much alarm in the town, that the little ones should have holiday to-day; but, class or no class, I will come. I do not wish your ladyship to go alone, for these lazy soldiers patrol all the streets, smoking and— Jacintito! Jacintito!"

"It is not necessary, I will go alone."

"Let Jacintito go," said his mother. "He should be up now."

They heard the hasty footsteps of the little lawyer coming downstairs from the higher floor. He came in, his face aflame, and out of breath.

"What is the matter?" questioned his uncle.

"In the Troyas' house," said the young fellow, "in their house—there."

"Finish at once!"

"Is Caballuco."

"He is there? In the Troyas' house?"

"Yes, sir. He spoke to me from the terrace, and told me that he was afraid he would be discovered there."

"Oh! how tiresome! This blockhead will allow them to apprehend him!" exclaimed Doña Perfecta, tapping the floor restlessly with her foot. "He might come here, and we could hide him."

"Here!"

Priest and niece stared at one another.

"Let him come down," said Doña Perfecta, vehemently.

"Here?" repeated Don Inocencio, looking annoyed.

"Here," replied Doña Perfecta. "I know of no other house so secure."

"He might easily go out by my bedroom window," said Jacintito.

"Well, if it is indispensable."

"Maria Remedios," said Doña Perfecta, "if this man is taken, all is lost."

"I am silly and simple," replied the priest's niece, putting her hand on her bosom, and heaving a sigh, which, doubtless, could be heard in the street; "but he shall not be taken."

Doña Perfecta went out quickly, and shortly afterward the Centaur was installed in the study, which was used only by the priest when writing his sermons.

We do not know how far Brigadier Batalla's ears reached, but it is certain that this diligent soldier had information whenever the Orbajosians varied their plans, and each day an addition was made to the prisons of those who in our rich insurrectional language are designated *caracterizodos*. The great Caballuco had, for a wonder, escaped by taking refuge in the Troyas' house; but, not believing himself secure there, as we have seen, he had gone to the holy, unsuspected house of the good priest.

At night the troops, distributed in different parts of the town, exercised the greatest vigilance on those who entered and sallied; but Ramos managed to evade the military precautions. He reanimated the people, and a multitude of men

gathered together in the villages round Villahorrenda, meeting at night to disperse again in the
daytime. To prepare the arduous business of an
insurrection, Ramos scoured the neighborhood,
collecting arms and men, and as the columns gave
way before the Aceros, in the land of Villajuan of
Nahara, our chivalrous hero performed much in
a short time.

At night he audaciously dared to enter Orbajosa,
sometimes by cunning, at others by bribery. His
popularity, and the protection that he received
within the town itself, served in a certain manner
as safeguard, and it might with truth be said that
the troop did not display the same rigor toward
this intrepid champion that it did toward the insignificant men in the locality. In Spain, and
chiefly in war time, which is always demoralizing,
one sees the infamous condescensions toward the
great, while unimportant people are persecuted
mercilessly. However it may have been, either
by audacity, bribery, or we know not what, Caballuco entered Orbajosa, recruiting more men, gath-
ering arms together, and collecting money. For
the greater security of his person, or, perhaps, to
disguise his intentions, he did not put foot in his
own house, scarcely went to Doña Perfecta's, and
then only to treat on important subjects, and partook only of supper in the house of one or other of
his friends, always preferring the respectable dom-

icile of some priest, and chiefly that of Don Inocencio, when to-morrow he might be receiving the dismal asylum of the prison.

Batalla had telegraphed to the Government saying that "he had discovered a factious conspiracy, and was apprehending the authors of it, and the few who managed to escape were dispersed and fugitive, actively pursued by our columns."

CHAPTER XXVI

MARIA REMEDIOS

NOTHING is more interesting than to seek for the origin of those successes which amaze and trouble us, and nothing more gratifying than to find it. When we see impetuous passions openly struggling and manifesting themselves, carried away by natural instinctive impulse, which always accompanies human observation, we desire to discover the hidden source from which such a turbulent river has drawn its waters; we experience a sensation very similar to the delight of geographers and seekers of lands.

God has conceded this delight to us now, for in exploring the hidden workings of those hearts which have palpitated in this history, we have discovered a fact which is surely the engenderer of facts more important than those we have narrated; a passion which is the first drop of water in the turbulent current whose course we have observed. Let us now continue the narration. We left the Señora de Polentinos without concerning ourselves as to what might have taken place on the morning of her dialogue with Maria Remedios. She hurried anxiously to her dwelling, where she was obliged to submit to Señor Pinzon's excuses and courtesies, who assured her that as long as he existed her house should not be surveyed. The señora replied in a haughty manner, without deigning to glance at him, which caused him to beg urbanely for explanations for such disdainful treatment; and for reply she told Señor Pinzon, arrogantly, that he might leave her house, as his conduct had been so perfidious while in it. He and Don Cayetano quarreled. However, as we are now interested in another subject, we will leave the Polentinoses and the lieutenant-colonel to settle their affairs as they can, and will examine another of those sources already mentioned.

We will take Maria Remedios, an estimable woman, to whom it is necessary to consecrate a few lines. She was a lady, a real lady; for in spite of her low origin, the virtues of her uncle, Don Inocencio, likewise of base origin, raised by his ordination as by his learning and respectability, had effused extraordinary splendor on the whole family.

Remedios's love for Jacintito was one of the most vehement passions that could exist in a maternal heart. She loved him deliriously; her son's welfare was to her of more importance than any other human affair; she believed him to be the most perfect model of beauty and talent created by God, and flattered herself that she would see him happy, great, and powerful all the days of his life, and he would then participate in eternal glory. Maternal sentiment is the only one that, with the very holy and noble, admits of exaggeration; the only one that delirium does not wear out. Nevertheless, a singular phenomenon occurs which is common in life, and this is, that if this exaltation of maternal affection does not coincide with absolute purity of heart, it only misleads and is converted into a lamentable frenzy, which may contribute the same as any other uncontrolled passion to great faults and catastrophes.

Maria Remedios passed in Orbajosa for a model of virtue, and likewise of nieces—perhaps she really was so. She was kind to all who were in need, never gave cause for spiteful report or murmurs, never meddled in intrigues. She was pious, without carrying it to hypocritical extremes, practised charity, ruled her uncle's house with supreme cleverness, was well received, admired, and courted everywhere in spite of an almost intolerable feeling of suffocation that produced a habit of sighing, and a dismal tone of voice.

But in Doña Perfecta's house this excellent woman suffered a species of *capitio diminutio*— brain fever. In remote times, and at an unlucky one for the good confessor's family, Maria Reme-

dios (if it is true, for so people said) had been a
laundress in the Polentinos house. And, no doubt,
on this account Doña Perfecta treated her haughtily; but no. She felt a truly sororal affection for
her; they dined together, prayed together, confided
their troubles, helping each other mutually in their
charities and devotions, as in the household matters—but there had always been an invisible line,
impossible to cross, between the parvenu and the
lady of birth. Doña Perfecta addressed Maria
familiarly, and always behaved with a certain for-
mality. The confessor's niece felt small in her
ladyship's presence, and her inborn humility took
a strange air of sadness. She saw that the good
priest was looked upon at the house as an infallible
counselor; she saw her idolized Jacintito in almost
friendly familiarity with the young lady, and notwithstanding the poor mother and niece frequented
the house as seldom as possible. Maria Remedios
felt slightly put aside in Doña Perfecta's house,
and found this disagreeable, for even in that sighing spirit, as in all living people, there was a little
pride. To see her son married to Rosarito; to see
him rich and powerful; to see him related to Doña
Perfecta, to a lady! Ah! this would be heaven and
earth to Maria Remedios, this life and the next,
the present and the future, the supreme totality of
existence. For years her heart had been full of
this sweet light of hope. For this she was good

and bad; for this she was religious and humble, or terrible and daring; for this she lived, for, without this idea, Maria, who was the incarnation of her project, would not have existed. Physically, Maria Remedios could not have been more insignificant. She was remarkable for a surprising vigor which made her appear younger than she really was; and she always dressed in black, although her widowhood had been of some duration.

Five days had passed since the entrance of Caballuco into the confessor's house. Night was falling. Remedios came into her uncle's room with a lighted lamp, and, putting it down on the table, confronted the old man, who since midday had sat on his chair immovable and meditative, as though he had been fastened to it. His chin rested on his palm, and his brown beard had not been shaved for three days.

"Did Caballuco say that he was coming here to sup to-night?" he questioned his niece.

"Yes, he will come. The poor fellow is most secure in these respectable houses."

"But I do not have them all here notwithstanding the respectability of my house," replied the confessor.

"How valiant Ramos exposes himself! And I am told that at Villahorrenda and in its neighborhood are many men—I do not know how many— What have you heard?"

"That the troops are committing all kinds of barbarities."

"It is a wonder that these cannibals have not searched my house. I swear to you, that if I saw one of those incarnate pantaloons entering my house, I should die without uttering a word."

"Willingly, we are willing," said Remedios, sighing from the depths of her soul. "I can not help thinking of Doña Perfecta's tribulation— Ah, uncle! you should go there."

"Shall I go to-night?— The troops are in all parts of the town. You think that the soldiery is but a caprice— Doña Perfecta is well protected. The other day her house was searched, and they apprehended the six armed men that were there, but have allowed them to return. We have no one to defend us in case of attack."

"I have sent Jacintito to the señora's house that he may keep her company for a short time. If Caballuco comes he will tell us what is passing there— I can not help thinking of these plots the marauders are preparing against our friend. Poor señora! poor Rosarito! When I think that this might have been prevented had Doña Perfecta followed the advice I gave her two days ago—"

"Dear niece," said the confessor phlegmatically, "we have done all that human beings could do to realize our holy purpose. We can now do no

more. We are ruined, Remedios. Rest assured of
that, and do not be obstinate: Rosarito can not be
our idolized Jacintito's wife. Your golden dream,
your happy ideal that at one time seemed possible
to us, and to which I have devoted all the forces
of my understanding, is now but a chimera; it is
dispersed like smoke. Grave stupefaction, one man's
wickedness, the undoubted passion of the young
girl, and other things have changed the order
of dreams. We were going to conquer, and we are
already conquered. Ay, my niece! Assure yourself of one thing. Henceforward Jacintito merits
much more than that mad girl."

"Caprice and stubbornness!" replied Maria,
with displeasure almost amounting to disrespect.
"What is the matter with you now, uncle? All the
great heads are becoming light. Doña Perfecta
with her sublimities, and you with your cavilla-
tions, are useful in some things. It is a pity that
God made me so silly, and gave me this brick and
mortar understanding, as the señora describes it,
for had it been otherwise I would have settled the
question."

"You?"

"If you and she would have left me alone, it
should have been already settled."

"With thrashings?"

"Do not alarm yourself, or open your eyes so
wide, for I do not wish to kill any one— See!"

"Beating," said the priest, smiling, "is like scratching— I know already."

"Bah! You would also tell me that I am cruel and sanguinary. I have not courage to kill a little worm; you know well enough— You may now understand that I desire no man's death."

"In short, my daughter, there are more things to consider than one; Don Pepe Rey will carry off the girl. It is impossible to prevent it. He is prepared to try all means, including dishonor. If Rosarito—how we have been deceived by that circumspect countenance and those celestial eyes, eh? —if Rosarito, I say, does not want him—we shall see—all might be arranged; but, ay! she loves him as the devil loves sin; she is ruined in criminal fire; fallen, my niece, fallen into an infernal libertinous trap. Let us be honorable and just; considering the ignoble pair, we can not think better of one than the other."

"You do not understand women, uncle," said Remedios, with fawning hypocrisy. "You are a holy savant; you do not understand that that is only a passing caprice of Rosarito's—one that can be cured by two blows on the mouth, or half a dozen lashes."

"Niece!" said Don Inocencio, seriously and sententiously, "when greater things have passed, little caprices are not called little caprices, by any means."

"Uncle, you do not know what you are saying," replied the niece, whose face had become suddenly inflamed. "How are you capable of supposing that of Rosarito? What atrocity! I defend her; yes, I defend her. She is as pure as an angel!— See! uncle, such things make me blush and treat you haughtily."

As she said this, the good priest's face was overshadowed with sadness, which made him look ten years older.

"Dear Remedios," he said, "we have done all that is humanly possible, and all that we could in conscience dare do. Nothing could be more natural than our desire to see Jacintito related to this great family—the first in Orbajosa. Nothing could be more natural than our desire to see him landlord of the seven town houses, of the pasture ground of Mundogrande, of the three orchards at Arriba and Encomienda, besides the outlying rustic farms that this young girl possesses. Your son is worthy of much—we all know it well. Rosarito liked him, and he liked her. It seemed an accomplished fact. Even Doña Perfecta, without being very enthusiastic—no doubt, owing to our origin—seemed well disposed, as she esteems and venerates me much as confessor and friend. But, unfortunately, that wretched young man turned up. Doña Perfecta told me that she had made an arrangement with her brother, and dared not with-

draw from it. Grave conflict! But what did I do
on sight of it? Ah! you do not know. I am frank
with you; had I found Señor de Rey a man of good
principle, capable of rendering Rosarito happy, I
would not have intervened; but the young fellow
appeared to me a calamity, and, as spiritual director of the house, I was obliged to take steps in
the matter—and I took them. I now know that I
placed the prow, as 'tis vulgarly expressed. I un-
masked his vices, discovered his atheism, revealed
to the view of the whole world the poverty of that
materialized heart; and the señora convinced herself that she was delivering her daughter up to
vice. Ah! how anxious I have been! Doña Perfecta vacillated; I fortified her wavering mind;
I advised her of the lawful means that she might
employ against her nephew, to get rid of him without scandal I suggested ingenious ideas to her, and,
when she showed me repeatedly her pure conscience bathed in tears, I tranquilized her, telling
her that any means were lawful to rid ourselves of
such a ferocious enemy. I never recommended
either violent or sanguinary measures, or any sort
of atrocity, only subtle stratagems that could not
be sinful. I am tranquil, dear niece. But you
well know how I have fought, that I have worked
like a negro. Ah! when I returned to my home at
night, and said, 'Mariquilla, we are doing well—
we are doing very well!' you were wild with de-

light, and kissed my hands a hundred times, saying that I was the best man in the world. Why are you now infuriated, spoiling your noble character and peaceful qualities? Why are you angry with me? Why do you say I am stubborn, and call me, in a polite manner, 'Juan Lanas'?"

"Why, because you," said the woman, her irritation in nowise diminished, "are so suddenly intimidated."

"It is because all is against us, woman. That wretched engineer, favored by the troop, is the cause of all. The little girl loves him—the little girl— I do not wish to say more. It can not be— I tell you that it can not be."

"The troop! So you believe, as does Doña Perfecta, that there will be war, and that to get rid of Don Pepito it is necessary for one-half of the nation to go to war with the other half. The señora has become mad, and you are following her example."

"I think with her. Given the intimate connections of Rey with the soldiery, the personal question attains force. But, ah! my niece, if our valiant men were only hopeful for two days, they might kick the troops out of the town, now that things have turned as they have. For I see that the greater part are surprised, even before fighting, and, as Caballuco is hiding and setting a trap for them, it discourages all of them. Good principles have not sufficient strong material to rout the ministers and emissaries of evil— Ah! my niece, resignation—resignation!"

Don Inocencio, following his niece's characteristic, sighed two or three times deeply. Maria, contrary to all that he might desire, maintained a profound silence. There was, or apparently was, no anger in her, nor even the ordinary superficial sentimentality natural to her; nothing but a deep and modest affliction. Shortly after her good uncle had concluded his harangue, two tears rolled down her rosy cheeks; she sobbed with little restraint, and little by little, more loudly, until it swelled into the tumult of a sea which commences to be turbulent, so boisterous was that wave of sorrow of Maria Remedios, relieving itself in such a waste of tears.

CHAPTER XXVII

A PRIEST'S TORMENT

"RESIGNATION! resignation!" Don Inocencio repeated.

"Resignation! resignation!" said his niece, drying her tears. "Then my dear son must always remain a cut-purse, for he may be that in time. Lawsuits decrease; the day may be near when he will be a lawyer to no purpose. Of what use is talent? What is the use of so much study and taxing one's brains? Ay! we are poor. A day will come, Señor Don Inocencio, when my poor son will not have a pillow on which to rest his head."

"Woman!"

"Man!— And if not, tell me; what heritage do you expect to leave behind you when you close your eyes? Four rooms, six little pamphlets, misery, and no more— We are going to see times— What times, Señor Uncle!— My poor son, whose health is so delicate, will not be able to work— He has headache now whenever he reads a book; he has always nausea and megrim when he works at night!—he is fated to beg from charity; I shall have to take in sewing, who knows—how shall we be able to beg an alms?"

"Woman!"

"I know what I am saying— Good times are coming," added this excellent woman, raising her voice with each word she uttered. "My God! what will become of us? Ah! A mother's heart alone feels these things. Only mothers are capable of suffering so much pain for a son's welfare. You! how can you understand? No; it is one thing to have sons and suffer sorrow for them, and another to chant in the cathedral and teach Latin at the institute. You see how much the fact of being your nephew is worth to my son; and his having been so successful in his studies; and being the glory and beauty of Orbajosa— He will die of hunger, for we know what law is worth, or he will be obliged to request a situation in Havana, where he will die of yellow fever."

"But, woman!"

"No, I will want, I will be quiet, I will molest you no more. I am very impertinent, very mournful, full of sighs, and I can not help it; for I am a tender mother and look to my beloved son's welfare. I shall die, yes, señor, I shall die, in silence and drown my sorrow. I shall swallow my sobs that I may not mortify Señor Priest— But my idolized son will understand me, and will not shut his ears as you are now doing— Ah, dear me! Poor Jacintito knows that I would become a martyr for him, and would afford him happiness at the cost of my life. Poor little child of my womb! He has so much merit, and to live condemned to a mediocre state, to a humble position; why, Señor Uncle, you will not be proud of him— For the more smoky we become, so will you be remembered as the son of Uncle Tinieblas, the sacristan at San Barnardo—and I shall only be the daughter of Ildefonso Tinieblas, your brother, he who sold pots; and my son will be Tinieblas's grandson— there will be darkness on our race, and we shall never overcome it; never shall we possess a foot of ground to enable us to say, 'That is mine,' neither shall we shear a ewe belonging to us; neither shall we milk our own goat; neither shall we be able to raise our hands to the cup to drink of our own threshing and winnowing—all this results from your little spirit, from your foolish outspoken heart."

"But—but, woman!"

The priest's voice was louder each time he uttered this sentence, and, with his hands to his ears, he shook his head from one side to the other with the sorrowful gesture of despair. The screaming song of Maria Remedios became each time more acute, and penetrated the unhappy stupefied priest's head like an arrow. But suddenly this woman's face was transformed; her plaintive sobs gave way to a harsh, crabbed tone; she became pale; her lips trembled; she clenched her fists; over her forehead hung some disordered locks; her eyes became still drier from the heat within her breast; she rose up, and, more like a harpy than a woman, shouted in this manner:

"I am going away from here, I am going with my son!— We will go to Madrid; I do not wish my son to remain in this town. I am tired of seeing my son sheltered under a cassock; and it shall be so no longer. Do you hear, Señor Uncle? My son and I are going! You will never see us again— never!"

Don Inocencio had crossed his hands, and received his niece's furious outbreak with the consternation of a criminal, to whom the presence of the hangman declares that it is useless to hope."

"For God's sake, Remedios," he murmured, in a dolorous tone, "for the Holy Virgin's sake—"

Such a crisis and horrible eruption, so unlike the niece's gentle character, was as strong as rare; and sometimes there was an interval of five or six years during which Don Inocencio did not see Remedios converted into a fury.

"I am a mother!— I am a mother!—and since no one else will look after my son, I will, even I," roared the lioness.

"For Holy Mary's sake, woman, do not alarm
yourself— Do you see you are sinning? Recite
the 'Lord's Prayer' and a 'Hail Mary,' and see if
you can not get over this."

So saying, the confessor trembled and perspired.
Poor chicken in the vulture's claws!

The transformed woman finished him with these
words:

"You are of no use; you are out of power— My
son and I will go away from here forever—forever!
I will secure a position for my son, I will seek
something profitable; do you hear? I would sweep
the streets with my tongue if I thought that by it I
should get something for him to eat; I would go
round the earth likewise to seek a position for my
son, that he might rise, be rich, a great personage,
a proprietor, a cavalier, a lord, anything that he
might possibly be—all—all."

"God will take care of me!" exclaimed Don
Inocencio, falling back in his chair, with his head
inclined on his breast.

There was quite a pause, during which the
deep breathing of the infuriated woman could
be heard.

"Woman," said Don Inocencio at last, "I have
lost ten years of my life—I have become mad—
my blood boils— May God grant me the serenity
to bear with you! Lord! patience, patience is what
I require. And you, niece, have done me the favor

of crying, sobbing, sighing, sniveling, and driveling for ten years; your cursed dexterity with pots, which so enraged me, is preferable to this wild anger. If I did not suppose you to be really good at the bottom— See! after having confessed and received Holy Communion this morning, you are not comporting yourself well."

"Yes, but it is your fault—yours."

"Because I say that in regard to Rosarito and Jacintito you must have resignation?"

"Because, when all was going well, you turned round and allowed Señor de Rey to take possession of Rosarito."

"And how could I prevent it? Doña Perfecta spoke truly in saying that you had a mind of brick. Do you wish I should take him by the shoulder and turn him out? Or must I go out with a sword and send away the whole troop, and then confront Rey, and say to him, 'Leave the young girl in peace, or I will cut off your head?' "

"No; but when I advised the señora to give her nephew a fright, you opposed me instead of supporting me."

"You are mad on this fright."

"Because by killing the dog an end is put to his madness."

"I could not recommend what you call a fright, but which might turn out to be something very serious."

"Yes, I am a murderer. Am I not, uncle?"

"I know that games with the hands are villainous games. Besides, do you think this man would allow himself to be frightened? And his friends?"

"He goes out alone at night."

"How do you know that?"

"I know all. I do not move a step without being thoroughly informed. The widow Cuzco reports all to me."

"See! do not send me mad. And who is to give this fright?— Are we?"

"Caballuco."

"Is he so disposed?"

"No; but he will do it if you order him to."

"See! woman, leave me in peace. I shall not order such an atrocity. A fright? And what is it? Have you mentioned it to him?"

"Yes, sir; but he took no notice, or, rather, refused me. In Orbajosa there are only two persons whose orders he will execute—you and Doña Perfecta."

"Then the señora may order him if she wishes. I will never advise her to employ such violent and brutal measures. Do you think that when Caballuco and his fellows were thinking of rising in arms that I would utter one single word to incite them to shed blood? No, no— If Doña Perfecta wishes it done—"

"She likewise does not desire it. I was talking
with her for two hours this afternoon, and she said
that people that preached war favored all means;
but that she would not order one man to hurt
another with the sword. She was right in op-
posing severe treatment—but I do not wish
him to be wounded. I only wish that he may be
frightened."

"Then, if Doña Perfecta does not desire to give
orders that he may be frightened, neither do I.
Do you understand? My conscience before everything."

"Good," replied the señora. "You tell Caballuco that he is to accompany me to-night— You
need tell him no more."

"Are you going out late?"

"I am going out; yes, señor. Well, did I not
go out last night?"

"Last night? I did not know. If you did go
out I am annoyed; yes, señora."

"You need simply say this to Caballuco, 'Dear
Ramos, I should be grateful if you would accompany my niece on a certain errand to-night, and
protect her in case of danger!'"

"I can do that. He is to accompany you—
to protect you. Ah! sly woman! you wish to
deceive me, to make me an accomplice in some
absurdity."

"I— What are you thinking of?" asked Maria

Remedios, ironically. "Ramos and I, together, will destroy many people to-night."

"No jests. I repeat that I shall advise Ramos in nothing wrong. I fancied he was here—"

They heard a noise at the street door. Then the sound of Caballuco talking with the servant, and presently Orbajosa's hero entered the room.

"News! give us news, Señor Ramos!" said the priest. "See! give us some hope in return for supper and hospitality— What is doing at Villahorrenda?"

"Something," replied the valiant man, sitting down and looking tired. "You will soon see if we are of any use."

Like all important persons, or those who wish to appear so, Caballuco displayed great reserve.

"To-night, my friend, I will give you, if you wish, the money that I have received for—"

"I can do well without it— Supposing the troop should not allow me to pass?" said Ramos, laughing brutally.

"Be quiet, man. We know now that you may pass whenever you wish. Then nothing further is wanting. The military are people with wide sleeves—and if they can weight them with two pesos, eh? Come, I see that you are not badly armed— You are only wanting in a cannon. Pistols, eh?— Knife also?—"

"With that one may manage," said Caballuco, taking the firearm off his girdle, and showing its horrible mouth.

"By God and the Virgin!" exclaimed Maria Remedios, shutting her eyes and turning her face away with fear. "Take care of that lumber. It horrifies me only to see it."

"If you do not mind," said Ramos, putting up the firearm, "we will sup." Maria Remedios prepared all quickly, that the hero might have no cause for impatience.

"Let me ask you one thing, Señor Ramos," said Don Inocencio to his companion, when they were taking supper; "have you much to do this evening?"

"Indeed I have," replied the other. "It is the last night that I am coming to Orbajosa—the last. I have to collect some young fellows who are faltering here, and we are going to see how we can transport the saltpetre and brimstone, which is at Cirujeda's house."

"I would say," added the curé, kindly filling his friend's plate, "that my niece would like you to accompany her for a short time. She has something or other to do, I know not what, and it is late for her to go alone."

"Is she going to Doña Perfecta's house?" questioned Ramos. "I have been there for a moment; and she did not wish to detain me."

"How is the señora?"

"Very well. To-night I am going to take the six young fellows who are with her."

"Man! do you not think that they are wanted there?" asked Remedios, anxiously.

"They are more needed at Villahorrenda. There are brave men in the houses, are there not?"

"Señor Ramos, that house must not be left unguarded," said the confessor.

"There are more than enough servants. But do you think, Señor Don Inocencio, that the brigadier will attack the houses in the neighborhood?"

"Yes; for you know that this engineer, with three thousand dozen of devils—"

"As to that—the house is not deficient in brooms," said Christobel, gaily. "They can but marry at last— After what has passed—"

"Señor Ramos," said Remedios, suddenly angry, "I fancy you do not understand much about people marrying."

"I tell you that I went to Doña Perfecta's for a moment to-night, and saw the señora and the señorita, and they were reconciled. Doña Perfecta embraced Rosarito, and continually addressed her tenderly."

"Reconciled! You have lost your head among all this warlike preparation— But, finally, will you accompany me or not?"

"It is not to Doña Perfecta's house that she wishes to go," said the priest, "but to widow Cuzco's. She was saying that she did not like to go alone, for fear of being insulted."

"By whom?"

"You know well enough. By this engineer with three or four thousand dozen devils. Last night my niece saw him there, and received some information about him, for which reason she wishes you to go with her to-night. The young fellow is revengeful and petulant."

"I do not know if I can go—" answered Caballuco, "I have to take care now not to be discovered. I can not defy Don José Pepita Cosa. If I were not as I am now, with half my face concealed, and the other half uncovered, I would have broken his backbone thirty times. But what would happen if I fell out with him? He would discover me; the soldiers would come down on me, and 'good-by' to Caballuco. To give him a blow in the dark does not suit me; it is unnatural, neither will her ladyship consent to it. Treachery does not suit Christobel Ramos."

"But, man, are you silly?—what are you talking about?" said the confessor, with undeniable symptoms of alarm. "I did not wish to counsel you to ill-treat this gentleman. I would rather cut out my tongue than advise such wickedness. The wicked fall, it is true, but God fixes the moment, not I. I do not recommend blows either. I would rather administer ten dozen to any Christian who would counsel such medicine. I only said to you," he added, looking at the man over his spectacles, "that as my niece is going there, as is probable, very probable, are you not, Remedios?—as she may have somewhat to say to this man, that I wished you not to abandon her, in case she might be insulted—"

"I have much to do to-night," replied Caballuco, laconically and dryly.

"You hear him, Remedios. Leave your errand until to-morrow."

"I can not. I will go alone."

"No, you will not go, my niece. We will keep the festival peacefully. Señor Ramos has plenty to do, and can not accompany you. Only fancy, you might be injured by that gross man!"

"Insulted!—insulted! He insult a lady!" exclaimed Caballuco. "Come, that can not be!"

"If you had nothing to do—bah! bah! I should be tranquil."

"I have plenty of occupation," said the Centaur, rising from the table, "but if it would oblige you—"

There was a pause. The confessor closed his eyes and meditated.

"It would oblige me, Señor Ramos," he said at last.

"Then there is no more to be said. We will go, Señora Maria."

"Now, dear niece," said Don Inocencio, half-gaily, half-seriously, "as we have finished supper, bring me the basin." He gave a penetrating look at his niece, and, accompanying these words with a corresponding action, said, "I wash my hands of it."

CHAPTER XXVIII

FROM PEPE REY TO DON JUAN REY

"ORBAJOSA, *April* 12th.

"DEAR FATHER—Pardon me if, for the first time, I disobey you by not leaving here, or renouncing my project. Your advice and entreaty are worthy of a kind, honorable father; my obstinacy is worthy of a foolish son, but a singular thing has taken place within me; obstinacy and honor are so intermingled and confounded that the idea of being dissuaded to forsake my cause confuses me. I am much altered. I do not recognize these attacks of fury that consume me. At one time I laughed at all violence, at impetuous men's exaggerations, as perverse brutality. Now nothing of this sort astonishes me, for I experience within myself at all hours a certain terrible capacity for perversity. To you I can express myself as I do alone to God and my conscience. I can tell you that I am a wretch, for he who is wanting in powerful moral strength to castigate the passions and submit to the hard rule of conscience is a wretch. I am deficient in Christian uprightness, which fills the spirit of an offended man with a beautiful sense

299

of elevation over the offenses received and over his enemies. I have been weak enough to abandon myself to a wild anger, letting myself down to the base level of my detractors; returning them blows equal to those received, and trying to confound them by means learned in their own unworthy school. How I feel it that I have not you by my side to help me on this road. Now it is late. Passions give no hope. They are impatient, and they hurry me along with shouts, and with the convulsion of a dreadful, deadly thirst. I have succumbed. I can not forget the many times that you have told me that anger is the worst of passions, for it unexpectedly transforms our characters, engendering all other wickedness, and lending to all its infernal fire.

"But I have not known anger alone, it is also a strong, expansive sentiment which has thrown me into this state; the deep and unalterable love for my cousin, the only circumstance that can absolve me; and, if not love, pity has led me to defy your terrible sister's fury and intrigues; for poor Rosarito, placed between her irresistible affection and her mother, is to-day one of those most disgraced beings that exist on the earth. Her love blinds me and corresponds with mine. Had I not the right to open, as I could, the doors of her house and draw her thence, employing the law where I could reach it, and using force where the law does not protect me? I believe that your rigorous, moral scrupulosity will not answer me in the affirmative to this question; but I am no longer that methodical, pure character conforming exactly to conscience. I am not he to whom an almost perfect education gave a marvelous regularity to his sentiments; I am now a man like any other. By one single step I have entered the common land of injustice and wrong. Be prepared to hear of some savage deed, which will be a work of mine. I will take care to let you know what I do.

"But the confession of my faults does not acquit me of the responsibility of those grave affairs that have occurred, and will occur, and which, though I am partly the cause, will not all fall on your sister. Doña Perfecta's responsibility is certainly immense. What will be the extent of mine? Ah, dear father, do not believe anything you may hear of me, but only what I reveal to you. If it is said that I have committed a deliberate villainy, answer that it is false. Difficult—very difficult—is it for me to judge myself in the present state of perturbation, but I can truly assure myself that I have not deliberately caused scandal. You well know how a favored passion is affected in its horrible growth by circumstances.

"The most bitter thing in my life is that I have employed fiction, deceit, and base dissimulation—

I, who was truth itself. I have lost my own form
—but does the soul incur this great perversity? Is
it now only commencing, or is it near the end? I
do not know. If Rosarito, with her celestial hand,
does not save me from this hell raging in my conscience, I wish you would come and save me. My
cousin is an angel, and, in suffering for me, has
taught me many things that I did not know before.
Do not wonder at the incoherence of what I write.
Divers sentiments inflame me. At times I am as-
sailed by ideas worthy of my immortal soul, but at
others I fall into a lamentable languor, and think
of weak and deceitful men, whose baseness you pictured to me in such lively colors in order to make
me detest them. This is what I feel myself to-day.
I am disposed for good and evil. I now know what
prayer is, a great reflective supplication; so personal that it can not be regulated by formulas
learned by heart; an expansion of the soul which
even dares to seek its origin; the opposite of remorse, which is a contradiction of the same soul,
wrapping it round and concealing it with the ridiculous pretension that no one can see it. May God
have mercy on me! You taught me many good
things, but I am now in practise, as engineers term
it. I have surveyed the land, so that my knowledge
is enlarged and settled— I am now fancying that
I am not as bad as I thought even. Is it so?

"I finish this letter hurriedly. I am going to

despatch it by one of the soldiers who is going to Villahorrenda, for I have no confidence in this people's courier."

April 14*th*.

"You would be much amused, dear father, could you understand what thoughts the people of this town have. You will now know that nearly all this country is in insurrection. It was a foreseen thing, and politicians have been deceived if they thought it was only a two days' affair. The hostility against ourselves and the Government, shown in the spirit of the Orbajosians, forms a part of them, like religious faith. As regards the particular question of my aunt, I will relate a singular thing to you. It is that the poor lady, who believes in feudalism to the marrow-bone, has fancied that I was going to attack her house to rob her of her daughter, as did the cavaliers of the Middle Ages, when they attacked an enemy's castle to perpetrate some act of injustice. Do not laugh, it is true; such are these people's ideas. You will excuse me telling you that I am looked upon as a kind of monster, as a species of Moorish heretical king, and the military men with whom I have become friendly here are considered as deserving of the same opprobrium. In Doña Perfecta's house it is a current topic that the troops and I have formed a diabolical, anti-religious coalition, in order to deprive

Orbajosa of its treasures, faith, and young girls.
It is certain that your sister believes literally that
I am intending to assail her house, and it is equally
certain that a barricade has been erected behind the
door.

"But that may not be by any means. They
retain the most antiquated notions here on society,
religion, state, and property. Religious exaltation
causes them to employ strength against the Government to defend a faith which no one has attacked,
and they maintain fiercely the spirit of vicious
feudal customs; and, as they resolve their questions
by brutal strength, blood and fire, they destroy all
who think differently to them, not understanding
that people in the world employ other means.

"Far from it being my intention to commit ex-
travagances in Doña Perfecta's house, I have done
my best that she should not be molested; whereas
the neighbors around her have not been free.
Through my friendship with the brigadier, she
has not been obliged, as was ordered, to make out a
list of all her men servitors who had gone to join
the faction; and, if her house was surveyed, I was
assured that it was only as a matter of form; and
if they disarmed the six men therein, they afterward allowed them to arm again, and took no steps
to prevent it. You may see by this how far my
hostility toward the señora extends.

"It is true that I have the support of the chief

military men, but I have only utilized it to protect myself from the insults and ill-treatment of these implacable people. My probabilities of exit consist in that the persons in authority, recently placed by the military chief, are all friends. They, and my moral strength together, are intimidating. I do not know but that if I should find myself in the house I might commit some violence, but assure yourself that the assault and taking of the house is a purely mad feudal assumption of your sister. Circumstances have placed me in an advantageous position. Anger, the passion that burns within me, induces me to profit by it. I do not know even when I shall go."

April 17th.

"Your letter has given me great consolation. Yes, I can attain my object, using the resources of the law alone, completely efficacious for this. I have consulted the authorities here, and all confirm me in what you indicated to me. I am content. I have now inculcated into my cousin's soul the idea of disobedience, which will, at least, be supported by social laws. I will do as you commanded me; that is to say, renounce the rather ugly collusion with Pinzon; I will destroy the terrifying consolidation that I established with the military; I will leave behind me the pride of being in power with them; I will put aside any adventures, and, at an opportune moment, will act with calmness, prudence, and all benignity possible. It is better so. My coalition half serious, half burlesque, with the army was with the object of shielding myself from the brutality of the Orbajosians and my aunt's servants and relations. Otherwise, I have always repelled the idea of an armed intervention.

"The friend who has favored me has been obliged to leave the house; I am, however, in slight communication with my cousin. The poor girl has displayed a heroic courage in the midst of her griefs, and will obey me blindly. You may rest tranquil as to my personal security. For my part, I have no fear, and am quite calm."

April 20*th*.

"I can not write more than two lines to-day. I have much to do. All will be finished in a few days. Do not write to me again here. You will soon have the pleasure of embracing your son,
"PEPE."

CHAPTER XXIX

PEPE REY TO ROSARITO POLENTINOS

GIVE Esterbanillo the key of the orchard, and charge him to be careful of the dog. The young fellow is mine, body and soul. Fear nothing. I shall be very sorry if you can not come down, as you did the other night. Do all you can to manage it. I shall be there about midnight. I will tell you what I have done and what I have to do. Be tranquil, my girl, for I have abandoned all imprudent and brutal resources. I will tell you all. It is long, and should be told verbally. I seem to see your alarm and anguish on not finding me near you. I have not seen you for eight days. I swear to you that this absence from you will soon end. My heart tells me that I shall see you. Unhappy me if I do not see you!"

CHAPTER XXX

THE ACT

A WOMAN and a man went into the widow Cuzco's house about ten o'clock, and came out of it about half-past eleven.

"Now, Señor Maria," said the man, "I will accompany you to your home, for I have much to do."

"Wait, Señor Ramos, for the love of God," replied she. "Why not go to the casino to see when he comes out? You heard just now. He was seen talking this afternoon to Esterbanillo, the little fellow from the orchard."

"But why do you seek Don José?" questioned the Centaur, in a very bad humor. "What does it matter to us? The nuptials with Señorita Rosarito seem to be just what should be, and there is nothing for Doña Perfecta to do but to let them take place. That is my opinion."

"You are a brute!" said Remedios, angrily.

"Señora, I am going."

"Then, you rude man, are you going to leave me in the middle of the street?"

"If you are not going at once to your house— yes, exactly so!"

"You leave me alone, exposed to insult! Listen, Señor Ramos, Don José will come out of the casino now, as usual. I want to know if he goes into his lodgings or not. It is a fancy, nothing but a fancy."

"I know that I have enough to do, and it will soon strike twelve."

"Silence," said Remedios; "let us hide ourselves in this corner. A man comes up this street of Triperia. It is he."

"Don José—I know him by his step."

They hid, and the man passed on.

"Let us follow him," said Maria Remedios, anxiously. "Let us follow him at a distance, Ramos."

"Señora—"

"Only to see if he goes into his lodgings."

"One minute only, Señora Remedios. Then I shall go."

They followed at about thirty paces, that the man might not discover them. The confessor's niece stopped, and pronounced these words: "He is not going into the house."

"He will go to the brigadier's house."

"The brigadier lives higher up, and Don Pepe is going further down, he makes for Doña Perfecta's house."

"Doña Perfecta's!" exclaimed Caballuco, walking briskly on.

But they were mistaken; the man they were

watching passed the Polentinos home and then went further.

"Do you see him now?"

"Señor Ramos, let us follow him," said Remedios, convulsively pressing the Centaur's hand. "I have a presentiment."

"We shall soon know, because the people will finish him."

"Do not go so fast—he can see us. I thought so, Señor Ramos; he is going in by the condemned door of the orchard."

"Señora, you are turning mad!"

"Go on, we will see."

It was a dark night, and the spies could scarcely see where Señor de Rey had entered; but a certain click as of a rusty lock, and the fact of their not meeting the young man all the length of the wall, convinced them that he must have gone into the orchard. Caballuco looked at his companion with an air of stupefaction. He seemed struck with amazement.

"What are you thinking of? Do you still doubt?"

"What can be done?" questioned the valiant man, full of confusion. "Shall we give him a fright? I do not know what Doña Perfecta will think. To-night, when I saw her, the mother and daughter appeared to be reconciled."

"Do not be stupid— Why not enter?"

"I wish those armed men were here now, for I told them to leave to-night."

"And no doubt this villain reckoned on that. Ramos, do not be a coward; go into the orchard."

"How; is not the door locked?"

"You can get over the wall— What a blockhead! If I were but a man."

"Then, higher up—there are some bricks by which the children mount to steal the fruit."

"Higher up, then. I am going to the principal door to wake Doña Perfecta if she sleeps."

The Centaur mounted, not without some difficulty. Soon his head rose above the wall, and he disappeared in the black density of the trees. Maria Remedios ran until she arrived in the Calle del Condestable, and, hammering at the door with the knocker, called—called three times with all her heart and soul.

CHAPTER XXXI

DONA PERFECTA

SEE how calmly Doña Perfecta is engaged in writing. We penetrate into her room, in spite of the lateness of the hour, and surprise her in a grave task; her mind divided between meditation and some long, conscientious letters, which she inscribes with sure pen and correct figures. Her face, hands, and bust are seen by the light from the lamp, while the shade leaves the rest of her person and nearly all the room in soft shadow. She looks like a luminous figure, evoked by imagination in the midst of vague shadows of fear.

It is strange that we have not, till now, made an important asseveration, and this is that Doña Perfecta was beautiful, or rather, she was still beautiful, preserving in her countenance traces of past beauty. Her country life, the absolute absence of conceit—for she neither dressed nor adorned herself; she abhorred fashion and despised vain ceremonies—were the cause of her native beauty not shining, or, at least, shining very little. The intense yellowness of her face, indicating a very bilious constitution, also deteriorated from it.

Her eyes were black, her nose fine and delicate, her forehead broad and clear; all who took much notice of her considered her a finished model of a human figure. There was now during these troubles an expression of harshness and stubbornness, which caused a feeling of antipathy. Her glance, though accompanied by kindly words, seemed to place an immeasurable distance between her and strangers; but those living in the house, that is to say, her near relations, felt drawn toward her by a singular attraction. She was a master in the art of governing, and no one equaled her in the art of speaking the language most adapted to each person.

Her bilious disposition and excessive intercourse with devout persons and things, which exalted her imagination fruitlessly, had aged her prematurely, and, though feeling young, she did not appear so. It might be said of her that, with her habits and system of living, she had covered herself with a crust, a stony lining, insensibility, and had shut herself up within, as does the snail in its portable house. Doña Perfecta seldom came out of her shell.

Her confirmed habits, and that general kindness that we have observed in her from the moment of her appearance in our tale, were the cause of her great prestige in Orbajosa. She still maintained relations with some excellent señoras in

Madrid, and by this means had caused her nephew's ruin. Now, at the moment of our history, we find her sitting before her desk, which is the only confident of her plans, and the depositary of her numerical calculations with the villagers, and her moral calculations with God and society. There, she wrote the quarterly letters received by her brother; there, she edited the notes to incite the judge and notary to entangle Pepe Rey in lawsuits; thence she flung the dart that was to cause him to lose the minister's confidence; there, she consulted Don Inocencio. But to become acquainted with the scene of other actions, the effects of which we have seen, we should be obliged to follow her to the Episcopal palace, and to the various houses of familiar friends.

We do not know how Doña Perfecta had been able to love. She detested with inflammatory vehemence, like to that of a guardian angel, hatred and discord among men. Such is the result produced on a hard character, not naturally kind, by religious exaltation, when this, instead of nourishing principles as simple as beautiful in the conscience derived from the truth revealed, seeks its sap from narrow formulas, which render it obedient only to interested priests. For, as hypocrisy may be inoffensive, that is the very reason why it exists in the purest hearts. It is true that in that case it bears no good fruit. But those hearts which are born without the seraphic chastity, which establishes on earth a premature Limbo, should be careful not to inflame themselves much by what they see on altars, choirs, in the pulpits and sacristies, if they have not previously erected in their own conscience an altar, a pulpit, and a confessional.

The señora, leaving off writing for a time, proceeded to the adjoining room where her daughter was. She had told Rosarito to go to bed; but she, already accustomed to disobedience, was up.

"Why are you not asleep?" questioned her mother. "I do not think of going to bed to-night. You know Caballuco has taken away the men that we had here. Something might happen, and I am watching. If I do not watch, what will become of you and me?"

"What time is it?" questioned the young girl.

"It will soon be midnight— You are not afraid —but I am."

Rosarito trembled, and all indicated that she was suffering the darkest anguish. Her eyes were raised to heaven as though she would pray, then she looked at her mother, expressing a lively terror.

"But what is the matter with you?"

"Did you say that it was midnight?"

"Yes."

"Then— But is it already midnight?"

Rosarito wished to speak, hung her head, in which was passing a world of thoughts.

"There is something the matter then—something has happened to you then," said her mother, fixing her sagacious eyes on her.

"Yes— I want to tell you," muttered the young girl. "I wish to say—nothing, nothing. I will sleep."

"Rosarito! Rosarito! your mother reads your heart like a book!" exclaimed Doña Perfecta, severely. "You are agitated. I have told you that I am ready to pardon you if you will repent; if you are a good, well-behaved girl."

"Well, then, am I not good? Ah, mama! mama! I shall die!"

Rosarito interrupted herself with a painful, sorrowful sob.

"Why these sobs?" said her mother, embracing her. "If these are tears of repentance, blessed be they."

"I do not repent, I can not repent," shouted the young girl, with the violence of desperation, which rendered her sublime.

She drew up her head, and on her countenance was suddenly depicted inspired energy. Her hair fell down over her shoulders. Never has been seen a more beautiful picture of an angel about to rebel.

"But you are mad; or what is this?" said Doña

Perfecta, placing both her hands on her daughter's shoulders.

"I am going, I am going," said the young girl, expressing herself with delirious exaltation.

And she threw herself across the bed.

"Rosarito! Rosarito!—my daughter— For God's sake! What is the matter?"

"Ah, mama, señora!" exclaimed the young girl, embracing her mother. "You frighten me."

"Truly, you deserve it— What madness is this?"

"You frighten me— I am going away, going with him."

Doña Perfecta felt as though a flame of fire rose from her heart to her lips. She felt suffocated, and only her black eyes, blacker that night, replied to her daughter.

"Mama! my mama! I detest all but him!" exclaimed Rosarito. "Hear me confess; for I wish to confess to all, and to you first."

"You are going to kill me, you are killing me."

"I wish to confess that you may pardon me. This weight, this weight bears me down and does not permit me to live."

"The weight of a sin— Add to it God's curse, and essay to walk under the burden, disgraceful girl! I alone can take it from you."

"No; you, no; you, no!" shouted Rosarito despairingly. "But you can listen to me, I wish to confess all—all. Then you may cast me out from this house where I was born."

"I cast you out?"

"Then I shall go."

"Never! I will teach you a daughter's duties which you have forgotten."

"Then I shall flee. He will take me with him."

"Has he told you so, has he advised you, has he commanded you?" questioned her mother, flinging out these words like lashes at her daughter.

"I advised it— We have concerted together to be married. That is it exactly, mama, dear mama. I would love you— I know that I ought to do so— I shall be condemned if I do not love you."

She opened her arms and, falling on her knees, kissed her mother's feet.

"Rosarito! Rosarito!" exclaimed Doña Perfecta in a terrible voice, "get up."

There was a short pause.

"Has this man written to you?"

"Yes."

"Has he been to see you since that night?"

"Yes."

"And you?"

"I likewise— Oh, señora, why do you look at me so? You are not my mother."

"Would to God I were not. You may rejoice in what you have done to me. I am being killed—

killed without remedy," shouted the señora, in the greatest agitation. "You say that this man—"

"Is my husband. I shall be his protected by law. You are not a woman. Why do you look at me in that manner and frighten me? Mother, my mother, do not condemn me."

"You have already condemned yourself; it is enough. Obey me and I will pardon you— Answer, when did you receive letters from this man?"

"To-day."

"What treason! What infamy!" exclaimed her mother, rather roaring than speaking. "Do you hope to see each other?"

"Yes."

"When?"

"To-night."

"Where?"

"Here—here. I confess all—all. I know it is a crime— I am an infamous girl, but you, who are my mother, will rescue me from this hell. You must consent— Say one word to me—only one."

"This man here in my house!" screamed Doña Perfecta, taking a few steps, one might say leaps, toward the centre of the room.

Rosarito followed her on her knees. At the same moment three blows, three reports, three cannonades were heard. It was Maria Remedios's heart knocking at the door with the knocker. The house shook with a terrible trembling. Mother and daughter remained like statues. Below, a servant opened the door, and shortly after Maria Remedios, more like a basilisk wrapped in a cloak than a woman, entered Doña Perfecta's room. Her face, inflamed by anxiety, appeared as though on fire.

"He is there! he is there!" she cried, on entering. "He has gone into the orchard by the small door which is condemned."

She had to take breath at each syllable.

"I understand now," repeated Doña Perfecta, uttering a cry like that of a wild beast.

Rosarito fell on the floor and became unconscious.

"Let us go below," said Doña Perfecta, taking no notice of her daughter.

The two women glided downstairs like two snakes. The women-servants and man-servant were in the gallery, not understanding what was the matter. Doña Perfecta passed through the dining-room and into the orchard, followed by Maria Remedios.

"Fortunately Ca-Ca-Caballuco is here," said the priest's niece.

"Where?"

"In the orchard likewise— He—he—he got over the wall."

Doña Perfecta explored the obscurity, with her

eyes full of anger. Rancor lent her the singularly acute vision of the feline race.

"I see something," she said. "It has gone underneath the bay trees."

"It is he!" shouted Remedios. "But there goes Ramos! Ramos!"

They could distinguish the colossal figure of the Centaur distinctly.

"Under the bay trees, Ramos! Under the bay trees!"

Doña Perfecta moved a few steps forward. Her menacing voice, which vibrated with a terrible accent, was heard to say:

"Christobel! Christobel! kill him!"

A shot was heard, and then another.

CHAPTER XXXII

THE END

FROM Don Cayetano Polentinos to a friend in Madrid:

"ORBAJOSA, April 21st.

"DEAR FRIEND—Send me without delay the edition of 1562, which you have found among the books that Corchuels left behind him.

"Obtain it for as much as it may be worth. For some time I have sought for it unsuccessfully, and shall be delighted to possess it. Have you met with a pot bearing on it the word 'Tractado,' and the X in the date MDLXII put on crookedly? If you should recognize it by these signs, telegraph to me, as I am very anxious—although I grant that the telegraph, by reason of these importunate and fastidious wars, does not now work well. I hope to receive a reply by post.

"I shall soon come to Madrid, my friend, with the object of printing this long-hoped-for work on the 'Lineage of Orbajosa.' I thank you for your benevolence, my dear friend, but I can allow no flattery. My work does not indeed merit the pompous qualifications which you accord it. It is a work of patience and study, a clumsy monument, but solid and extensive, and intended to celebrate the greatness of my beloved country.

"Poor and ugly in its form, I hold the idea that engendered it a noble one. One which intends it to open the eyes of this unbelieving, stubborn generation to the marvelous feats and refined virtues of our ancestors. God grant that the studious youth of our country may interest themselves in this work, to which I have devoted all my strength! God grant that the abominable studies and intellectual habits introduced by licentious philosophy and erratic doctrines may be consigned to oblivion! God grant that we may employ our wisdom to the contemplation of these glorious ages, and that, penetrated by the substantial and beneficent sap of modern times, this mad solicitude for mundane matters, and ridiculous mania for appropriating strange ideas, may disappear, with which our fine national organism combats!

"I am much afraid that my desires will not be fulfilled, and that the contemplation of past perfections will be circumscribed to the narrow circulation met with to-day, through the whirlwind of mad youth which runs after vain chimeras and barbarous novelties. What things these are, my friend! I believe that some time hence our poor Spain will be so disfigured that she will not recognize herself when glancing into the mirror of her pure history.

"I do not wish to conclude this letter without informing you of a disagreeable affair—the disastrous death of an estimable young man well known in Madrid, the road engineer, Don José de Rey, my sister-in-law's nephew. This sad affair took place last night in the orchard adjoining our house, and no one seems able to form an exact opinion as to the causes which induced the unfortunate Rey to such a horrible and criminal determination. According to what Perfecta told me this morning on my return from Mundogrande, Pepe Rey went into the orchard at twelve o'clock (midnight) and drew a pistol at his right temple, intending to kill himself. You may imagine the consternation and alarm produced in this peaceful, honorable house.

"Poor Perfecta was so afflicted that we have been frightened, but she is now better, and this afternoon we have persuaded her to take a soporific. We employed all means to console her, and she, being a good Christian, knows how to support the greatest misfortunes with edifying resignation.

"I will tell you here, my friend, in confidence, that, in this attempt on his life, the young man

Rey must have been greatly influenced by a contrary passion, remorse for his conduct, and a state of hypochondriacal bitterness which he manifested.

"I liked him very much. I believe he was not deficient in excellent qualities, but here he was not esteemed much, for not once have I heard him well spoken of. According to what was said, he held extravagant opinions and ideas; scorned religion; entered the church smoking, and with his hat on; respected nothing, and for him there was nothing in the world, of power, virtue, soul, ideal, faith; nothing but squares, lines, machines, planes, picks, spades, and theories. For truth's sake I would say that in his conversations with me he always dissimulated such ideas, doubtless fearing that he would be confounded by the grapeshot of my arguments; but in public there are a thousand accounts of his heresies and stupendous acts of injustice.

"I can not continue, dear friend, for at this moment I hear gunshots. As I am not enthusiastic about combats, nor am I a warrior, my pulse beats no faster. I will send you a few particulars about this war.

"Yours affectionately," etc., etc.

April 22d.

"MY EVER-REMEMBERED FRIEND—There has been a bloody affray to-day in the neighborhood of Orbajosa. The large body that was at Villahorrenda has attacked the troop with great courage. Many have fallen on both sides. The brave partizans are dispersed, but are still full of spirit, and perhaps you may hear of some marvels. Caballuco, son of that eminent Caballuco who was so prominent in the last war, commands them, in spite of a wounded arm. He it is who directs their movements, and he is honorable and simple. As we shall at last try to make a friendly compromise, I presume that Caballuco will be the general of the Spanish army, by which much would be gained. I deplore this war, which will attain alarming proportions; but I know that our country braves are not responsible for it, having been provoked to it by the Government's audacity; by the demoralization of its sacrilegious delegates; by the angry system with which the representatives of the state attack those things most revered by the people's conscience, religious faith and purified Spanish, that by fortune is preserved in those spots not affected by destroying pestilence.

"As to a town, the soul of which they wish to destroy in order to infuse another which they wish to degenerate, we will say this—that it is as natural such a town should wish to protect its sentiment, customs, and ideas from change, as he who is beset by infamous robbers in the middle of a solitary road. Let the sphere of the Government's spirit be raised by the pure, healthy substance of my 'Lineage' (pardon my vanity), and then we shall have no wars.

"I have here to treat of a very disagreeable question. The priest, my friend, had refused to inter the unhappy Rey in consecrated ground. I intervened in this affair, impressing it on the bishop that there would be a curse on such a refusal; but I could do nothing. We have at last buried the young fellow in the field of Mundogrande, where my patient researches have brought to light the rich archeology that you are acquainted with. I passed a very sad visit there, and even now the painful impression I received lasts. Don Juan Tafetán and I were the only mourners. Shortly after came (strange thing!) those who are known as the Troyas, and prayed for a long time by the rustic tomb of the mathematician. Although it seemed a ridiculous officiousness, I felt touched by it. Respecting Rey's death, public rumor runs that he was assassinated—I do not know by whom. It is asserted that he declared it, as he lived for an hour and a half afterward. He kept the name of his murderer secret, so 'tis said. I repeat this version without adding to or curtailing it. Perfecta does not like to be spoken to on the subject, and is always much afflicted when it is mentioned.

"The poor little girl had scarcely recovered from the effects of one disgrace when another happened, which tries us much. My friend, another victim is added to the inherited funest infirmity of our family. Poor Rosarito, from whom our care has, till now, warded it off, has become mad. Her incoherent words, her frightful delirium, her mortal pallor recall my mother and sister to my mind. This is the most serious case that has been in my family, for it is not simple frenzy, but real madness. It is sad—very sad; and I am the only one who has escaped, and preserved my judgment sane and entire, totally free from this evil.

"I can not give your messages to Don Inocencio; he has suddenly taken a dislike to us, and will not receive even his most intimate friends. But I am sure he will wish to be remembered to you, and, doubtless, will take in hand the translation of the various Latin epigrams which you send him—Again I hear shots. It is said there will be a fight this afternoon. The troop begins to march."

BARCELONA, *June 1st.*

"I have come here to place my niece, Rosarito, in St. Baudillo de Lobregat. The director of this establishment assures me that hers is an incurable case. She will receive admirable assistance in this large asylum. My dear friend, should I likewise fall at any time, take me to St. Baudillo. I hope soon to receive the proofs of my 'Lineage.' I thought of adding six sheets, for it would be a great oversight not to publish the reasons for maintaining that Matthew Diez, colonel, author of 'Metrical Praise,' was descended, by the maternal side, from the Guevaras, and not from the Burguillos, as the author of 'Floresta Amena' has declared. I write this letter chiefly to inform you of an incident. I have heard several people speak of Pepe Rey's death here, who seemed to know how it took place. I revealed that secret to you when I was at Madrid, telling you what had transpired shortly after the affair. It is very strange that, as I only mentioned it to you, people here should know all particulars; how he had entered the orchard, how he had discharged his pistol at Ramos when he saw the latter attack him with a knife, how Ramos despatched him cleverly— In fact, my dear friend, this must have been spoken of unthinkingly to some one. I only told you this family secret, thinking it would be safe with one as prudent and discreet as yourself.

"Good news! good news! I read in a newspaper that Caballuco has defeated Brigadier Batalla."

ORBAJOSA, *December* 12*th*.

"I have some touching news to give you.

"We now have no confessor; not precisely that he has passed to the better life, but that, since the month of April, the poor man has been so afflicted, so melancholy, so taciturn, that one scarcely recognizes him. There is none of that Atticism, of that correct, classic joviality which rendered him so pleasing. He shuns men, shuts himself up in his house, receives no one, scarcely takes any food, and has broken off all relations with the world. If you were to see him you would not know him, for he is only skin and bone. The strangest thing is that he has quarreled with his niece, and lives alone—entirely alone—in a miserable hut at Badajoz. He has renounced his chair in the choir, so 'tis said, and is going to Rome. Ah! Orbajosa loses much in losing its great Latin scholar. It seems to me that years upon years will pass, and we shall never have another. Our glorious Spain is falling—is being annihilated—dies!"

ORBAJOSA, *December* 23*d*.

"The young man who brings a letter of recommendation to you is our dear confessor's nephew, a lawyer, likewise an author. He has been admirably educated by his uncle, and has sensible ideas.

He will indeed be sensible if he be not corrupted in that muddy place of philosophy and incredulity! He is honorable, a worker, and a good Catholic; and will, I believe, make his way at his desk, as your son did! Perhaps he is a little ambitious in regard to politics (like your son), and I think that he will not do badly in the cause of order and tradition, in this day when youth is perverted and made unstable by malcontents. His mother accompanies him, an ordinary woman of no social standing, but who has an excellent heart, and is very pious. Maternal love in her takes the form of worldly ambition, and she says her son will become a minister. Perhaps he may.

"Perfecta wishes to be remembered to you. I do not know what is the matter with her, but she requires our greatest care. She has lost her appetite in an alarming manner; yet I hear of no pains, but am a little afraid she has jaundice. The house is very dull since Rosarito left; she enlivened it with her smile and angelical goodness. Now a dark cloud seems to overshadow us. Poor Perfecta frequently mentions this cloud, which becomes blacker, while she becomes more yellow each day. The poor mother obtains consolation in her sorrow in religion, and she becomes more exemplary and edifying. She passes nearly the whole day in church, and spends her large fortune on special prayers and services. Thanks to her, religion has regained the splendor of former days in Orbajosa. This should console us in the midst of the decadence and falling away of our nation.

"To-morrow my proofs will go. I will add two other sheets, for I have discovered another illustrious Orbajosian—Bernardo Amador de Soto—who was the Duke of Osuna's chaplain, whom he served during the viceroyship of Naples, and who appears to have done nothing—absolutely nothing —in the conspiracy against Venice."

CHAPTER XXXIII

L'ENVOI

IT is finished. You are now able to decide if those persons who seemed good were really so.